JACKPOT!

ROBIN BELL

BALBOA.PRESS
A DIVISION OF HAY HOUSE

Balboa Press books may be ordered through booksellers or by contacting:

Balboa Press
A Division of Hay House
1663 Liberty Drive
Bloomington, IN 47403
www.balboapress.com.au
AU TFN: 1 800 844 925 (Toll Free inside Australia)
AU Local: (02) 8310 7086 (+61 2 8310 7086 from outside Australia)

Front cover painting copyright © acknowledged to Diane Judge

Print information available on the last page.

ISBN: 978-1-9822-9265-2 (sc)
ISBN: 978-1-9822-9266-9 (e)

Balboa Press rev. date: 11/22/2021

CHAPTER 1

JANUARY - FEBRUARY

MELBOURNE

Kate Rayne rarely purchased Tattslotto tickets, so when on the spur of the moment she joined the multitude and purchased a quick pick for that evening's three hundred million dollar super jackpot draw, she put the ticket in her wallet, then promptly forgot all about it.

It wasn't until a fortnight later, when Kate was reading the local paper while on her coffee break that she noticed an article stating that the uncollected winning ticket had been purchased at the local newsagency, where she had bought her ticket.

When her shift ended she looked up her ticket number on the 'check your ticket' web site and was flabbergasted to find that she had the six winning numbers! At first, Kate couldn't believe what she was seeing, then eventually decided to ring the phone number listed for potential winners to find out what percentage of the first prize amount she had won.

The lady who answered Kate's phone call asked for the ticket number, then agreed that it was indeed a winning ticket, but was non-committal when Kate asked how much she had won. She explained that Kate would have to take her ticket and some ID, such as her licence or passport, plus bank details, to the Melbourne Head Office, before the amount could be disclosed.

Kate spent the evening in a daze, wondering just how much she might have won. Obviously, it must be more than just a few thousand dollars!

Having two rostered days off later in the week, Kate rang the Tattslotto office in Melbourne to make an appointment for the following Thursday morning, at a time that allowed her to catch the early train from Shepparton to Melbourne. During the trip to Melbourne, Kate wondered what it would be like to win a million dollars. The total jackpot was three hundred million dollars, but a record number of people had apparently bought tickets, so who knew how many others shared the winning numbers?

When Kate arrived to the Tattslotto Head Office she was ushered into a large, airy office and offered a cup of tea or coffee, while a very pleasant lady named Joan scanned her ticket and passport. With a wide smile Joan looked at Kate. 'Congratulations Kate. I think you should put your mug down, because you are the sole winner of the entire three hundred million dollar jackpot!'

Joan had seen a variety of reactions from recipients who had won large sums of money, though nowhere as much as Kate had just won, and wondered how she would react. At first Kate just stared at Joan, then leant back in her chair, took a deep breath, and exhaled it slowly. 'What on earth does one do with that amount of money? I thought maybe a million dollars would be more than enough for me to deal with!'

'Have you spoken to anyone about the possibility of having a winning ticket Kate?'

'No. You are the only person who knows that I bought a ticket Joan, let alone a winning one, and I would prefer to keep it that way; at least until I have had time to come to grips with the magnitude of the amount. I opened a new bank account this morning before I came here, and indicated that there might be a sizable instalment later today. I don't want my local bank to know until I'm ready to move some money there. Being a country town, the news of a local winner would spread like wildfire and I don't want every Tom, Dick & Harry calling in for a handout.'

'That's very sensible Kate. However, before we transfer the money to your account, might I suggest that you meet with our financial advisor Geoff Rowe, who can help you deal with your newfound wealth? He can advise you of various ways to spread your wealth, so that you don't have all your eggs in one basket.'

When Kate nodded Sally spoke on the intercom and asked Geoff to come to her office. Moments later, a middle-aged man wearing a dark suit and a welcoming smile walked into the office and shook Kate's hand. 'So, you are our mystery multi-millionaire Kate. Congratulations!'

Once they were seated and Kate had explained her wishes for anonymity, Geoff nodded. 'Considering the sum that you have won Kate, I think you would be wise to open up a couple more accounts at other banks, and spread your money. That way it would be harder to associate your deposits as part of the recent jackpot. If you like, I could go with you to open the accounts, then we will electronically transfer money straight into each account. Walking out of this building with a cheque for such large amounts would be a bit daunting! Also, when the banks receive money transferred from us, they immediately ring to verify the amount, and the name of the account holder.'

By the time Kate and Geoff finally finished lodging her money into four different banks, it was mid-afternoon and she was feeling quite exhausted. As she and Geoff walked out of the last bank, he looked at her. 'If you don't have to travel home tonight Kate, why don't you book into a hotel and try to relax?'

Kate was about to say that it would cost too much, when it dawned on her that she could afford to stay wherever she wanted to!

She laughed. 'I think I might just lash out tonight Geoff, and see what it feels like. Where do you suggest I try?'

'Why not the Langham on South Bank? It would pay to buy yourself a small case, so that they won't query your lack of luggage!'

When Geoff left to return to his office, Kate purchased an airline cabin case, plus some night attire and toiletries, then crossed the Yarra River via Princes Bridge, and walked along the riverbank to the Langham Hotel. At first when she entered the impressive lobby she nearly turned around to leave, but then squared her shoulders and walked over to reception, where she arranged to stay for the night.

A young bellboy, whose nametag revealed that his name was Graham, cheerfully took her key and case and led the way to the lifts. As Graham unlocked the door to her room on the fifteenth floor, Kate wondered should she tip him. But when he opened the door and said, with a sweep of his arm 'Welcome to the Langham, Ms Rayne,' she gasped at the large, elegantly furnished room, and forgot the bellboy as she stood transfixed, looking out of the large window overlooking the city, and only turned when she heard the door quietly closing.

After taking a long, refreshing shower in the beautifully appointed bathroom, Kate spent the remainder of the afternoon sitting out on the balcony, watching as the city lights came on and reflected on the river below her. Finally, Kate decided to ring room service to order her dinner, as she didn't think her casual attire would be suitable for the Melba Restaurant downstairs.

She was surprised when her dinner was wheeled into her room on a small table draped by a starched white linen cloth, with dishes covered by domed silver covers, and her place setting of silver cutlery arranged as in the restaurant. When the liveried waiter seated Kate and placed her serviette on her lap with a flourish, he removed the cover from the oysters, poured a glass of wine then left, after advising her to ring the restaurant, should she require further service.

Following a delicious dinner of natural oysters, a beautifully cooked sirloin steak with a Greek side salad, followed by a delicious salted caramel éclair, Kate curled up on the king-sized bed and tried once again to come to terms with the unbelievable amount of money that she had won. What on earth should she do with all that money, and how would it change her life? While the experience of staying in a five-star hotel was extraordinary, it wasn't how she wanted to live her life, nor spend her money. Upgrading to business class, or even first class on a flight maybe, but she couldn't think of anything else that she wanted to do to change her life. However, whatever she did with it, she was determined that she wasn't going to just squander the money.

Kate was a senior paramedic based in Shepparton where she had worked for the past three years, following several inner suburban appointments after her change from nursing to paramedics seven years ago. She loved working in a large country town, but had to admit that she and her colleagues were finding some callouts much more challenging these days, especially when dealing with some drug induced cases. The unpredictable behaviour of some patients and, worse still, some bystanders, could be quite confronting and at times undeniably dangerous.

Maybe it was time to do something different with her life, as she would no longer have to rely on her salary for an income, although she knew that she wouldn't be able to just swan around doing nothing for long, and she loved her work. Wishing to keep her win anonymous for as long as possible, Kate decided not to do anything too hasty, and resolved to keep working until she had a clearer idea about what she might do.

While still working her regular shifts in Shepparton, Kate used most of her rostered days off to travel to Melbourne to meet with Geoff, to plan how to best utilise her wealth. They discussed many ways of dealing with such a huge sum of money, and the legal implications of gifting sums of money to individuals and to various charities.

Eventually, by the end of February they had resolved to form a holding company, into which $200,000,000 would be allocated. Kate applied for three months long service leave, to allow her time to help Geoff with the development of *Windfall Holdings*. It was decided that Kate would invest $60,000,000 to accumulate interest for her future, give $5,000,000 each to her father and her sister Julie, who both ran the family property in East Gippsland, and $1,000,000 to each of her two aunts. The remaining money was to be deposited in the four different bank accounts opened soon after her win, to be used use as Kate felt fit.

After much discussion and many sleepless nights, Kate decided that she wanted *Windfall Holdings* to be primarily involved in assisting the homeless, animal shelters, plus guide dog and service dog training. However, before any money was distributed, she was determined to speak to as many of the organisations as possible, to find out how best to assist them.

CHAPTER 2

———⟫◉⟪———

JANUARY

HINNOMUNJIE

Kate and her younger sister Julie had grown up on *Glen Rayne,* the family's 500–hectare cattle property near Hinnomunjie in North Eastern Victoria, under the loving care of their father and his older sister Margaret. Tragically, when Kate had just turned five and Julie was almost three, their mother Jean had developed preeclampsia in the final weeks of her third pregnancy, and she and her unborn son had died when she suffered a fatal seizure while travelling in the ambulance to Bairnsdale hospital.

Initially, their Aunt Margaret had intended to drive to *Glen Rayne* for her sister in law's funeral, but had ended up leasing her house in Bairnsdale, and moved back to her old home, where she looked after her brother and her two young nieces for the next ten years until Julie had completed grade six at the Omeo primary school.

Kate and Julie adored their aunt, and grew up helping her in the house and their father out on the property. Both girls learnt to ride ponies at an early age, swam in the large, river fed lake below the homestead, and had plenty to occupy their days, but it was Julie who became her father's little helper, working with him whenever she could. Kate was more studious, and was quite happy with the long-held plan to leave the district when she had completed her primary schooling, to attend her mother's old school, Presbyterian Ladies College in Burwood. Jean had lived in Burwood and attended PLC for her entire education.

While she was at Teachers College, one of her school friends had invited her to attend a Batchelor & Spinster ball held in a shearing shed near Bairnsdale. There, Jean met Gregory Rayne, the only son of a long-established pastoralist family at Hinnomunjie, a small settlement in the Victorian Alpine country, about 140 kilometres north of Bairnsdale. Six months later, Greg and Jean were married in Melbourne at the Scotch College Littlejohn Chapel, and she left her suburban life to live in the remote area of Eastern Victoria. Greg's parents, happy to see their only son married, retired to Lakes Entrance, bought a house in Bairnsdale for their daughter Margaret, and left their property *Glen Rayne* to Greg.

Due to the remoteness of *Glen Rayne*, both Greg and Jean had agreed that as Margaret and Greg had done years before, their two girls would attend boarding school in Melbourne for their secondary schooling.

Kate couldn't wait to finish primary school and move to Melbourne, to commence her secondary schooling. While she loved living at *Glen Rayne,* she wanted to see more of the wider world that she so enjoyed reading about. Jean's sister Jane and her family lived within easy walking distance of PLC, so instead of becoming a boarder, Kate went to live with her Aunt Jane, Uncle Malcom, and teenage cousin Melonie, who was already enrolled at PLC as a day girl.

Julie, on the other hand, dreaded the thought of leaving the district, and as her final year at primary school drew to a close, she became quite distraught. After much discussion, it was finally decided that Margaret and Julie would live in Margaret's house in Bairnsdale so that Julie could attend Bairnsdale Secondary School during the week, then spend the weekends at home working with her father.

This arrangement worked reasonably well, although Julie was nowhere near the enthusiastic student that her sister was, and she was determined to leave school as soon as she could. Her wishes came true not long after her sixteenth birthday when her grandfather had a bad fall, and Margaret left Bairnsdale to look after her parents at Lake's Entrance.

Julie quickly proved to her father that she had the skills and determination to carry out both the house work, as well as the cattle and farm work required on the property, and he finally agreed to allow her to leave school to become a fulltime worker on *Glen Rayne*. When Margaret saw how well Greg and Julie were coping, she agreed to stay on with her parents, for as long as they needed her.

Julie was passionate about the stud Hereford cattle breeding program that Greg had embarked upon a few years earlier, and he was impressed with her commitment to researching the program and in her record keeping, being fully aware of his younger daughter's lack of interest in studying at school.

During the following eleven years Greg and Julie formed a close working partnership, utilising the strengths of each other. Together, they developed the respected Glen Rayne Hereford Stud, breeding much sort after prize bulls and cows, and *Glen Rayne* produced prime cattle, in great demand for the overseas markets.

Throughout these years, father and daughter respected each other's private lives, and Greg ensured that Julie had time away from the property on a regular basis, to meet up with friends, and he hoped possible suitors. However, Julie's commitment to her work, and the isolation of *Glen Rayne* ensured that such encounters were quite brief.

Greg spent occasional weekends away, but never brought women back to *Glen Rayne*. Therefore, on an early January morning while Greg was out moving cattle, Julie was flabbergasted when an immaculately dressed, middle aged woman drove into the yard, bluntly announced that she was Greg's fiancé, and then walked uninvited into the house where she deposited her cases in Greg's bedroom.

Finally, in response to Julie's demand to know who she was, she snapped 'My name is Velma Naughton, and I have come to live with

Gregory.' Looking Julie up and down she sneered 'So, you must be his 'oh so perfect daughter', who he never stops talking about. We will see how long that lasts now that I'm here.'

Julie couldn't believe what was happening and stormed out of the house to look for her father. When she told him about Velma's arrival, he stared at her for a moment, then abruptly jumped into his ute and drove back to the house, leaving Julie coughing in his dust. When she arrived back in the house yard, Julie could hear raised voices coming from the house, so continued driving to the front gate, then on to Omeo. Julie texted her whereabouts to Greg, a practise that they had implemented soon after Julie began working on the property and added that she would stay in town with a friend and return in time for work in the morning.

Julie was shocked when she saw her father the next morning. He looked as though he hadn't slept at all, and he'd lost his usual cheerful disposition. He muttered an abrupt greeting, then mumbled that he was going fencing. Entering the house to change her clothes, Julie noticed that Velma was still in her father's room, and that the bed in the spare room was dishevelled, so she assumed that her father had spent the night there. After a quick shower Julie ate a bowl of cereal and drank a cup of coffee, then left to find her father.

At first Greg wouldn't speak to her but eventually, when they had a break and sat in the shade of the trees near the fence line, he turned to Julie. 'I'm so sorry lass. Velma and I first met when I was a school lad in Melbourne, and I haven't seen her since, until we bumped into each other when I was away last weekend. We were getting on fine, until I realised who she was, and what she was after. I left town straight away and had no idea that she would turn up here.'

'But she told me that she was your fiancé Dad!'

'Um, yes, well, I'd had a few drinks, and I can't remember some of our conversation that night. Let's just leave it for a bit, and I will soon persuade her to go.'

Unfortunately, things didn't turn out that way, and Velma quickly established herself in the house, taking over the cooking and housework. At first she spoke quite civilly to Julie in front of her father, although when they were alone she was vindictive and merciless in her criticism of her. But it wasn't long before she treated Julie the same way, whether her father was present or not.

A few weeks later, Greg and Velma went away for a few days, and on their return at lunchtime Greg stormed straight out to the shed, while Velma gleefully waved a piece of paper at Julie, and smirked. 'Greg and I were married yesterday!'

Unable to find her father to speak to him, Julie rode up into the ranges to check the young steers. When she returned later in the afternoon, she found all of her belongings stuffed into black garbage bags dumped out on the verandah. Velma stood at the front door, hands on her hips. 'This is my house now Miss High and Mighty, and you are no longer welcome to live here. I'm sure that your father will soon decide that he is quite capable of doing without your interference on the property any longer!' Totally nonplussed, Julie stared up at the wild-eyed woman, then quickly began to gather up her possessions when Velma hissed 'Get all this rubbish off my verandah before I burn it!'

Julie piled the bags onto the back of her ute and drove over to the empty workman's cottage, unable to believe what was happening. That night, after she cooked herself a couple of eggs collected from the hen house, she wondered why her father wasn't standing up for either her or for himself? She had expected him to come looking for her, to say that it was all a big mistake. But, although she heard Greg and Velma shouting at each other, she saw no sign of her father that night. When they met the next day, Greg assured Julie that he still wanted her to work with him on *Glen Rayne*, but he was unable to convince Velma that Julie was his partner in the business. From that day, the only room in the house that Julie entered was the office, via the verandah door, and Velma began to lock the outside doors whenever she was away from the house.

Julie wondered if Velma held something over Greg. Could she possibly be blackmailing him? But what? He'd become a shadow of his former self, but hadn't discuss the issue with Julie; in fact, he rarely spoke, other than to talk about the cattle or jobs to be carried out.

He and Velma spent very little time together. Greg was always up at dawn, eating breakfast and leaving the house before Velma emerged from her bedroom. He often ate lunch with Julie, and the only meal that Greg and Velma shared was dinner at night. After dinner he'd sit out on the front verandah to drink a mug of coffee, then he went to bed in the spare bedroom, while Velma made herself a hot chocolate, took a sleeping tablet and retired alone to the main bedroom.

Two weeks after Julie's ejection from the house, Greg and Julie went to Bairnsdale to watch a pen of their steers being sold, and to stock up on groceries. After the sale, while Julie shopped, Greg went off by himself for an hour. On the drive home, he obviously had something on his mind. Eventually he spoke. 'Jules, if anything happens to me, don't let Velma get her hands on the stud cattle. They're yours and mine and have nothing to do with her.'

Stunned by this statement, Julie stared at her father, but she knew that there was no point in badgering him to explain what he meant. When he had more to say, she was sure that he would do so in his own time. Julie spoke to Kate about what was happening at *Glen Rayne*, but she was as much in the dark as her sister about their father's odd behaviour.

Kate visited once not long after Velma's arrival and had been appalled at the way she treated her father and sister and was sure that the woman was a charlatan. But unless their father discussed the situation with them, she had no way of proving it.

CHAPTER 3

FEBRUARY

WOOLGOOLGA

Flicking through the pages the recent Coffs Coast Advocate that her friend Lynn had sent her, Kate noticed a 'for sale' notice for a property in Woolgoolga that she had often admired when visiting Lynn, who lived near the small seaside township, north of Coffs Harbour in New South Wales.

Kate immediately rang Geoff, who was now employed as *Windfall Holdings'* financial advisor, to tell him about the property, and of her desire to buy it using money from her personal account. He agreed to fly up to Coffs Harbour with her the next day to have a look at the property, and to discuss the terms with the vendor's real estate agent, if needs be.

The vendors were a couple who were desperate to move to New York to be with their daughter who had just given birth to triplets, and they were offering the property for sale on a walk-in walk-out basis. They were thrilled at the prospect of a quick sale, and were happy to accept the lower price that Geoff managed to negotiate when he indicated the possibility of an instant transfer of the full amount into their account that day.

The following day Kate had the keys to her new, fully furnished house, and after dropping Geoff off at the Coffs Harbour airport and doing a grocery shop, Kate drove back to Woolgoolga to take possession of her property.

The impressive white house was positioned on a double, slightly sloping block overlooking the Solitary Islands and Woolgoolga Beach. The bitumen Esplanade separated the front of the block from a narrow grassy verge that bordered the steep cliffs, where the rolling waves crashed and swirled on the rocks below. The house was built into the slope, with a seven metre rectangular inground swimming pool near the side fence, surrounded by decking and a high clear plexiglass fence in a sizable front garden.

The ground floor of the house was designed to be two self-contained two bedroomed flats, each with a carport. The second and top levels each had a wide balcony extending the entire width of the front of the house. A covered brick path led up the left side of the building to the top floor, where the front door opened into a large lounge and dining area, with the kitchen, walk in pantry and breakfast bar on the left, and the master bedroom, dressing room and ensuite on the right side. Floor to ceiling sliding glass doors in the bedroom and lounge area opened onto the balcony.

At the back of the lounge was a smaller room, with a large skylight and side window that was set up as an office. Seven steps near the front door went down to the middle level, which had two double bedrooms with ensuites and a lounge opening onto the balcony as on the level above.

A hallway at the back of the top lounge led to the laundry that opened out to a large gently sloping lawn, enclosed on each side by high wooden fences and a high metal grill fence, shutting the property off from the lane bordering the back of the property.

A solar gate of the same design as the back fence was next to the left boundary fence as you looked up to the gate, and there was a gravel drive running down beside the fence to a large gravel turning area in front of the wide roller door that opened into a sizeable double garage. An internal door opened from the garage into the end of the hallway opposite the laundry door.

The following morning Kate was sitting out on the top balcony enjoying her early morning coffee, admiring the magnificent vista in front of her, when she was startled to hear a dog yelping in pain. Looking down across the road to the wooden bench near the cliff edge, she saw a woman hunched over what appeared to be a small brown and white dog on her lap. As she watched, the dog gave another loud yelp and the woman staggered to her feet, looking towards the cliff edge, about ten metres from the bench.

Kate immediately rushed downstairs, crossed the road, and managed to restrain the woman before she took the last couple of steps to the cliff edge. Kate held her arm firmly. 'Please come back to the bench with me, and let me help you.'

'You can't help us. Just let me end our torment, here and now!'

Shocked, Kate gently lowered the woman back onto the bench, and saw to her horror that one side of her face was bruised and puffy, and her left eye was swollen shut. Glancing down at the little dog hugged to her chest, she noticed its misshapen face and damaged front leg.

'Please let me take you to the doctor, and your dog to the vet.'

'I can't afford to take Hugo to the vet, nor myself to the doctor. My son will murder me if he finds out that anyone knows what he did to us!' The woman sobbed as Kate sat down beside her, and placed her arm around the shaking shoulders. When the woman had calmed down a little Kate stood up. 'Come over to my house, and we will see what needs to be done.'

As if in a trance the woman, supported by Kate and still hugging her dog, staggered across the road and into the front yard. It was only when they started to walk up the path that the lady looked around. 'Who are you? Is this really your home?'

'My name is Kate Rayne and I have just bought this property and moved in last night. You and Hugo will be my first visitors.'

'I'm Jessie Martin.'

Kate led Jessie straight through the house into the garage, and sat her in the front passenger seat of her car, before she realised where she was. 'I'm happy to pay Hugo's vet bill Jessie, if you show me where the clinic is. He obviously needs attention as quickly as possible, then I will take you to see a doctor.'

As soon as they entered the vet clinic the shocked receptionist led them into a side room where a vet nurse gently laid the whimpering Hugo on the consulting table. She placed a warm blanket over him, before turning to Jessie. 'What in the world happened Jessie?'

'It was that lousy son of mine Tracey! Poor little Hugo just walked past him to go out into the garden, and Karl kicked him into the wall. Then he kicked him again while he was lying on the floor.'

Before Kate or the nurse could reply the vet, who had been standing at the doorway when Jessie spoke, strode into the room. 'Jessie, you need to report this to the police straightaway. Karl has gone too far this time!'

He bent over the little dog lying on the table, and patted him gently. 'What has he done to you my little Hugo? I will need to x-ray his jaw and leg, and do a thorough check for any other injuries. Leave him with us Jessie, and get your self seen to as quickly as possible.'

He glanced at Kate. 'I'm Kate Rayne Dr Heslop. I'm taking Jessie to the doctor's as soon as we leave here, then I will call the police. I will leave my phone number with your receptionist, in case you need to call Jessie about Hugo.'

When Kate and Jessie left the doctor's surgery, with strict orders for Jessie to rest quietly for the next week, Jessie began to sob. 'How can I rest quietly? Karl will still expect me to have his dinner ready tonight, and will also insist that I clean up after him, as though nothing's happened.'

'I'm not taking you home Jessie. You and Hugo will stay with me until you are ready to decide what to do next. I will call the police, and ask them to take your statement at my house.'

'My life won't be worth living when Karl finds out that I have reported him to the police.'

'He won't know where you are staying Jessie. I'm new in town, so who is going to tell him where you are?'

Once Jessie was settled in bed in one of the bedrooms Kate rang the local police station to explain what had occurred, and gave them her address. She was surprised to hear a muffled exclamation when Karl Martin's name was mentioned, and had not long hung up when a police car pulled up in front of her house. A policewoman quickly strode up to the front door where she was met by Kate.

Introducing herself, Kate explained what had happened since she first saw Jessie and Hugo, then Sergeant Sally Everton and Kate went into the bedroom to see Jessie. When the policewoman saw Jessie she stopped and stared. 'My God, Aunty Jess! What in the world has happened to you?'

Jessie peered at the tall policewoman standing beside her bed. 'Sally, is that really you? I thought that you were stationed somewhere down in Sydney.'

'I was promoted to the sergeant position at Coffs Aunty Jess. I was visiting the local police station when Kate's call came through, and I heard her mention Karl's name.' Sally turned to Kate. 'Mum and Jessie have been best friends for years, and I have called her Aunty Jess since I could talk. Mum will be thrilled to know that you are still in town, rather than in Western Australia Aunty Jess. But first, tell me how you received those injuries.'

'Karl did it Sally! I should start at the beginning for Kate's sake. Sam and I moved into our house near the Headland not long after our wedding 35 years ago Kate, and we lived there for our entire married lives. Our son Karl was born a year after the wedding, and was a gorgeous little lad, and his sister Julie was born two years later. We were a close and loving family, until Karl joined a gym in Coffs Harbour when he was 16. Sam and I couldn't understand how our loving, happy son could so quickly change into such a surly, aggressive, and abusive individual, until we found out that he was using steroids and a concoction of illicit drugs.

Julie was terrified of Karl and his friends, and went to England when she was fifteen to live with my Aunt Joan, and she has never returned. When Karl was eighteen, he punched Sam over some minor disagreement, and stormed out of the house, and we heard nothing of him for the next sixteen years.

My Sam died suddenly five months ago, and I was just beginning to recover from the shock of his death, when Karl turned up six weeks ago, saying that he needed somewhere to stay. Karl is a big man, scary to look at with his shaven head and muscular body covered in tattoos, and he has a vicious temper. A few days after his arrival, when I asked him not to wear his muddy boots in the house, he grabbed me by the throat and pinned me up against the wall so that my toes only just touched the floor. When I began to choke, he glared at me and growled 'Listen to me you old bitch, if you know what's good for you, you will do whatever I tell you to do from now on. You will cook and do the housework without any complaint. You won't leave the house, and you will sleep out in the garage from now on.' He let go of my neck just as I started to black out, then he kicked me in the ribs as I lay gasping on the floor.'

Jessie closed her eyes for a moment then continued. 'The past six weeks have been utter hell Sally. Karl takes great delight in slapping me around, frightening me and threatening Hugo. I'm not allowed to go outside; Karl even hangs out the washing to make sure that I'm not seen by the neighbours. At first, a few of my friends called to see me not long after Karl moved in, but he was really rude to them. He told them that I had gone to stay with friends in Western Australia, and he didn't want anyone else calling around asking for me. I was too afraid to call out or to let them see me, as I was terrified what Karl would do to me, or to Hugo when they left.

Hugo and I have to sleep in the garage that's full of his junk, and there's only just enough room near the door for an old mattress on the floor. The wind and rain constantly blow in through the window that Karl broke not long after he arrived, so the mattress is often damp, but Karl locks me in there every night regardless. I'm only allowed to wear an old tracksuit day and night; all my other clothes are locked in one of the spare bedrooms.

Karl makes me work until I'm exhausted, and I live in a daze most of the time. One day he grabbed me and held a knife to my throat, to force me to sign a piece of paper that he put in front of me. It turned out that I signed over power of attorney to him, with a knife held to my throat!'

Kate and Sally looked at Jessie in horror as she continued. 'This morning he told me that he has sold my house and contents, emptied and closed my bank account, and that I have to find somewhere else to live now, because the new owners are arriving in a couple of days! As he left the house, he kicked Hugo and broke his jaw and front leg. When I bent over Hugo, he kicked me in the face, then kicked me again as I lay on the floor, then he laughed and drove off in my car. For once he forgot to lock the door, and I somehow managed to stand up and carry Hugo away from the house. That was when Kate rescued us.'

As Jessie lay back exhausted, Sally patted her hand. 'Thank you, Aunty Jess, you've given me a lot to work on. This, on top of other information that we received from the Victorian Police yesterday regarding Karl, should see him locked away for some time.' Quickly she left the room and rang through the registration number of Jessie's Datsun.

Kate followed Sally out of the bedroom. 'Thank you for your assistance Kate. Until we apprehend Karl, I think it would be wise to keep Aunty Jess's whereabouts as quiet as possible; I won't even tell Mum. If anyone queries my visit today, just tell them that I was paying a curtesy call to a new resident to check your security system.' She smiled and added 'We actually did a check not long before you purchased the property, and found the security system to be well and truly appropriate.

Would you mind accompanying me to Aunty Jess's house to collect her personal possessions and clothing? I will arrange for a colleague to stay here with Aunty Jess while we're away.'

When the two women entered Jessie's house, it looked neat and tidy, testament to Jessie's housekeeping prowess. They quickly packed all of Jessie's clothes into the boxes that Sally had collected from the Woolgoolga Police Station. Going through the house room by room, they collected ornaments, trinkets, paintings, and anything else that they agreed would not be considered to be contents. Karl's belongings were also packed in a couple of boxes that Sally was going to take to the Police Station. Before they finished packing a small removal van arrived, in response to a call from Sally, and arrangements were made for everything to be offloaded into Kate's garage.

Both women were appalled when they saw the conditions that Jessie had been forced to sleep in each night, and Sally took a number of photos, as evidence of the cruelty that Jessie had been subjected to.

The next day, when Kate was sure that Jessie was content to be left alone in the house, she made quick trips to the local supermarket, the vet clinic to check on Hugo, and also to the local library, to sign up as a member, and to borrow some books for Jessie to read.

The vet was pleased that Hugo's surgery had gone well, and that he'd had a peaceful night. His broken jaw was wired, and his leg was splinted and bandaged from foot to shoulder, but he still wagged his tail when he saw Kate. Assuring the vet that she was happy to look after Hugo until Jessie was able to, Kate arranged to collect the little dog the next morning. She went home with a new pet bed, bowls, and packets of pet food that the vet recommended for Hugo until his jaw healed.

Jessie slept most of the time in the extremely comfortable bed. When not sleeping, she lay looking out at the magnificent ocean view. Both she and Hugo were thrilled to be reunited when Kate brought him back from the vets, and he wouldn't settle until he was allowed to lie on the bed beside Jessie.

Not long after lunch that day, Sally rang and asked if she could meet with Jessie again. When she arrived, she sat out on the upper balcony with Jessie, Kate, and Hugo, who was soon snuggled up on Sally's lap.

'I'm pleased to see that you and this little chap are recovering from your injuries Aunty Jess. However, I'm afraid that I must inform you that Karl was killed yesterday, when his car skidded on a dirt road near Bathurst, and hit a tree.'

Jessie let out a gasp, her hand going to her mouth; then, after a moment of reflection she turned to Sally. 'I know that this will sound awful, but that monster living in my house was no longer my son, and I'm relieved that I won't have to worry that he could return at any time in the future. I just hope that no one else was involved in the crash.'

'No Aunty Jess, he was alone in the car, and no other vehicle was involved. But unfortunately your car is a write off. The officers investigating the crash found many legal documents, some pertaining to the sale of your house, and statements for your bank account. Unfortunately, because Karl still held the signed power of attorney, the house sale was legal, but the payment for the sale was deposited into your bank account. I know Karl told you that he'd closed it, but he hadn't. He was using it as his own account, so any money in it is legally yours!

There was also a large quantity of illegal drugs in the boot, along with a considerable amount of cash, causing us to believe that Karl was a drug dealer. Did he have many visitors at your house Aunty Jess?'

'I never saw anyone Sally, but he had a lot of visitors most nights. That might explain why Hugo and I were locked in the garage at night, not, as I thought, to stop me leaving the house when he was asleep. I knew when people arrived and left, but I never saw them, nor heard their conversations clearly. Some people stayed longer than others, and I always had to clean up the mess when Karl dragged me back into the house each morning to cook his breakfast.'

'Ok, thanks Aunty Jess. Now, do you feel up to a visit from Mum this afternoon? I'm sure she will be over in a flash when I tell her that you are still in town.'

'I would love to see Elizabeth again, if it's okay with you Kate? I am, after all, a visitor here too.'

'You invite whoever you like to Jessie, though I think it might be wise to limit the numbers until you are feeling stronger.'

By the end of a week Jessie was feeling much better, and was able to take Hugo out onto the back lawn where he was still learning to cope with his bandaged front leg. Sally's mother Elizabeth had called soon after being informed where Jessie was staying, and was upset to hear what her friend had been forced to endure; but she was relieved that Kate appeared to have taken her friend under her wing.

CHAPTER 4

———————⟨⟩———————

MID-FEBRUARY

WOOLGOOLGA

A fortnight after their first meeting, Kate began to feel that Jessie was becoming concerned that she might be outstaying her welcome, and was worrying about where she was to live. While she and Jessie were sitting out on the top balcony after dinner, watching an electrical storm far out to sea, Kate turned to Jessie. 'Did you enjoy cooking and housekeeping, before Karl turned up Jessie?'

'Oh Kate, I love cooking, and was always trying out different recipes for Sam and myself, and for our numerous friends who used to drop in for meals. I often won prizes at the local shows for my cakes, preserved fruits, and vegetables. I adored my house, and took great pride in keeping it looking spick and span. That's why it hurt so much to be forced to do what I used to love doing, then to be criticized that it wasn't good enough. If only Karl had realised that I would have willingly cooked and cleaned for him, instead of throwing his weight around and enjoying domineering and frightening me.

I liked to keep busy and being involved in community activities. I played bowls, was a CWA member and a regular Meals on Wheels volunteer. Until Karl turned up, I had many wonderful friends who really helped me cope when Sam died. But Karl soon scared them off. If it hadn't been for little Hugo, I don't think I could have kept going.'

Kate sat back and looked out to sea for a moment longer, then turned to face Jessie. 'Now that I have this house, I intend to employ some permanent staff Jessie, to live here whether I am staying here or not. Would you be interested in being my live-in cook/housekeeper here? There are two self-contained flats downstairs in the front garden. You and Hugo could have one, and the driver/maintenance man I intend to employ, would have the other one.'

Giving Jessie time to think over her offer Kate went to the kitchen and made two cups of coffee. Handing a cup to Jessie, Kate sat back in her chair.

'I can cook Jessie, but I don't enjoy it like you obviously do. I eat most things, except curries and baby veal. I love roasts – beef, lamb, pork, poultry, though when I cook for myself, it's mainly steak or lamb chops with vegetables. I will eat salads if someone else prepares them, and the same goes with pasta and seafood.'

Jessie laughed, a sound that was music to Kate's ears. 'You sound just like my Sam. No meal was complete for him without meat! Kate, I would love to work for you in this wonderful house, with that magnificent view to look at every day.'

'Thank you Jessie, that's wonderful news. But you won't be starting for a few days yet; not until you are fully recovered. That goes for you too young Hugo. You are going to be our back up security system! 'Tomorrow I'm meeting a gentleman who has been recommended as a potential driver/maintenance man. If I decide to employ him, I will bring him here to see where he will be working, and also to meet you Jessie. You will have some say in who I employ, as you will both be working and living here, whether I'm staying here or not.'

Jessie gave Kate a questioning look. 'I live and work in Victoria Jessie. I bought this property to escape the colder weather down south!'

The next day Kate met Donald Campbell at one of the local coffee shops, to interview him for the driver/maintenance job.

Donald was of medium height and quite lean, with a tanned face and short dark hair showing a few grey hairs at the temples. He was quietly spoken, and on the resume he handed Kate, she noted that he was 54 years old.

'Having the surname Campbell, my father couldn't resist calling me Donald, especially when I was born when Donald Campbell held both the land and water world speed records!' he joked. As they talked, Donald regularly stroked the ears of a small cream whippet sitting by his side. 'Chloe is my little mate, who goes everywhere with me. Would that be an issue regarding the position we are discussing?'

'I don't see a problem Donald. She appears to be a friendly, well trained little lass. Providing that she and the Jack Russell living at the house get on, she should be fine.'

Donald was a qualified mechanic who had worked for many years in the family garage in Lismore. When his wife died ten years ago, he'd left the garage and become a driver for a large interstate haulage company, then two years ago he moved to Darwin to drive the large livestock road trains. A few weeks ago Donald had decided to use his leave to catch up with his sister in Woolgoolga, but on his arrival he was disappointed to hear that following her husband's death she had left town. Despite this sad news, he had decided to remain in the area to look for a job, so put his name down with the local job agencies.

On completion of the interview Kate closed her folder. 'Let's walk up the lane to the back of my block and I will show you the house, and introduce you to my new housekeeper. Also, we will see how Chloe and Hugo get on.'

When they reached the high metal fence Donald exclaimed in amazement. 'Wow! That's a great lawn. You could run all day in there Chloe. Is this the back yard of the double balconied house overlooking the cliff?'

'Yes, it is. Part of your job will be to keep this lawn mown, and to make sure that the gate and everything else are in working order.' As she turned from shutting the gate, Kate noticed Jessie pegging some washing on the fold down washing lines attached to the side fence near the laundry. 'Let's go down and I will introduce you to Jessie.'

Kate was astonished when Donald turned to her. 'Did you say Jessie?' He looked back towards the house. 'My God it is!' then he ran down to where a startled Jessie looked up, then smiled, and clung to Donald as he hugged her.

Reaching the excited pair Kate smiled. 'I take it that you know this man Jessie!'

'Know him Kate? Donald is my brother!'

Nodding his head, Donald looked at his sister. 'What are you doing here Jess? I was told that you had left town.'

'Why don't you take Donald inside Jessie, and explain what has been going on? I will hang out the rest of the washing, then, if you let Hugo out, I will introduce him to Chloe and they can spend some time together out here with me.'

For the next half hour Kate lay on a sunlounge watching the two dogs. When they first met, they had sniffed noses and circled each other a few times, then both walked together around the boundary of the large yard. Hugo was still adjusting to walking with a straight leg, and Kate was amused to watch Chloe walk more slowly to stay beside him. They both stood for a while, looking through the metal fence as people and cars went past, then came down to lie beside Kate. Occasionally Chloe would get up and go for a quick scamper around on the grass, then return to give Hugo a lick on the nose and lie down beside him again.

Finally, Kate and the dogs walked to the back door and went into the house where Jessie and Donald were sitting chatting on the balcony. 'Would you two like a cup of tea, coffee or a cool drink?' When Jessie started to get up, Kate held up her hand. 'Stay there Jessie, I will get whatever you want.'

Soon Kate, Jessie and Donald were sitting in the lounge chairs drinking tea, with the two dogs lying at their feet. 'Do I take it that you would be happy to work with Donald Jessie?'

'I would really enjoy working here with my younger brother Kate.'

'Only by twenty minutes!' Donald gave Jessie a gentle punch on the arm. 'We always got on well together when we were youngsters, so I don't see why we couldn't work together here, if you employ me Kate.'

'Well, the dogs get on well together too, so consider yourself employed Donald!

There may be times when my friends or relatives come up here for a holiday when I'm not here Jessie, but you won't be required to cook and clean for them. They'll cater for themselves and will be expected to restock the pantry and clean up before they leave. You will just need to deal with the laundry when they depart. I plan to open a debit account with a card for each of you, to use for food, housekeeping, maintenance supplies, fuel, tools etc, and I will expect you both to keep account of your purchases. Talking of purchases, what type of car do you prefer to drive Donald?'

Donald looked mystified. 'You are to be my driver, and I need to buy a car for use when I'm here. Like I prefer someone else to cook for me, I can drive, but will need a driver to ferry me to and from the airport, and to also to share the driving in some long-distance trips that I may need to make from here in the future.'

'Having been a truck driver, I prefer to sit up higher than in the typical sedan Kate. If I was buying a car, I would be interested in looking at the new Rav4 hybrid. It's a small SUV, but has a lot of good features.'

'Great minds think alike Donald. I have an Escape at home, but have been thinking of getting a Rav4. Maybe we should go shopping tomorrow. Actually, where are you living now, and where is your car?'

'I'm staying in a cabin at the caravan park, and my van and boat are parked there.'

'Donald is a mad keen fisherman Kate.'

'Maybe I should add supplying the household with a plentiful supply of fish to your job description Donald! As Jessie doesn't have a car at the moment, you can park your van and boat in the double carport downstairs. Would you like to take Donald down to the flats Jessie, and choose which ones you want to put your gear in?'

When Jessie, Donald and the two dogs went downstairs, Kate lay back in her chair and thought about the events of the past few weeks. She certainly hadn't expected to be involved in such dramatic events, nor to have found a housekeeper and a driver so quickly. Even after such a short time, she felt comfortable to leave Jessie and Donald to look after her property.

The day before Kate was due to fly back to Melbourne, she and Donald went to Coffs Harbour to look at cars. Kate was delighted to discover that the Toyota dealer had just received a new delivery of Rav4s, and quickly arranged to buy the only vehicle not on back order. Arrangements were made for the car to be registered and delivered to the airport the next morning for Donald to collect after he drove Kate to the airport and returned the hire car that Kate had been using during her stay at Woolgoolga.

Kate was sorry to be leaving her new house and acquaintances, but she was also looking forward to being home again after a longer than usual visit up north. Apart from the purchase of her new property, employment of two staff and a new car, the only other outlay that Kate had made on her newfound wealth was travelling business class when flying, and staying in more upmarket accommodation when staying overnight in Melbourne.

CHAPTER 5

———⟨ ✦ ⟩———

MARCH

MELBOURNE

In March, Kate's new company *Windfall Holdings* took control of the administration of a newly completed twenty-floor high building in Spring St, opposite the Treasury Gardens. The front of the ground floor was occupied by a coffee shop, and Gaspare's Italian restaurant, with the swimming pool and fitness centre at the rear. The first five floors were assigned for office space, while the upper fifteen floors were exclusively for accommodation, with a range of two and three bedroomed apartments, plus a four-bedroom penthouse on the twentieth floor, with a roof garden.

Located within a fifteen-minute walk to the centre of the CBD, both the office space and apartments were in great demand, and were already paying their way. The new company offices were on the third floor, while the four apartments on the sixth floor were reserved solely for company staff accommodation. There was an underground car park for residents, with two parking spaces designated for the penthouse.

Kate applied for a transfer to the Metropolitan Ambulance Service, leased her flat in Shepparton and after considerable persuasion from Geoff, she moved into the beautifully furnished, fully serviced penthouse, on the understanding that she would be paying the full rental back to *Windfall Holdings*.

Towards the end of a late March Monday afternoon, Kate was sitting in her office, wondering how much longer she should wait for the late applicant for the PA position that she had advertised, when she heard a soft knock on her door. Walking to the door, she opened it to find a medium height man, with short brown hair standing in front of her. 'Mr Mansfield, I assume?'

'Yes Ms Rayne, I am Scott Mansfield. I'm very sorry that I'm late for my interview. Do you still wish to see me?'

'Come in and be seated Scott. Fortunately, you are the last on my list of interviewees for the day.' Kate turned and led the way into the almost empty office. The man hesitated, glancing down at the small red and white, short haired Border Collie standing by his side. 'Is it alright for George to come in with me?'

'Please come in Scott, and bring George with you.' Looking down at George she noticed a tag on his collar indicating that he was a PTSD service dog. 'What a beautiful dog you are George.' She looked at Scott. 'May I pat him?'

George looked at her, then at Scott. When he nodded his head, George sat down and held out his right paw for Kate to shake. Laughing, Kate shook the offered paw. 'Nice to meet you George,' then she went back to sit behind her desk.

When Scott sat down on the chair facing the desk, Kate noted that he looked very ill at ease, sitting on the edge of his chair, with beads of perspiration forming on his forehead. 'Before we start, would you like a drink Scott? I wouldn't mind a cup of tea myself.'

At first Scott looked a bit unsure, then answered 'A cup of white tea, no sugar would be lovely, thank you Ms Rayne.'

'Great. Why don't you sit over near the window and observe the splendid panorama that I pay an arm and a leg for.' Kate laughed as she moved to a bench, where a kettle and coffee machine sat on a tray. After handing Scott his tea, they both sipped their hot drinks. 'You seem concerned about coming to see me this afternoon Scott. Do you mind telling me why?'

Scott fondled George's head, then looked at Kate. 'This is the fourth interview that I have been instructed to attend today Ms Rayne. The previous three appointments I didn't even get past the introduction. 'No dogs allowed in offices' appeared to be the rule, even for service dogs. I guess it just made it easier for them to reject my application, without actually acknowledging that I have PTSD. I went to the park across the road, and just sat, wondering why I was even bothering. Eventually George calmed me down, and here I am.'

Shocked by this statement, Kate leant forward. 'Scott, both you and George will be most welcome to work in this office if you satisfy the criteria for the advertised position. As George hasn't shown any inclination to bite me he's okay, and you will soon have the chance to prove your suitability!'

From the resume that Scott had enclosed with his application, Kate knew that he had joined the army when he left school, and had gained his Bachelor of Office Management Degree after doing his initial army training. Following his graduation, Scott was assigned to the Army Medical Corps to serve as the adjutant to the Commanding Officer Colonel Peters.

After twelve years in the army, Scott had attained the rank of Captain, and had served on several mercy missions to Asia and the Pacific Islands when the Medical Corps was sent to help, following earthquakes, tsunamis, and typhoons. He had also served in Iraq and Afghanistan. On return from his second tour of Afghanistan two years ago, he was suffering from PSTD and had recently been medically discharged from the army at the age of 30.'

Colonel Peters wrote Scott a glowing reference, commending him on his efficient office management skills, and his commitment to his job. The Colonel had also added that he would be happy to speak further on Scott's behalf, so Kate had rung him two days ago.

Colonel Peters thanked her for calling, and explained that he felt some extra clarification was needed on Scott's situation. 'Captain Scott Mansfield was an exceptional adjutant, with an instinctive sense of office organisation and personnel management, and I feel confident that he will be a real asset to whoever employs him, providing that they are aware of his PSTD, and are prepared to let him work without too much bureaucratic supervision.

Scott was severely wounded when our medical centre in Afghanistan came under fire from a Taliban machine gun, mounted on a small truck. Scott grabbed a medical bag and raced to the aid of four wounded Australian soldiers, who were trying to shelter behind a low mud wall, receiving three bullet wounds to his legs in doing so. He managed to staunch the soldiers' wounds, saving them from bleeding to death, then tended his own injuries. All the time, the wall was being strafed by the machine gun, causing it to begin to disintegrate.

When one of the wounded soldiers handed Scott a grenade, he flung his helmet out onto the street to distract the machine gunner, then threw the grenade at the truck. Being a keen cricketer with a good throwing arm, he managed to land the grenade in the truck where it exploded, destroying the truck and its occupants.

Scott and the wounded soldiers were medivacked back to the base hospital in Kabul, where they were stabilised, then on to a US military hospital in Germany. By the time he returned to Australia, Scott's physical wounds had healed, but he was suffering from severe post-traumatic stress disorder, and spent further time in rehabilitation, before he was medically discharged from the army. The introduction of George into Scott's life has helped him to feel ready to attempt to join the civil workforce. However, finding a suitable job is proving to be quite difficult and depressing.'

With all this in mind, Kate ran the interview informally while sitting in the armchairs near the window, overlooking the gardens across the road. It didn't take long for her to decide that, of the half dozen applicants she had spoken to, Scott was the one most suitable for the job. When she offered him the job and told him the annual salary that he would receive, Scott looked quite astonished, and was even more so when Kate added 'There is also a fully serviced, two bedroomed apartment upstairs Scott, available as part of your remuneration providing that you don't mind living in the same building as your office. And before you ask, George will be most welcome to live in the apartment with you.'

'Thank you, Ms Rayne. I am overwhelmed by your offer, both for the job and the accommodation. I will do my best to justify your faith in me.' As Scott's voice broke on the last word, George stood up and put his paws on Scott's knees, allowing Scott to place his head against the dog while he fought to regain his composure.

'Would you like to have a look at the apartment before you make up your mind Scott?'

'That would be wonderful, thank you Ms Rayne.'

'As we will be sharing this office and working together Scott, I would prefer that you to call me Kate from now on.'

Kate led Scott and George to the lift and exited on the sixth floor, where she unlocked the door to one of four fully furnished apartments on that level, and led Scott into the open spaced lounge room, kitchen, and dining area. There were two good sized bedrooms, one with an ensuite, the other next to the bathroom and toilet, plus a small laundry, with a chute for larger items to be laundered in the basement. The far wall of the lounge room consisted mainly of a large glass feature window, with sliding glass doors opening onto a wide balcony. Scott was pleased to see that it had a higher than normal see-through barrier; safe for George to sit outside with him. The panoramic view looked out across the city towards the bay sparkling in the late afternoon sunshine.

'A housekeeper will come in each day Scott, and there's a pool and a fitness centre on the ground floor for residents to use.'

'I really am lost for words Kate. I am currently staying in a YMCA hostel, as my army veteran's pay doesn't cover the high rents asked for by most landlords these days, especially when they know that I have George.'

'Scott, as it is getting late, would you care to join me for a meal at the restaurant downstairs, then you and George can spend the night in your new apartment? The cupboards are well stocked so you will just have to buy some milk, bread, and butter for the morning. Spend tomorrow collecting your gear and settling in, then be ready to start work on Wednesday at 9.00am. I will let Mrs Nash, the housekeeper, know that you will be moving in tonight, and I will tell her about George living with you. I'm sure she will adore him, as she has two very spoilt dogs of her own.'

Kate was a regular patron at the Italian restaurant on the ground floor of the building, and was greeted warmly by the proprietor Gaspare, who led her and Scott to a reserved table near the window. When she informed Gaspare that George was a service dog, he placed a bowl of fresh water beside Scott's chair. 'Is George allowed to have a small bowl of spaghetti Sir?'

Scott and George were waiting outside the office when Kate arrived at 8.45am on Wednesday. While Scott made a cup of tea for both Kate and himself she looked around the large, rather empty office space, and wondered how best to set it up for Scott, a receptionist and herself to work in.

'Did you and George get settled in okay yesterday Scott?'

Sitting beside her Scott smiled. 'Yes, thank you Kate. Mrs Nash arrived while I was having breakfast, and she was very welcoming. She and George get on well, and I felt quite relaxed leaving him with her while I went to the YMCA hostel to collect my belongings. Everything fitted easily into the taxi you sent, thank you. George and I went for a run in the park this morning, and I feel like a new man, raring to get to work.'

'That's good to hear Scott. How would you feel being put in charge of setting up and organising the office? I began making a list of the equipment that I thought we will need, but as you will soon learn, I'm not an office person. I much prefer to be out and about, meeting people.'

'We should get on well then, as I really enjoy running an office. One of my many duties in the army was to set up the office wherever our unit was based, then to supervise the office staff.' Scott looked around the room. 'Are we permitted to put in partitions Kate?'

'Yes, we can add to, but not knock down existing walls. What do you have in mind?'

'Well, I think your desk, and these armchairs should be separated from the reception area and my workspace, plus the photo copier, printer/scanner and filing cabinets that we will require. To start with, I will work in the front area until you appoint a receptionist/typist, as you mentioned on Monday.'

Kate handed Scott a plastic card. 'Here's a debit card for the office account. You will need this to purchase everything that you think we will need. I have my own laptop, but you must get one for yourself, for when you work away from the office, plus desk top computers for yourself and the receptionist. The rest I will leave up to you.'

Seeing the big grin on Scott's face Kate smiled. 'Just remember, that this doesn't have to be finished today! If at any time you feel you need a break, take George out for a walk, or go back to your apartment to sit on the balcony for a bit.'

'Do you know Kate, this morning I feel better than I have since before my last tour of duty. My head is clear, and I'm really enjoying the sense of having something positive to do, and to plan for.'

'Okay, just don't overdo it. I plan to head up north for a few days to check out a couple of organisations asking to meet me, so could you please contact Qantas to book me a return business class ticket to Coffs Harbour. I will give you the dates, my Frequent Flyer number and bank details when I open up my computer. While I'm away, you will have free range to plan and equip the office to your specifications. Geoff Rowe will deal with the accounts for you.'

CHAPTER 6

LATE MARCH
MELBOURNE

During breakfast the morning after her arrival for meetings near Woolgoolga Kate received a disturbing phone call from Julie, who was so distraught that it took Kate some time to calm her down enough to explain what was wrong. Kate was horrified when she heard that their father was in a critical condition in the Bairnsdale Hospital, suspected of attempted suicide. Julie and their Aunt Margaret were currently waiting for an air ambulance to fly him to the Alfred Hospital in Melbourne.

Luckily, following Julie's frantic phone call, Kate managed to purchase a ticket on a direct flight to Melbourne later that morning. When she arrived at Melbourne Airport Kate rang Julie and discovered that she and Aunt Margaret had just arrived in Melbourne, having been forced to drive the four-hour journey to Melbourne because Velma had insisted that, as Greg's wife, she alone would accompany him on the helicopter flight to Melbourne.

Kate took a taxi straight to the Alfred Hospital, and met her sister and aunt at the front entrance. When they were taken to the Intensive Care Unit waiting room, they found Velma infuriated because she wasn't allowed to be in the ICU with her husband, and she was even more incensed when Kate, Julie and Margaret entered the waiting room. A ward sister who knew Kate from her nursing days saw her in the waiting room and beckoned for her to join her in the corridor. 'What's with that crazy woman in there Kate? Is she a relative of yours? We're getting very close to requesting that Security remove her from the floor.'

'She is a bit overwrought, isn't she? I have only met my step mother once before, and I must say, once was quite enough!'

'The medics on the helicopter said that when she spoke, or tried to hold your father's hand, his pulse rate and blood pressure spiked.'

'Well, they are not what you would call a loving couple, but I can't understand why hearing Velma's voice, or her holding his hand should cause Dad's vital signs to rise. Though, if he was aware of her presence, maybe he isn't as deeply unconscious as we thought.'

'Maybe, maybe not. But remember Kate, he is still critically ill.'

Kate took her aunt and sister to the canteen, and over a coffee she explained that Greg was in a critical condition, as he was suffering from hypothermia, as well as from the drugs in his system. She waited for Julie to calm down before asking 'What happened Jules?'

'I haven't a clue Kate. I went out before breakfast, intending to check some cows and calves, and found Dad unconscious just inside the shed near the tractor. Chief and Bluey were both lying against him, and the doctors think that they may have saved him from dying of hypothermia during the night. But they also said that he appears to have overdosed on sleeping tablets!'

'Dad doesn't use sleeping tablets, does he?'

'Not that I know of Kate, but Velma uses them every night and has a stash in her bedroom. So, I suppose he might have taken some of those.'

While Julie went to the bathroom to freshen up, Margaret looked at Kate. 'I just can't imagine that Greg would ever try to end his life Kate. I understand that things weren't going well out at *Glen Rayne* following Velma's arrival, but suicide? I know it happens, but I just can't believe it of my brother.'

'Julie told me that it was Velma who suggested to the paramedics that Dad might have tried to commit suicide.'

After a long pause Margaret looked at her niece. 'Julie also said that Velma uses sleeping tablets. You don't think she might have put some in his food, then tried to insinuate that Geoff took them voluntarily, do you?'

'Who knows Aunt Meg? Unless Dad recovers, we will never know for sure.'

'Do you think we should warn the staff not to let her near Greg, just in case?'

Kate thought of her friend's comments about Greg's reaction to Velma's presence on the helicopter. 'I guess it's worth thinking about Aunt Meg. Here comes Jules. I'm just going to make a phone call.'

Kate rang a lawyer friend, and told him of the situation, and Margaret's concern. Simon told her that he would look into it, but agreed that nothing could be proved unless Greg recovered and could point the finger at his wife, if needs be.

Determined to keep Velma away from Greg, Kate went to see Sarah Hamilton, the Director of Nursing, who she had trained with, and told her of her growing unease regarding Velma. Sarah had been informed of the commotion in the ICU waiting room, and when Kate told her of her father's reaction to Velma's presence on the flight, she agreed to make sure that the staff continued to forbid Velma from entering the ICU.

That night Kate took Margaret and Julie home to her penthouse, hoping that the revelation of her newfound wealth would alleviate their shock and concern about Greg, who was still seriously ill. When Julie had completed her second tour of the luxurious apartment, she joined Kate and Margaret out on the balcony overlooking the flood lit MCG. 'How in the world can you afford to lease a place like this Kate? Have you hocked your share of *Glen Rayne* or something?'

'More like the 'or something Jules,' Kate laughed. 'A couple of months ago I bought a Tatts ticket, which to my amazement was the winning ticket!'

Margaret and Julie stared at her. 'Don't tell me you've won a million dollars Sis!?'

'A bit more than that actually Jules! I won the entire jackpot, lock stock and barrel! You two are the first to know, other than the Tatts officials and my financial advisor. I haven't told anyone because I have been concerned that when word gets out, I will be besieged by people wanting handouts or more! The new property that I bought at Coffs Harbour is a bit of an unknown bolt hole, I guess.'

Margaret gazed at her niece. 'Do you mind telling us what the actual jackpot was worth Kate?'

'Three hundred million dollars!'

Margaret and Julie sat back in their chairs and stared at Kate in astonishment. Finally Julie gasped 'Holy moly Sis!! You're kidding!'

'I see your dilemma Kate.' Margaret stood up and hugged her niece. 'I am so pleased for you darling. Thank you for trusting us with your astonishing news. I assume that you still want to keep it quiet?'

'If possible, for the time being at least, Aunt Meg. I am still trying to work out what to do with it, yet not let it change my life too much.'

Julie looked around the opulent apartment. 'Surely a posh place like this is a bit of a change for you though, isn't it Sis?'

'I'm trying hard not to get too used to it Jules! Now, what about dinner at the restaurant downstairs, then bed?'

The next morning Kate, Margaret and Julie took a taxi to the hospital where, to their delight, Greg was slowly showing signs of recovering consciousness. One by one, Kate, Julie and Margaret were allowed to spend a short period of time sitting with Greg. While she was holding her brother's hand as she spoke to him, Margaret noticed that Greg was beginning to grip her fingers. Slowly he opened his eyes and whispered 'Thanks for coming Mags. How are my girls?'

When she answered, 'They're fine Greg,' he smiled and shut his eyes again. The nurse on duty quickly checked the equipment attached to him. 'He's sleeping naturally now Ms Rayne, which is a good sign.'

Greg woke up again mid-morning, and once his vital signs had been checked and recorded, Kate and Julie were allowed to sit with him for a short time. Velma was informed that she could go in after lunch.

Chewing her lip, Kate looked at her father. 'Do you feel up to telling us what happened Dad?'

'There's not much to tell Kate. I remember that Velma made my coffee and her hot chocolate before she went to bed, and I went out onto the verandah to watch the moon rise over the lake. I had only taken a few sips of coffee when Chief and Bluey ran up to join me. I thought that you had tied them up for the night Jules, but as you obviously hadn't I walked over to their kennels in the shed. I remember bending over to grab Chief's chain, but that's the last I recall.'

'Did you take your coffee with you to the shed Dad?'

Greg looked puzzled. 'Yes, I had a couple more mouthfuls while I was walking. Why Kate?'

'Nothing for you to bother about Dad. I was just wondering where to look for your mug. You know how Velma hates having anything missing from the kitchen!'

While Julie remained with their father, Kate went outside and rang Simon. When she repeated what Greg had told them, he rang the police, who immediately contacted the Omeo Police Station and asked them to send someone out to *Glen Rayne* as quickly as possible to look for a coffee mug near or in the tractor shed. Within half an hour, the broken coffee mug had been found lying under the tractor near the shed door and was immediately dispatched to the Bairnsdale Hospital to have the dregs in the bottom of the mug analysed.

When Velma arrived back at the hospital after lunch, demanding to see her husband, she was met by two policemen who escorted her from the hospital and transported her to the nearest police station, where she was to be questioned about her husband's suspected suicide.

CHAPTER 7

LATE MARCH

HINNOMUNJIE

Senior Constable Dale Hopkins, an off-duty country policeman visiting his hospitalized colleague, recognised Velma as she was being escorted from the hospital. He showed his police identification card to the receptionist at the front desk and asked 'Who was that woman being escorted outside?'

'Mrs Rayne. Her husband is a suspected overdose in ICU. She has been creating such a fuss up in ICU she has been removed.'

Dale didn't recognise the name, but he remembered Velma's face. He had been stationed at Halls Gap three years ago, when grazier Neil Naughton fell to his death when he and his wife were visiting Halls Gap. She claimed that he had slipped and fallen down the cliff, although his landing point away from the cliff base indicated that he had either been pushed or had jumped.

With no witness to contradict her story, Velma Naughton wasn't charged with any crime, even when it came to light that she and Neil had only recently been married, and Neil's will had been changed just before their arrival in Halls Gap. Despite strong opposition from his children, Velma became the sole owner of Neil's extensive property near Wangaratta, and her son had taken over as manager.

Quickly Dale caught a taxi and followed the police car to the St Kilda Police Station, where he introduced himself to the desk sergeant, and explained why he was there. Soon after, he was sitting in the Superintendent's office explaining his previous contact with the lady calling herself Velma Rayne, who had just been brought to the police station.

While Velma was held in custody awaiting questioning, two detectives from Bairnsdale were sent out to *Glen Rayne* to search the homestead, especially Velma's room. On their arrival, they parked next to the Omeo Police squad car near the garage at the back of the house. After introducing themselves to the constable, who had been instructed to remain at the house, the two detectives quickly checked each room, then spent time thoroughly searching Velma's bedroom, bathroom, and the kitchen.

They bagged up a considerable quantity of sleeping tablets and other medications, and also found a laptop and briefcase in the bedroom wardrobe. Amongst the contents of the brief case were two plastic folders. One contained Velma and Neil Naughton's marriage certificate, Neil's death certificate and his will. There was also the title for a large rural property near Wangaratta, and details of a bank account in her name, containing more than five hundred thousand dollars. The other folder contained a birth certificate in the name of Christopher Durie, declaring his parents to be Velma Isobel Durie and Gregory Rayne, Velma and Greg Rayne's marriage certificate, and a copy of Greg's will, leaving his share of *Glen Rayne* and the contents of his bank account to his wife Velma.

There was also a two-year-old cutting from an agricultural magazine, featuring the *Glen Rayne* Hereford Stud with two photos, one of a youthful Greg with his school rowing crew, and a more recent one of him standing beside one of his prize-winning Hereford bulls at the Royal Melbourne Show.

When they opened Velma's laptop, the detectives were surprised that there wasn't a password and they were able to gain access to all of her emails and documents. While his partner continued to search the house, Inspector Hogan began to scan the emails, and quickly found a file of emails from Velma to her son Chris Durie. Velma's most recent message to her son read, 'Greg is getting harder to manage since I made him change his will. I think we will have to proceed sooner than planned. Any bright ideas Chris?' Chris had replied 'Farm accidents are commonplace Mum. Suicide is another option. Just stay away from high cliffs this time!!!'

'Wow! Max, come and look at this.'

As his partner read the email he whistled. 'We need to get this back to Melbourne as quickly as possible. I notice that her emails date back a number of years. I wonder if there's any reference to her previous husband's death.'

Inspector Hogan rang his superior at Bairnsdale and read the email and reply to her. 'Can you copy all of the emails to her son onto a USB James? If not, take some photos of that email and reply, just in case her son erases the emails before he is apprehended. Leave the Omeo lads to tape off the house, arrange a twenty-four-hour watch and advise them to detain anyone who tries to enter the house, especially her son. You and Max head straight back here, and I will see if a helicopter can meet you at the airport. The sooner the IT experts look at that laptop, the better.'

James and Max had just finished loading everything into their car when they heard the dogs bark, then the sound of a car slowly driving up the road towards the homestead. Gesturing to Max and the constable to be quiet, James peered around the corner of the house and watched a sturdy, dark haired man step from the grey car parked beside the front steps, stretch his arms above his head, look around, then walk up to the front door.

James quietly instructed the constable to wait near the front door to stop the man if he tried to escape. Beckoning to Max to follow him, they quietly entered the back door just as the man disappeared into Velma's bedroom. He was about to open the wardrobe when James entered the bedroom 'Can I help you sir?'

The man whirled around, his right hand moving towards his trouser pocket as James leapt forward and grabbed his arm. Both men crashed against the wardrobe, and James managed to twist the man's

42

right arm behind his back whilst pushing his head hard up against the mirror on the door.

Max entered the room, and swiftly handcuffed the man's wrists behind his back. He then pulled on his disposable gloves and gingerly removed a small handgun from the man's pocket, and a mobile phone from the other. He looked closely at the weapon, then unloaded it before placing the phone and gun into separate plastic specimen bags. 'Not the safest place to carry a loaded gun mate! Do you have a licence for this nasty little firearm?' The man just scowled at him, saying nothing.

James turned the angry man to face him. 'So, who might you be sir?'

The man glared at James. 'I could ask you the same thing! This is my mother's house, and you are trespassing. I'm going to report you for assault, and illegal entry.'

'Oh, so you must be Christopher Durie. I am Inspector Hogan and this is Sergeant Smith.' The two men showed their badges. 'Why are you here?'

'I have come to visit my mother.'

James laughed. 'What, did you expect to find her in the wardrobe? Come on buddy, don't put yourself deeper into the hot water you're already in.'

Angrily Chris stared at the policemen. 'My mother is in Melbourne with my father, who is in a critical condition in hospital. She rang to ask me to collect her some clean clothes.'

'Okay, let's pack a bag for her, and we will take you to Melbourne to be with her.'

'How can I pack with these f****** cuffs on?'

'Sorry mate. They have to stay on, because I'm arresting you for carrying an illegal weapon, and for attempting to draw it on Inspector Hogan.'

Finally the unmarked police car drove out through the gates of *Glen Rayne* and headed for Bairnsdale, the handcuffed passenger strapped into the backseat, with Max sitting beside him. James contacted Chief Inspector Graham to inform her that they had arrested Velma's son, and also had some interesting messages on his phone to show her.

On arrival at the Bairnsdale airport, they were met by Chief Inspector Graham, who informed them that the police helicopter was only a few minutes away. By the time it arrived, she had read some of the messages on Chris's phone, and was particularly interested in a voicemail left earlier that morning.

"Chris, where the hell are you? Greg is still hanging on, and they won't let me near him. I'm not sure if they suspect something, but I'm getting really concerned. You must drive to *Glen Rayne* immediately, and remove the laptop and briefcase from my wardrobe, plus any medication you can find, especially the sleeping tablets. I don't want anything left there that can possibly incriminate us, whether he dies or not!"

The police interviewed Greg when he was deemed well enough, and he tried to explain how Velma had managed to have such control of him. Becoming quite distressed, Greg told them that he had left a letter with his solicitor Jack Snellings, to be opened on his death, as he had come to fear for his life soon after he married Velma. He had signed a letter to Jack, authorising the police to collect the letter, swab, and hair sample from his safe.

> *My darling Jules,*
>
> *When you read this, I fear that I will be dead. I need to write this down, to try to provide you with some understanding of why I have treated you in such a shameful way over the past months, and the reason why I allowed Velma to upset our lives.*
>
> *When I first met Velma, I was a naïve sixteen-year-old country boy at Scotch College in Melbourne. Three friends and I were at an end of year celebration at a city nightclub, following our final exams, and after a few drinks I'm afraid I was easy prey for the likes of Velma.*
>
> *Before I understood what was happening, I found myself alone in a backroom with her and she had stripped off all*

*my clothes. Before long, Velma and I were both on a bed,
and I am afraid to say that my first sexual encounter was an
embarrassing, painful, and totally futile event. Velma was
most disparaging, dressed and left immediately, and that was
the last I saw or heard of her, until we met again a couple
of months ago.*

*At first I didn't recognise her, though she obviously knew
who I was, and we spent a couple of days and nights together.
It wasn't until she commented on the improvement of my
performance, that I realised who she was!*

*Velma claims that she became pregnant from our first
encounter, and has a son who she insists, as my first-born
child, should have the right to claim Glen Rayne as his
inheritance! Remembering my humiliating performance on
the night in question, I just laughed at her and came home!*

*I had no idea she would turn up like she did, and I
am truly sorry I let her treat you so appallingly. The night
she arrived, she showed me her son's birth certificate, with
my name as father, and she threatened to have me charged
with rape, and refusal to recognise my son, plus to sue me
for unpaid child support during his first eighteen years, if I
didn't marry her. It was blackmail, pure and simple, but I
was so shocked, that I'm afraid I lost the plot for a while.
The thought of the damage a rape charge, no matter how
false, would do to my standing in the community and worse
still, to our stud's name, made me give in to her demands.*

*However, after our marriage at a registry office in Sale,
when Velma demanded that we meet with her solicitor to
rewrite my will to make her my sole beneficiary, I began to
seriously worry about my future, and how my demise would
affect you.*

*Velma doesn't know that when you and I went to the
sale in Bairnsdale, I met with my solicitor Jack Snellings,
and wrote a new will, making you and Kate my only*

beneficiaries, and you Julie, the sole owner of the Glen Rayne Hereford Stud.

As my wife, Velma is legally a partner in Glen Rayne, but she can't easily sell her half share of the property if I die, because my share is left to you two girls. She isn't entitled to any share of stud cattle sales, and unless she's prepared to pay the considerable cost of having Glen Rayne resurveyed, to reallocate her half, and to restock that area, I can't see her staying around for long!

However Jules if her 'son' arrives to claim anything, demand an immediate DNA test, and speak to Jack Snellings. I have left a cheek swab and some hair in his safe. Also, be aware because Velma is dangerous, and could be a threat to you too.

Well my love, I'm very proud of you, and am happy to know that Glen Rayne will be safe, left in your capable hands.

All my love to you and Kate

Your loving father
Gregory Rayne

When the police read Greg's letter, Chris Durie's DNA was tested, and the results totally exonerated Greg of his parentage, and further examination of Chris's birth certificate showed it to be a forged document. The police interviewed one of Greg's schoolmates who had been at the club on the night in question, and he informed them he knew of at least two boys who had been with Velma that night.

The information downloaded from Velma's computer, and her son's mobile phone was a real revelation. Not only was Velma's attempt to murder Greg, and her son's involvement in her plans confirmed, but there was further information that implicated both mother and son in the murder of Neil Naughton. Velma and Chris were both remanded in custody, and were awaiting trial, Velma on charges of murder and attempted murder, and Chris on being an accessory to murder and attempted murder.

CHAPTER 8

EARLY APRIL

MELBOURNE

Three days after being flown to Melbourne, Greg recovered enough to be moved from ICU to a private room, then two days later he was released from hospital, on the proviso that he stayed with Kate for at least a week, before returning to *Glen Rayne*.

Julie and Margaret returned to East Gippsland when Greg was moved to the private room, both keen to relieve their neighbours, who had been feeding the cattle and keeping an eye on *Glen Rayne,* and on Margaret's parents in their absence.

Although Greg missed *Glen Rayne* and his cattle, he knew that he would be more of a hindrance than help to Julie until he regained his strength, so he happily accepted Kate's offer to look after him until he felt fitter. He was delighted to be spending some time alone with his elder daughter as, since Kate had left Hinnomunjie in her early teens to live in Melbourne, they had seen little of each other, except for brief holidays, and he was hoping to rekindle the rapport that they had experienced before she left *Glen Rayne*.

When Greg first entered the penthouse he just stood and stared, then turned to Kate with a quizzical expression on his face. 'You don't really live here, do you lass?'

Kate hugged her father. 'Yes, I do Dad. Let's go out onto the balcony, and I will explain everything that has been happening in my world this year.'

Half an hour later, Kate went into the kitchen to brew some coffee, while Greg sat staring out over the city to Port Phillip Bay, slowly digesting the fact that his elder daughter was now an extremely wealthy lady, and was the CEO of a company devised to aid not for-profit charities. He was proud to think that she was keen to share her wealth, and not squander it on gratuitous commodities.

While Kate was occupied with her father in hospital, and her aunt and sister had been staying with her, she hadn't been near the office, other than to ask Scott to recruit a receptionist. So, the morning after Greg moved to her apartment, Kate took him down to her new office and introduced him to Scott and George, and Scott introduced them both to the new receptionist.

Belinda Turner was a young woman who had been an army administration assistant for most of her career. Scott's and her paths had crossed several times over the years, and their last meeting had been at an RSL dinner on the previous ANZAC day, where Belinda told Scott that she had left the army to care for her aged mother, until she died earlier in the year. When Kate asked him to find a receptionist, Scott had thought of Belinda and rang her to see if she would be interested in the job.

Kate was amazed at the transformation of the large empty office area that she had left nearly a month ago. Her desk now occupied a smaller, more welcoming area, with the two comfy chairs still in front of the big feature window. A smaller office to the side had been created for Scott, with a door opening into Kate's office, and also one into the reception area. Both Scott and Belinda had a desktop computer, with double screens and a printer on their desks. Kate was pleased to see a fleece dog bed and water bowl beside Scott's desk. An enclosed area to the side of the receptionist's desk was set aside for the photocopier, scanner, filing cabinets and office supplies.

The office next door had been established for Geoff Rowe, now the company financial officer. Kate had informed Geoff that she was happy for him to have private clients until *Windfall Holdings* was fully functional.

When Scott took Greg downstairs to show him the swimming pool and fitness centre, Kate went to the area to the side of the reception area, where a sink and bench was set up with a kettle, coffee machine, a small bar fridge and shelves for cups and mugs. 'Would you like a hot drink Belinda – Coffee, tea or Milo?'

'White tea, no sugar please Ms Rayne, although I should be getting your drink.'

'Rubbish!' Kate carried the mugs through into her office. 'Come in, sit down and relax while the men are downstairs.'

Belinda sat down in the chair next to Kate and sipped her tea. 'I don't know how much Scott has told you about *Windfall Holdings* Belinda, but I think that you will find working here somewhat different to the regimentation you would have been used to in the army. You and Scott are both experienced in your roles, and as you will soon realise, I don't have conventional management skills. I would prefer the three of us to work as a team, utilising our strengths to enhance those of the others. Now, to start with Belinda, please call me Kate. When I hear Ms Rayne, I think you're referring to my Aunt Margaret.'

'Thank you, Kate. Scott has only told me that you founded *Windfall Holdings* earlier this year. Your unconventional management style certainly appears to be working wonders for him. I haven't seen him show such joie de vivre for years. Between you and George, I think he's beginning to overcome his PTSD.'

'I would like to think so Belinda, but we both need to make sure that he doesn't push himself too far, too quickly. A little R & R every so often should help. Now, tell me a little about yourself.'

'When I left school my parents enrolled me in a secretarial course, then I worked in my father's office until he retired five years later. When my parents moved to the Gold Coast I joined the army, where I became an administration assistant. We all underwent basic army training, and occasionally were sent out to 'play soldiers', but I was never posted overseas.

My mother's health deteriorated a few years ago, and my father became her primary carer. Last year, not long after my thirty first birthday, my father suddenly died, so I left the army and went up to look after Mum, who in turn died early this year. Since then, I have been getting temp jobs wherever one was available. I couldn't believe it when Scott asked me if I would like to work full time for you.'

'Where do you live now Belinda?'

'When Mum died, my brother and sister, who both live in Western Australia, came over for the funeral and insisted that our parents' house had to be sold. Due to the mortgage that my father had taken out to pay for Mum's medical care, there wasn't much left to be divided between the three of us. I came down to Melbourne to stay with a friend, until I rented a small flat in Bundoora, near to where I was working at the time. Now I have this job, I will need to look for something a bit closer.'

'Has Scott told you about his apartment?'

'Yes, he has. In fact, I slept in his spare room last night after we worked late, cleaning up after the builders and painters had packed up. Scott wouldn't allow me to travel back to Bundoora by myself, so late at night.'

'Very sensible. There is a similar apartment on the same floor as Greg's, if you would like it Belinda.'

Belinda stared at Kate. 'I would love to live upstairs Kate, but at the moment, I couldn't afford the rent.'

'Sorry, I should have added that the apartments on the sixth floor are reserved for our company employees, rent free.'

Tears suddenly started to run down Belinda's cheeks and Kate handed her the tissue box from the side table. 'I'm sorry, this is all just too good to be true.'

Kate stood up and went to her desk, where she took a set of keys from the top drawer and handed them to Belinda. 'Why don't you go up to the sixth floor and have a look at number three. It is a serviced apartment Belinda; Mrs Nash the housekeeper will come in once a day.'

When Belinda left the office, Kate washed the mugs then sat

down, and looked out of the window until Scott and her father returned. 'I have just offered Belinda the apartment next to yours Scott. She's a bit overwhelmed, so why don't you and George go up and welcome her to her new apartment. Tell her that you have my permission to hire a small removal truck tomorrow, to collect her possessions.'

She turned to Greg who was watching her. 'Dad, do you feel well enough to fly up to Coffs Harbour, to spend some time at my house at Woolgoolga?'

'I would love to Kate. I feel stronger every hour. City living, even in a penthouse, isn't really my thing!'

'Great. Scott, before you go up to Belinda's flat, could you please book two return tickets to Coffs for the day after tomorrow, to return a week later? Dad and I will look after George while you help Belinda tomorrow.'

Kate and Greg went back up to the penthouse and took their pre-dinner drinks out on the balcony. 'You really enjoy helping people, don't you Kate?'

'Yes, I do Dad. Having the means to help a lot more is wonderful. The hardest thing is trying to decide who would benefit most.'

'You remind me so much of your dear mother now that you are older Kate; both in looks and deeds.'

CHAPTER 9

EARLY APRIL

WOOLGOOLGA

Sitting at the front of the Qantas plane in the wider, more comfortable seat, with his legs stretched out in front of him, Greg sighed and looked at his daughter, who was seated beside him. 'I could get used to this luxury you know Kate.'

'I know what you mean Dad. I am trying hard not to let my values change too much, but travelling business or first class is one thing that I am becoming very used to, and I would hate to go back to sitting in economy again! Remember Dad, whenever you are travelling from now on, I will happily upgrade your ticket. You know, helping people and all that!!'

On arrival at the Coffs Harbour Airport, Kate and Greg were met by Donald who, after being introduced to Greg, collected their luggage, then drove them to Woolgoolga. Greg was fascinated by the shape of the hills, some still displaying small banana farms, unlike in earlier years, when the hills were covered by banana plantations. Blueberry and raspberry farms now seemed to be more common. The semi tropical vegetation along the side of the highway intrigued Greg, used as he was to the alpine vegetation of home.

As they neared Woolgoolga, Kate pointed out the white Sikh

Temple on the hill in front of them. She explained that there was a large Indian population in Woolgoolga, as well as it being a popular tourist destination, especially when the whales were migrating north, then travelling back to the Southern Ocean after calving.

By the time they arrived at the house, Greg was feeling quite fatigued, so after a quick introduction to Jessie and the two dogs, Kate showed him to his room, and left him to sleep for the rest of the afternoon.

While Jessie and Donald knew that Kate was a wealthy woman, they had no idea, nor wished to know, where her wealth came from. They were thoroughly enjoying being employed together and took great care of her property. Jessie had re-joined some of her previous social and community groups, and was delighting in reconnecting with her old friends, especially Elizabeth. Donald soon made friends with fellow fishermen, and after seeking Kate's permission, he joined the local SES.

The day after their arrival, Donald took Greg out for a short trip out in the bay in his 5.5m boat, and Kate was surprised how enthusiastic her father was to go out fishing with Donald the next morning. Kate had rarely seen her father fishing, and then only from the side of the *Glen Rayne* lake.

When the two men arrived back mid-morning, Greg was tired but thrilled to have caught a number of fish, and told Kate that he couldn't wait to go out again the next morning. That evening, following an entrée of fresh oysters and prawns, everyone enjoyed a delicious meal of grilled schnapper and salad.

After dinner, while Donald attended an SES meeting and Jessie went over to visit Elizabeth, Kate and Greg sat out on the balcony, enjoying the balmy evening. 'This is a beautiful place Kate. I never thought I would find anywhere to compare with *Glen Rayne,* but by golly, this comes awfully close!'

'It is rather special, isn't it?' Don't forget Dad, you, Jules, and Aunt Meg are welcome to come up to stay here any time you want to, whether I'm here or not. Jessie and Donald would love to look after you.'

'You were lucky to come across them. They're friendly people.'

Greg sat looking at the lights around the bay for a while. 'How are you getting on with your plans to distribute your money Kate?'

'Slowly Dad. It's becoming quite frustrating actually. Every time I think I have made up my mind, something else comes up.'

'Don't be in too much of a hurry. Stick to the groups that you originally thought of. There will be exceptions I'm sure, but don't feel compelled to help everyone who asks, or looks needy.'

'I know, but after what you and Scott have gone through, I think I will add Air Ambulance Victoria, Suicide Prevention Australia and Fearless-PTSD Australia New Zealand to the list.'

'Very commendable lass. Are you thinking of one-off donations, or smaller annual amounts?'

'Geoff and I agree that smaller annual amounts would be better, especially if the money can be put towards a specific project. For example, paying for the training of maybe half a dozen service dogs a year. That way, the money invested in *Windfall Holdings* will increase, meaning the endowments will continue for longer.'

'Talking about endowments Kate, your planned handouts to the family are way beyond generous. I know that you can afford it, and those of us who know of your win are just thrilled for you, but none of us expect you to give us anything.'

'I don't want to keep it all for myself Dad. But I have been advised not to make the amounts too large, which could adversely affect people's lifestyles and tax obligations.'

'Well, my lifestyle is going to change from now on. I am going to employ a couple of farm hands to take the pressure off Jules and myself, and maybe a housekeeper as well.'

Kate lifted an eyebrow. 'Don't look at me like that Kate! Maybe I should employ a married couple, and build them a cottage nearby!'

'Have you mentioned these plans to Jules?'

'Yes, I have. She agrees, and has asked me to try to employ her a future husband!'

'That means you would have time to come up here every so often, to go fishing with Donald!'

After breakfast the next morning Greg sat out on the balcony attempting to complete a newspaper crossword, absentmindedly stroking Chloe's head. When she moved her head, he glanced down and thought about the dogs that he'd had at home on *Glen Rayne* over the years.

His father, Phillip Rayne, had always insisted that their dogs were purely for cattle work, and would be ruined if Greg treated them as pets, so dogs had never been allowed in the house. Greg realised now that he had continued that doctrine with his daughters, but now he was beginning to wonder how right that had been.

He enjoyed having Hugo and Chloe for company when he sat as he was now, or when he went for walks along the beach. He always had dogs with him when he was out working, but he rarely handled them. Yet it seems that he owed his life to Chief and Bluey, who had remained close to him all night to keep him warm.

Hugo accompanied them in the boat, when he and Donald went out fishing each morning, and was perfectly behaved, even when a fish flapped in front of him. Greg commented on this to Donald. 'Kate told me that you are well known for your dog training skills Greg. You train them to be good cattle dogs, but I will bet, to begin with, you teach them basic obedience, to come, stay, sit etc before you teach them more complicated skills.

The same goes for any dog, large, small, pet or working dog. They enjoy learning and pleasing their trainer. Hugo wants to be with me, so he quickly learnt the behaviour that I expect when he is with me in the boat. I will bet that those dogs of yours at *Glen Rayne* would remain good workers, even if they spent some time inside with you, like Hugo does here.'

'It certainly gives me food for thought.' Greg grinned. Just then his phone rang. 'It's Julie.'

'I will leave you to it mate.'

Greg pushed receive on his phone. 'Hello love, how are things on the ranch!'

'Just fine Dad. How's the seasickness?'

'I don't get seasick – I'm always too busy reeling in fish!'

'Great to hear. Now, seriously, everything is fine here. Tony's nephew has been looking after *Glen Rayne* while we were away. He seems to be a pleasant, competent bloke Dad, and from what I saw when we went out this morning, he's done a great job. I thought about what we spoke of before I came home, so I hope you don't mind; I have offered him a job.'

That's wonderful news Jules. We both need to cut back our workloads a bit. Is he tall, dark and handsome?'

Julie laughed. 'Not particularly, but his horse is!!'

'I assume that he .., Never mind. What's his name?'

'Tom Marsden.'

'Oh, Tony's sister Glenys's son. I remember when he used to visit next door for school holidays. Nice lad.'

'What do you assume Dad?'

'That he's staying in the workman's cottage, and you've moved back into the house!

'Yes Dad! Though I have told him that he can eat his meals with us. Have you any idea when you are likely to be home?'

'Why? Are you planning a little 'while the cat's away, the mice will play!?'

'Julie laughed. 'I think it's time you came home. The sun is really starting to affect you!'

'I will be home within the week love. If we are going to have a sale before Christmas, we need to get our heads together sooner rather than later. See you soon.'

'Love you Dad.'

Putting his phone down on the coffee table Greg sat back and thought '*Tom Marsden eh? He must be about thirty now.*'

When Kate came home, Greg told her of his phone call from her sister. 'I vaguely remember Tom. He often spent his school holidays with Tony and Jill, and we met a few times when I was home. He's a bit younger than me, but older than Jules, I think.'

'Yes, I think you're right.' Greg stretched in his chair. 'This has been the most wonderful break, but I think I should head home soon.'

'To chaperone Jules and Tom?'

'Maybe! No really, there's a fair amount of stud work that needs working on. I have also decided to start looking for a boat like Donald's to moor at Lakes Entrance. I really enjoy fishing, and the Gippsland Lakes are a great place to fish, plus there are also the Tambo and Nicholson Rivers nearby.'

'You could take Aunt Meg to bait up for you!'

'Not on your nelly! Mags would be too busy reeling in her own fish to bother helping me. She's become a keen wharf fisherman – fisherwoman? – herself, since she discovered Dad's rods in their garden shed.'

'Ok, I will see if there are a couple of seats available on a flight to Melbourne tomorrow afternoon. We will stay overnight in Melbourne, and drive home the day after if you like. I will spend a couple of days with you and Jules, then I will need to get back to work.'

'Kate, I have been thinking about our stud bull sale later in the year. I need to run this past Jules, but I have been thinking that if the sale goes well, I will make a sizable donation to Beyond Blue, and the Black Dog Institute.'

'What a wonderful idea Dad.'

'Oh, I'm full of ideas these days Kate. It's amazing what you think of while waiting for those little fishes to bite!'

CHAPTER 10

———— ⟫⟨ ————

EARLY APRIL

HINNOMUNJIE

Julie and Margaret left Melbourne to drive home after they had said goodbye to Greg on his discharge from the ICU. Both women were keen to get home after their sudden, unplanned departure from their homes. On the drive home they discussed Kate's bombshell revelation about her colossal win, and her disclosure of the monitory handouts that she proposed to give them.

'Far too generous, if you ask me Jules. I couldn't spend what she's given me if I live to be one hundred. I like my current lifestyle and don't plan to change too much.'

'Me too Aunt Meg. Well, maybe I will change a few things. Dad and I have discussed employing some workers and maybe a housekeeper, so I might have more time to visit other stud farms, and maybe even travel to Herefordshire in England, where the Hereford cattle originated.'

After dropping Margaret off at Lakes Entrance, Julie continued on to Bairnsdale, where she stopped to do a big grocery shop, then finally drove through the front gate of *Glen Rayne*. The first thing she did, after she had withstood the ecstatic greeting from Chief and Bluey, was to cheerfully go through the house, and stuff all of

Velma's belongings into the black rubbish bags that she had bought in Bairnsdale, and then dump them out on the verandah! Feeling truly vindicated, she ate some toast and drank a cup of tea, then happily retired to bed back in her own bedroom.

The next morning, while Julie was cooking breakfast, she heard the dogs bark and a vehicle drive into the yard. Looking through the kitchen window, Jules saw a tall man in moleskins and a bluey coat walk over to let Chief and Bluey off their chains. Quickly she took the pan off the stove, grabbed her coat and boots, and hurried outside. Before she could speak, the man looked up. 'Hi, you must be Julie. Don't worry, I'm staying with your neighbours Tony and Jill, and have been coming over here each day to keep an eye on your place. Jill thought that you might be home later today, so I just came over to feed the dogs and let them off for a run.'

By this time Julie had put on her boots and coat and stopped in front of the man. 'Yes, I'm Julie Rayne. And you are?'

'Oh sorry, I'm Tom Marsden.'

'I arrived home last night, and I'm just cooking some breakfast. Would you care to join me, and tell me what's been going on while I have been away?'

'Sure, that would be great, thank you. By the way, we are all delighted to hear that your father is recovering.'

As they stepped onto the verandah Tom cocked an eyebrow and chuckled. 'I see that you have already been doing a bit of spring cleaning.'

'Yes, I have been reclaiming my home!'

'Tony is my uncle, and I was visiting them when your father was taken to hospital. Your neighbours were planning to make up a roster to look after *Glen Rayne* while you were away, but I told them that I would be happy to come over here each day. I have been employed on cattle properties since I left school, and am quite capable of working cattle on my own.'

'Thank you, Tom. It was a great relief to know that our cattle were being looked after during our rather traumatic time in Melbourne. Was everything okay?'

'Sure, there weren't any problems. I hope you don't mind, but I left my stock horse here, so that I could ride around the cattle. I much prefer to use a horse where possible, rather than the universal quad bike.'

Julie sat down to eat the cooked breakfast that she had placed on the table for Tom and herself. 'My sentiments exactly. The quad and ute are handy when you have to go a fair way in a short time, or when you have a lot of equipment or tools to carry, but the cattle remain much calmer when you are on horseback.'

'Would you like me to come around with you today, to explain what I have been doing, and to show you where the various mobs are at the moment?'

Julie looked at the broad-shouldered, friendly man sitting at her table and thought that it would be nice to have company today. 'That would be a good idea, thanks Tom.'

As they walked out to the horse paddock, Julie was interested to watch the rapport that Tom had with Greg's and her two Blue Heeler dogs Chief and Bluey. Both were excellent, reliable cattle dogs, but they were working dogs, not family pets. Yet here they were, both jumping around Tom, seeking his attention.

Tom noticed Julie's frown at the dogs' behaviour. 'I'm sorry, I love dogs and they seem to respond well to me. Tony warned me to be careful with these two, but a few minutes after I met them, they both just sat and waited for a pat.'

'I like dogs too, but we have never had anything other than working dogs on the place. Dad has always been responsible for their training, and ensured that they weren't treated as pets.'

When they reached the paddock gate, a magnificent black gelding trotted over and stretched his neck over the gate so that Tom could scratch his ears. 'Meet Cole, Julie. That's C.O.L.E, meaning coal black.'

Julie held out her hand for Cole to sniff. 'Hello Cole, you are a beautiful lad.'

Julie's grey mare Misty, and Larry, Greg's roan stock horse both came up to share the attention. 'These two seem to be quite happy to have Cole in their paddock. I must say, it will be great to be back on Misty again.'

'Does Larry need to be ridden while your father is away Kate?'

'He should be Tom, but he can be a bit of a handful for anyone other than Dad.'

'Would you like me to take him out today while you are on Misty. I'm sure that Cole won't mind a bit of time off today.'

'That would be great, if you are happy to put up with some fireworks for a while.'

Ten minutes later, both horses were saddled and led out of the paddock. Julie watched as Tom stood beside Larry, talking quietly to him as he fondled his head. Gathering up the reins, Tom placed his left foot in the stirrup and slowly lifted himself up and swung his right leg over Larry's back and sat gently down in the saddle. Larry twitched his ears a couple of times, but made no further movement until Tom gave him a slight squeeze with his legs. Delighted to see Tom's quiet handling of her father's often feisty horse, Julie swung herself onto her saddle, and nudged Misty forward to walk beside Larry.

'I have been checking the stud cows and bulls each day and making sure that the troughs and fences for each paddock are okay. I moved each group when I felt they needed a fresh paddock. The store cattle up in the hills have been regularly moved and I was planning to head further out today.'

Throughout the morning Julie and Tom rode through the various mobs of cattle, checking the animals, their water and feed supply. 'I must say, you have some beautiful cattle Julie. Your young bulls are certainly going to draw a crowd when you sell them.'

'I hope so. We are hoping to have a bull sale later in the year, but I'm not sure that Dad will be up to the work required to help get everything ready.'

As they began to ride back to the homestead Julie turned to Tom. 'How long are you staying with Tony and Jill, Tom?'

'Maybe a couple more weeks. I came up here between jobs, so I will have to start looking for a new place to work pretty soon.'

Julie thought about the conversation that she had had with Greg before driving home, about possibly employing some farm hands. Now, thanks to Kate, they had more financial security, and could afford to employ a couple of workers and take the constant pressure off her father and herself.

'Would you like to work here full time Tom? Dad and I both agree that we should employ a worker or two.'

'Would I ever! While I have been helping out here during the past few days, I have often thought how much I would love to work here on a permanent basis.'

Julie laughed. 'You don't know what sort of employers Dad and I will turn out to be.'

'I have worked for a few different employers Julie. I don't think I would have too much to worry about here.'

'Great, then consider yourself to be a full time *Glen Rayne* employee Tom Marsden.' Julie shook his hand. 'There is a workman's cottage near the shed that you can move into when you're ready. There are basic cooking facilities, but you're welcome to have meals at the house.'

'Thank you. I assume that Cole can stay, but can I also bring Brodie my Border Collie? She's a great little cattle dog, and I'm sure that she would get on with Chief and Bluey.'

'Sure, that would be fine. Why don't you go back to Tony's to collect your gear after lunch, and I will look up some bedding for you?'

CHAPTER 11

———⟫●⟨———

APRIL

HINNOMUNJIE

K ate and Greg arrived back in Melbourne late in the afternoon and were joined in the lift by Scott, Belinda, and George, who had just finished work for the day.

'Would you two like to come up for a drink in half an hour?'

Scott looked at Belinda who nodded. 'Thanks Kate, that would be great. See you in half an hour.'

'You are very casual with your staff Kate. Aren't you worried that they will take advantage of your informal authority?'

'I want them to feel part of a close-knit team Dad. If anyone doesn't pull their weight, I will deal with it, but I think the people that I have employed so far will give their all.'

Soon everyone was sitting in the penthouse lounge with a glass of wine or a beer. 'You are certainly looking much better Greg.'

'I'm feeling much better thanks Scott. I don't think I have ever spent such a laidback week in my life.'

'Dad has become an avid fisherman Scott. His Herefords might soon be taking second place! How have things been going here?'

'Belinda and I have finally managed to get everything organised in the office Kate and are ready for business.'

Glancing at Greg Kate laughed. 'You sound like you have been busy.'

'Well, Scott's been a lot busier than I have Kate. I hope you don't mind, but I have been doing some admin work for Geoff, when not working with Scott. Geoff said that he would ensure that I will be paid separately for any work that I do for his private commissions.'

'I don't mind at all Belinda. Geoff works for *Windfall Holdings,* and until his office staff are appointed, by all means do admin work for him, if you have the time. Dad and I will be driving to *Glen Rayne* tomorrow, and I plan to be back by the end of the week. Scott, can you please research the prison dog training programs in Victoria and send the info to me? Also, if you can arrange an appointment for me with the Fulham Prison Governor on my way home, I would like to discuss the possibility of setting up such a program there. There are also some Animal Aid centres down that way that I wouldn't mind contacting as well.'

'Not a problem Kate. I am sure that Belinda and I can get onto that first thing in the morning.'

Once Kate had negotiated the city traffic, and they were out on the Princes Freeway heading towards Sale, Greg turned to her. 'I think I need to take back what I said about your employees Kate. I don't know if it's their army training or what, but I reckon that Scott and Belinda would give an arm and a leg for you, if needs be.'

'Thanks Dad, I might soon have to watch that they don't put me out of a job!'

'No, I think you will all complement each other.'

'Talking about working together, are you and Jules back on side again after the Velma incident?'

'I think so lass. I have been thinking of making her a full partner in *Glen Rayne*, if you don't mind.'

'Me? I don't have any entitlement to *Glen Rayne* Dad, especially now that I have all this money. Yes, I love the place and I'm sure that you and Jules will still have me to stay when I hanker for a bit of solitude, but I effectively left the place when I went away to school.'

Greg nodded his head. 'I want both Jules and me to ease back a bit, instead of trying to do everything by ourselves. Thanks to your generosity, we can afford to employ a couple of workers to do most of the daily checking and repairs, giving us extra time to concentrate on the stud work, and more time off. I really am keen to get that boat as soon as possible, and if I moor it at Lakes Entrance I will be able to call in on Mum and Dad a bit more often.'

'I wonder how Jules and Tom are getting on.'

'We will find out when we get home.'

When they reached the front gate to *Glen Rayne,* Kate pulled up and Greg went over to check the mailbox, then they continued up the drive. 'It's so good to be home at last. You know Kate, for a while there, I wasn't sure that I would ever see this place again. I have spoken to a lawyer about my rights to divorce Velma, especially if she is convicted for trying to kill me.'

Kate agreed wholeheartedly with her father but said nothing. She knew that the family of Velma's first husband were suing her for obtaining their property near Wangaratta by unlawful means.

No dogs met them when Greg stopped in front of the house, so they assumed that Julie was out working. Sure enough, when they entered the kitchen, there was a note on the table, propped up against the pepper mill.

> *Hi Dad and Kate. WELCOME HOME!*
>
> *Tom is out checking the cows and calves, and I'm fixing a fence on the second river. Hope to be home by mid-afternoon. Lunch is in the fridge if you haven't already eaten.*
>
> *Love Jules*

Julie had made her father's and Kate's beds in their old rooms. After putting their cases in their rooms, Greg joined Kate in the kitchen for a much needed cup of tea, and to eat the salad that Julie had left in the fridge for them. After their late lunch, Greg went out to check his bulls, and Kate walked down to the large lake below the house. Sitting on the small jetty that her father had built when she and Julie were little, Kate thought of how her plans were slowly starting to be realised.

Her reflections were ended when she heard the sound of hooves on hard ground, and she opened her eyes to see a tall man on a striking black horse ride into view on the house side of the lake. There appeared to be something red slung across the horse's withers, which Kate assumed must be a calf when she saw a large Hereford cow trotting close behind the horse, and a border collie following her. The horse and cow appeared to be heading for the yards, so Kate quickly ran back to the house, then down to the stockyards, careful not to startle the horse or cow, and opened the gate for the rider and cow to enter the yard.

While shutting the gate Kate was amazed to see the man remove his feet from the stirrups, then the horse sat down while he was still sitting in the saddle. Shooing the cow away with a wave of his hat, he stepped off the horse, then gently lifted the calf into his arms and carried it over to the yard fence and put it on the ground for the cow to lick, while the horse stood up again.

Leading the horse, the man walked over to Kate and smiled. 'Thank you. I assume you must be Kate. I'm Tom Marsden.'

'Nice to meet you Tom. That was certainly an extraordinary way to dismount!'

'Lucky for me, Cole's previous owner was quite short, and taught him that trick so that he could get on without a mounting block! When I found this little calf with a broken leg, I didn't want to destroy him without first trying to fix his leg nor to leave him for longer than necessary by coming home to get the ute. I had Cole sit down so that I could place the calf across his withers, as you saw, then I sat in the saddle and he stood up, and home we came, with the worried mother keeping close behind.'

'Are you going to try to splint the leg Tom?'

'If I can. I generally cut a suitable diametre piece of poly pipe in half, lengthwise, pad it well, then bandage the two pieces around the leg, after making sure that the bones are in alignment.'

'Do you have all the materials available? I have a first aid kit in my car, with a range of elastic and self-adhesive bandages if you want any?

'That would be a great help thanks Kate. I know where there is some poly pipe and cotton wool, but I'm not sure about bandages, and I would prefer to get that leg set as soon as possible.'

It wasn't long before Kate and Tom were back at the yards, Kate carrying her large first aid backpack, and Tom some half pieces of black plastic pipe, a hacksaw, and some rolls of cotton wool. Tom whistled when he saw Kates first aid kit. 'Is that your work pack Kate? I remember now, Julie told me that you are a paramedic. We should get this little fellow fixed up in no time flat! Though first, let's get his mother into the next yard; the last thing we want is a nudge in the back, or worse, while we are setting his leg.'

Half an hour later the calf was standing with its front leg wrapped from shoulder to hoof by a green self-adhesive bandage, happily feeding from his mother, taking tentative steps as needed. Julie and Greg had arrived just as Kate finished bandaging the splints in place. 'Hi Sis, glad to see that you haven't lost the touch, while you've been on leave!'

Greg went over to shake Tom's hand. 'Hi Tom, I gather that you have come to work for us. Looks like you are on the ball with that one. How do you think he broke his leg? Not wild dogs chasing the cattle I hope.'

'Hello Mr Rayne. No, I don't think it was dogs. Brodie showed no signs of sensing their presence. She really lets me know if she does. I think the cow might have trodden on him.'

Leaving the cow with some hay to eat, Greg and his two daughters walked back to the house, while Tom unsaddled Cole and took him back to his paddock. Julie turned as they stepped onto the back verandah. 'Come and have a cuppa with us when you let him go Tom.'

Chief and Bluey stood at the bottom of the steps as usual, and Greg whistled to them. 'Come inside and see how you like it you two.' Both dogs walked hesitantly through the door, looking up at

Greg; but when he walked past them to the kitchen they happily followed.

Julie stared at Kate in amazement. 'You will notice a few changes in Dad Jules. He has discovered that he has a softer side after all. Also, he has decided that he is no longer going to be a workaholic, and doesn't want you to be one either.'

'Having Tom here has been a godsend Kate. He really knows his stuff, and I can leave him to work on his own, no worries, as per today's example.'

When Kate and Julie walked into the kitchen, Greg had put the kettle on, and Chief and Bluey were happily lying on an old blanket that he had put near the back door. Just then Tom arrived on the veranda and Julie called out to him. 'If you want to bring Brodie in with you Tom, she's welcome to join the boys.'

'She'll love it Julie. She's used to being in the cottage with me.'

CHAPTER 12

APRIL

MELBOURNE

K ate was determined to remain impassive when she was shown through the dog holding enclosures at the third animal shelter that she visited on her way back to Melbourne. She had succeeded until she was about to leave the room where dogs recovering from treatment were held. She heard a faint whimper, but when she looked at the end cage all she could see was a rumpled rug. As she turned to walk away, she noticed a slight movement in the back corner amongst the bedding.

'What's in this cage Tanya?'

The vet nurse showing her this area looked sad. 'That's our poor little Mitty. She's a tiny Chihuahua puppy, but I'm afraid that she will have to be euthanised before we leave tonight.'

Kate looked at Tanya in horror. 'Why? What's wrong with her?'

'Mitty was found in a cardboard box left in a council rubbish bin earlier this week. The lady who brought her to us said that she heard a sound when she put her rubbish in the bin, and was appalled to find a tiny puppy in the box. We think Mitty is about eight weeks old and she appears to have been dropped or trodden on, we're not sure, suffering trauma to her head, lower back, and pelvis.'

'Can't anything be done for her? Is she in pain?'

'From the tests that we've done, and the pain medication she's receiving, we don't think she's in pain. She may be lonely, missing her mother or litter mates. The operations that Mitty requires to have any chance of recovery are only carried out by a few specialist veterinary surgeons in Melbourne. I'm afraid that the cost involved in her treatment, and our lack of being able to ensure a successful recovery, has deterred potential adopters, and we can't leave her untreated for much longer.'

'May I have a closer look at her please Tanya?'

When the tiny black pup with a white throat and chest, plus white front feet, was gently placed onto Kate's outstretched hands, she fitted easily on one of Kate's palms. Mitty looked so pitiful, and when Kate held the shivering pup to her cheek, she was smitten, and her resolve immediately disappeared.

Kate made an instant decision. 'Tanya, if I undertake to pay for whatever treatment Mitty requires, would you be able to arrange her referral to the appropriate specialist in Melbourne?'

Tanya gave her a questioning look. 'I assure you, I can afford her treatment Tanya, and I will give her a loving home when she recovers.'

Tanya smiled when she noticed that Mitty had nestled under Kate's chin, and was no longer shivering or whimpering.

'There's a specialist at a veterinary hospital in Mount Waverly, who is aware of Mitty's condition and has told us that he would be willing to admit her as his patient if a suitable owner is found. You must realise though, it's not just the cost of the surgery that's involved. Mitty will require long term rehabilitation if the surgery is successful.'

'She will have whatever therapy is required to enhance her recovery. If I need to, I will employ the appropriate people to help assist her recuperation.'

Half an hour later Kate drove off on her way to the Waverley Animal Hospital, with a slightly sedated Mitty asleep in a small dog carrier strapped to the front passenger seat. Arrangements had been made for the specialist to examine Mitty on arrival, with provisions made to operate immediately, if he felt that it was still a viable option.

Following a sleepless night after dropping Mitty off at Mount Waverly, Kate went down to the swimming pool to spend some time doing laps, before going back up to her apartment for breakfast. The surgeon rang just as Kate finished her second cup of tea, to inform her that Mitty had survived the anaesthetic and operation, and that he was cautiously optimistic that the procedures were as successful as could be expected, on such a tiny pup. By the end of the call Kate didn't really know how well Mitty could be expected to recover, however she was still alive, so only time would tell.

Kate rang Scott to tell him that she would be spending the day at Mount Waverley, explaining quickly about Mitty. She packed her laptop and notes from her appointments during the week and drove to Mount Waverley, where she spent the day sitting on a mat in the recovery room, with Mitty cuddled up beside her hip. Even though still very sleepy, Mitty seemed to sense Kate's presence, and noticeably relaxed when Kate stroked her. Seeing how the pup responded to Kate, and learning that she was a paramedic, the surgeon agreed to allow Mitty to go home with her, with strict instructions on how and when to medicate her, and what indicators of deterioration to be aware of.

For the next three days and nights Kate, Scott and Belinda took four hourly rotations to nurse Mitty in Kate's apartment, allowing each other to sleep and also to carry on with their work. When George first met Mitty, he sat and stared at the tiny bundle on the mat in front of him, looking at first as though he was trying to decide whether she was for him to eat or to play with. Finally, he lay down with her lying tucked in between his front paws. From then on, whenever Mitty spent time in the office, she slept close to George on his bed.

CHAPTER 13

LATE APRIL

MELBOURNE

Since moving to Melbourne Kate went for a run early most mornings, usually through the Treasury Gardens across the road from her apartment, and occasionally she went further into the Fitzroy Gardens. If it was too wet or cold, she swam in the pool downstairs.

One cool late April morning, while Scott had Mitty in his apartment, Kate was jogging back up towards Spring Street when she heard someone running behind her, then a red faced, heavyset man passed her, puffing heavily. About twenty metres further on, he suddenly staggered and fell face forward onto the grass beside the path.

Running up to him, from habit Kate quickly assessed the area for danger, then crouched down to see if the man was still breathing. Noting that his chest was no longer moving, Kate felt for a pulse at his neck. Feeling no pulse, she rolled him onto his back, and opened his mouth to check that there was nothing obstructing his airway. After placing a disposable CPR face mask, from the small first aid kit she wore clipped to her waist band, over the man's open mouth, Kate glanced at her watch, then tilted his head back and commenced CPR.

As she rhythmically compressed the man's chest, a tall, fair headed man, with his left arm in a sling, walked rapidly towards her. 'Is there anything I can do to help?'

Kate continued the compressions while talking. 'Ring 000 for an ambulance. Suspected heart attack. Then please wait up on pavement and show the ambos where we are.'

As Kate kept up the steady chest compressions, followed by a couple of breaths, she noted the man using his mobile as he walked back towards Spring Street. Ten minutes later Kate heard a siren approaching and was relieved to see two paramedics carrying their packs, walking towards her. As the female paramedic took over the chest compressions, Kate stood up to allow the other paramedic to attach a defibrillator to the man's chest.

Stepping back to regain her breath, Kate was thrilled to see the man begin to respond to their efforts. After an oxygen mask was placed over the patient's mouth and nose, and ECG pads were attached to his chest, the female paramedic looked closely at Kate. 'Kate Rayne! I thought it was you when we arrived. How long were you working on him?'

'Ten minutes Mel. I'm sure glad that you came when you did!'

'What are you doing down here in the big smoke? I thought you were well established with the Shepparton ambos.'

'I have transferred down here to the city, and was out for an early morning jog when this chap collapsed in front of me. When he ran past, he was red in the face and puffing profusely, evidently pushing himself beyond his limit.'

'He's a lucky man that you where nearby when he collapsed.'

After the patient was loaded into the ambulance and driven to the Royal Melbourne Hospital, Kate turned to the man who had called the ambulance. 'Thank you for your help. Thank goodness that ambulance was close by. I don't think I could have kept going for too much longer.'

'I'm sorry I couldn't help you more. Are you going to continue your run, or can I shout you a coffee over the road at Ben's?'

After a moment's hesitation Kate nodded. 'Thank you, I would love one.'

Before they crossed Spring Street, the man held out his free hand. 'My name's Arthur Thompson. I have become one of Ben's regulars since I moved into my apartment upstairs a fortnight ago.'

Kate shook his hand. 'I'm Kate Rayne. I know I shouldn't undo the good work my morning runs are meant to achieve, but I don't often forgo one of Ben's coffees on my way home.'

While Arthur was at the counter ordering their coffees, Kate scrutinised him – over six feet tall, broad shoulders, short wavy blond hair, quite good looking with a square jaw line. '*Not Bad*' she thought as he sat down at their table.

'What did you do in Shepperton Kate?'

Kate laughed. 'I'm actually a paramedic Arthur, based down here now!'

'No wonder you knew what to do, and looked pretty proficient while you were dealing with that poor chap.'

'It's never pleasant to do, but at least he has a chance of survival. What do you do?'

'I am a corporate lawyer, making my way slowly back to the office, after being on a couple of days leave following a backyard cricket injury!'

Just as Arthur was about to ask Kate where she was staying his mobile rang. Excusing himself, he answered the phone, and after a short reply hung up. Standing up he turned to Kate. 'I'm sorry, I have to get to the office as quickly as possible. A project that I was working on has gone pear shaped, so I need to get back to the office asap. Maybe we will meet here again one day.'

'Possibly. Thanks for the coffee Arthur.'

Slowly finishing her coffee, Kate wondered whether they would meet again. Living in the same apartment block, and frequenting Ben's coffee shop, the odds were high that they would. He seemed a nice, friendly chap, and although Kate was still single at twenty eight, she wasn't averse to male company.

Waving goodbye to Ben, Kate went back to her apartment for a shower and some breakfast, then went down to the office. Mitty sat up and gave an excited yip when she saw Kate, then took a couple of her crablike steps before Kate picked her up to give her a quick cuddle. She then lay quietly on Kate's lap while she opened her computer.

The veterinary surgeon was thrilled to see the progress that Mitty was making since her operations. She was bright and alert, and the damage to the side of her skull had healed well and appeared not to have affected her sight. According to the last x-rays, Mitty's lower spine and pelvic surgery was healing satisfactorily. She was still learning to coordinate her back legs, and had trouble walking in a straight line. Three mornings a week, a veterinary nurse took Mitty for hydrotherapy and physiotherapy sessions, which were increasing the mobility of her hind quarters.

Before they commenced work, Belinda stopped at Kate's desk. 'Did you notice the ambulance across the road when you were out this morning Kate?'

Kate's reply was brief, and she kept looking at her computer. 'A runner collapsed and needed treatment.'

Scott glanced at Belinda, and he fleetingly shook his head. He sensed that there was more to it than Kate was disclosing, and that in some way, Kate had been involved. But she obviously wasn't prepared to reveal anything yet.

Later that morning Kate had an appointment in Doncaster to discuss her future with the Metropolitan Ambulance Service. Although she knew that she no longer had to work for an income, she enjoyed working as a paramedic, and wanted to find out if she could put her paramedic skills and experience to use in the city. Now that *Windfall Holdings* was operational, and Geoff, Scott and Belinda were working so efficiently, Kate, who didn't enjoy being office bound, was looking for something more to do. By the time she left the meeting in Doncaster, it had been agreed that Kate, being such a highly qualified paramedic, would be transferred to the Metropolitan Ambulance Service, in a part-time position, to be rostered on three mid-week afternoon/evening shifts. Without disclosing her exact role in *Windfall Holdings,* she had explained her need to live in Melbourne and her desire to keep working part time with the service.

The next day she drove to Shepparton to say farewell to her colleagues, then she went to her flat to collect her remaining possessions left behind when she went on leave. The flat was to be cleaned professionally, then was to be let at a reduced rent to paramedics working from Shepparton.

CHAPTER 14

MID-MAY

MELBOURNE

Early one morning Belinda paused at Kate's desk. 'Kate, a close friend of mine is the victim in a nasty domestic violence situation. Last night her husband thumped her because he stubbed his toe on the tool bag he'd left in the hallway, and she thinks that he has broken her arm and nose.'

'Has she seen a doctor Belinda?'

'No she is too scared to defy Clive in any way these days.'

'Could she go to a women's refuge?'

'There aren't many that accept pets Kate, and she won't leave her dog behind, because she believes that Clive will take his anger out on him. Do you mind if I spend some time this morning researching women's refuges prepared to take dogs?'

'I don't mind at all Belinda. Where does Celia live?'

'In Ringwood.'

'Do you think she will leave home if we find somewhere for her to stay?'

'Like a flash, if she can take Chas with her. While the children lived at home, Clive was cunning in the way he abused Celia, making sure that he didn't mark her face. Unfortunately, now that their children have left home, he hits her wherever, and whenever he feels like it. She rarely seeks medical treatment and tells people who see her bruises the usual 'I fell over, ran into a door etc'.

'Before you start researching refuges Belinda, why don't you take my car to collect Celia and Chas, then bring them back here. I'm sure that we can conceal them for the short term, until more suitable accommodation can be found.'

Belinda hesitated. 'Is Clive likely to be home mid-morning?'

'He is a builder's labourer and is generally away from early morning to late afternoon. However, one of his neighbours keeps an eye on whatever Celia does, and rings him if she goes out or has visitors, so he sometimes comes home during the day.'

'Would you like me to come with you?' Belinda nodded. 'Just give me time to make a couple of phone calls, and we will be on our way.'

An hour later, Kate and Belinda were at the Ringwood Ambulance Station, Kate wearing her paramedic uniform and Belinda a white lab coat. They travelled to Celia's house in the back of an ambulance, while Scott drove Kate's car along the back lane, and stopped at Celia's back gate.

Belinda had spoken to Celia and advised her that an ambulance would call at her house later that morning. She told her to pack a suitcase with as many of her clothes as possible, plus her laptop, important documents such as passport, bank details, insurance papers etc and leave them just inside the unlocked back door.

When Celia opened the front door to let Kate, Belinda, and the other paramedic into her house, they were shocked when they saw the condition she was in. Her nose was crooked, both eyes almost swollen shut, and her cheeks and chin were covered in dried blood. Her right arm hung limply at her side, and she was struggling to stay upright.

Immediately Kate sat Celia on a chair in the hallway, then she and her fellow paramedic went out to the ambulance to get the stretcher, while Belinda comforted her sobbing friend. Chas, her little white Maltese Terrier, lay beside her, with his nose resting on her foot.

While Celia was placed on the stretcher, Belinda put Chas into his dog carrier and took him out to the car, where Scott was loading the meagre possessions that Celia had struggled to collect. Scott removed the SD card from Celia's mobile phone and left it under the bench in the garden shed before he drove off.

As Belinda climbed into the back of the ambulance, she noticed a curtain in the front window of the house next door pulled back, showing an elderly woman peering out of the window. '*I wonder when she'll ring Clive?*' she thought as the doors shut behind her.

Due to the seriousness of Celia's facial injuries, she was taken straight to the Ringwood Hospital emergency ward, rather than back to the ambulance station as had originally been planned. When the doctors heard how Celia had received her injuries, the police were notified, and two officers arrived to take Celia's statement before she was taken into the operating theatre. Belinda remained at the hospital, while Kate, Scott and Chas travelled back to the city.

Later that night, Belinda rang Kate to inform her that the police had arrested Clive at his worksite, and had taken him straight to the hospital. He hadn't been allowed into Celia's room when she returned from the operating theatre, but he'd seen her through the glass window next to the door.

'Would you believe it Kate, he tried to bluff his way out of it by telling the police that Celia had fallen down the steps. The doctor laughed at that suggestion, saying that he could make out fist marks on her cheek. Plus, Clive has freshly bruised knuckles. Currently he is being questioned by the police about this assault, and previous incidents relating to the scars and recent bruises all over Celia's body. She really is a mess Kate. Broken nose and eye socket, broken arm and cigarette burns on her back that she declared Clive gave her the night before last!'

'Use your company card to pay for a room at the nearest motel Belinda, and stay with Celia for as long as she is in hospital. Then we will bring her here, while we find her and Chas a secure home. He's a lovely little dog and gets on well with Mitty.'

'Thanks Kate. Would it be possible for me to have my laptop and briefcase couriered here, so that I can work while Celia is asleep?'

'No worries Belinda. I will get onto it first thing in the morning.

The next morning Kate was told that Clive had been remanded in custody, on the serious charge of causing grievous bodily harm to his wife, and he had been refused bail while awaiting trial.

Scott took Belinda's laptop and brief case to Ringwood, then they both went back to Celia's house to pack more of her possessions. Scott noticed the neighbour watching through her side window, so when they went into the house, he went through to the garage and opened the roller door, then parked his car next to what he assumed was Celia's car and closed the door. He made a note to check at Clive's workplace for his vehicle.

The police had advised Kate to have the external locks on Celia's house changed, in case Clive had given the neighbour or friends a copy of his keys, so a local locksmith had been booked to do the job while Scott and Belinda were at the house. Five minutes after being notified that they were at the house, he arrived and changed all the locks, while they packed more of Celia's belongings.

While Belinda sorted out Celia's personal property, Scott went to the office and quickly went through the papers and bills on the desk, then searched the drawers for any of Celia's personal documents. The larger bottom drawer was locked, but after a quick search, Scott found some keys stuck to the bottom of one of the other drawers and opened the locked drawer.

It contained life insurance documents for both Clive and Celia, the title for the house, interestingly in Celia's name, plus house insurance, their birth certificates, passports, and marriage certificate. In a bulky large envelope, there were numerous bundles of one hundred and fifty dollar notes. Scott added the two laptop computers and a box of USBs in the office to the items to go out to the car. Before leaving Scott went out to the back shed and retrieved Celia's phone card, reasoning that while Clive was in custody, he couldn't easily locate Celia through her phone.

When Celia was released from hospital a week later, she and

Chas became Kate's guests in the penthouse. Kate planned to take Celia and Chas up to Woolgoolga to complete her recovery when she felt stronger. The police retrieved Clive's truck from his worksite, and discovered a bong, a packet of marijuana, plus a small packet of white powder and a drug injection kit wrapped in a chamois, behind the driver's seat. So, it appeared that Clive's stay in custody could be extended considerably.

As Kate surmised, it wasn't long before she and Arthur Thompson crossed paths again. One morning, not long after Celia's release from hospital, Kate was in the lift on her way down to the office, when it stopped at the tenth floor and Arthur stepped in when the doors opened.

'Kate, what a surprise! Don't tell me that you live in this apartment block too?'

'Good morning Arthur. Yes, I do. How's your arm?'

'Itchy! Hopefully the cast comes off next week. I had no idea my arm would get so dreadfully itchy. My mother's knitting needles have certainly come in handy!'

Kate laughed as the lift stopped at the third floor, and she stepped out when the doors opened. 'See you again sometime Arthur.'

Belinda was already in the office when Kate arrived, and soon after Scott arrived with three cups of coffee from Ben's. 'I went down for a paper and couldn't resist getting us all a coffee. While I was there, I met a chap called Arthur Thompson, who's moved into an apartment on the tenth floor. Seems a friendly sort of bloke.'

'We shared the lift down this morning. It's interesting that although we three all live and work in this building, I can't say I know too many of the other occupants.'

Belinda put down her coffee cup. 'Me neither. I recognise a few who frequent Ben's and Gaspare's, but I can't say that I know them.'

'I first met Arthur that day the jogger collapsed in the gardens across the road. He called the ambulance, while I did CPR on the man, then we had a coffee at Ben's, once the ambulance left. He told me that he is a corporate lawyer, I assume somewhere in the city.'

'Have you heard how the chap who collapsed is Kate?'

'I gather he's recovering after having a triple bypass Belinda.'

Kate threw her coffee cup into the rubbish bin. 'The other day, Geoff and I were discussing the company's need to employ a lawyer sometime soon. I wonder if it would be worth looking into this Arthur Thompson's credentials?'

'Do you want me to look into it Kate?'

'Thanks Scott, I will leave it to you. Now, Belinda you and I are due to meet with those ladies in Toorak, who are interested in learning what we do at *Windfall Holdings*. Let's go now, before we get caught up with other issues.'

When they arrived at the venue where the meeting was to take place, they were introduced to the wives of ten of Melbourne's successful entrepreneurs. These women were keen to hear about the organisations that *Windfall Holdings* was working with, as they wanted to make sizable donations to some lesser known organisations.

One of the older women put her hand up. 'Kate, how do you choose the organisations that *Windfall Holdings* supports? Many of them appear animal orientated.'

'When we first started, I was advised not to try to help everyone. Before we make the decision to help, we find out as much as we can about the group, their management and accounting practises, and above all, their dedication to those receiving their assistance. I love animals, so I guess I'm a bit biased, but regardless if it's animal or human aid, we tend to work with those bodies not receiving Government subsidies or those without a large annual donation input.'

Belinda stood up when Kate finished speaking to the women. 'Have you thought of helping to form more women's refuge shelters that accept pets, especially dogs? There is a great need for such refuges, and at present they are few and far between.' That suggestion caused quite a lot of discussion and note taking.

As they were leaving the venue following a delicious luncheon, a silver haired, impeccably dressed lady with a double string of pearls around her neck, took Kate aside. 'Kate, I am Lady Frances Smythe, wife of Sir Eric Smythe. Are you the lady who saved my husband's life in the Treasury Gardens?'

Kate blushed. 'I only did what I have been trained to do, to try to help your husband until the ambulance arrived Lady Smythe. I am just delighted to hear that he is recovering.'

'So am I my dear, so am I! I was told that a paramedic called Kate had saved Eric, but until you walked through the door today, I didn't connect the name with my brother Malcolm's niece. I met you once when you lived with your Uncle Malcolm and Aunt Jane, while you attended PLC.'

'Uncle Malcolm is your brother? Good grief, isn't it a small world!'

'I must say, Eric certainly chose the right person to collapse in front of! Sorry, I'm embarrassing you Kate. Would you care to visit us sometime next week? I know that Eric would like to thank you personally.'

'I would love to Lady Smythe. Thank you.'

Before she and Belinda took their leave from the group, Kate left her card with Lady Smythe. 'I will call to arrange a suitable date and time for you to visit, my dear. Eric will be thrilled.'

On the way back to the office Belinda joked 'You sure know how to make friends and influence people Kate. Sir Eric Smythe is one of Melbourne's most notable philanthropists. Don't tell me you don't know of the Smythe dynasty!'

'I must admit that I don't Belinda. What do you know about them?'

'Well, I think it was Sir Eric's great grandfather who made his fortune at Ballarat, during the gold rush in the 1850s. He bought some land about nine kilometres south east of the CBD, at what is now Elsternwick, and built a substantial mansion there. His youngest son, who inherited *Smythe Park* after his three elder brothers were killed during the first world war, was a shrewd businessman who, during his lifetime, increased the family's wealth and standing in the community.

The family fortunes were further augmented when much of the

land was sold for development after the second world war. By the time Sir Eric inherited from his father in the late seventies, most of the farmland had been sold, but the mansion was still surrounded by an impressive garden, and the family fortune was intact.'

'I thought Lady Smythe said that she lived in South Yarra.'

'I'm not sure when they moved from *Smythe Park* Kate, but I know that Sir Eric and Lady Frances Smythe have lived in South Yarra for a number of years now. Their adult son and daughters live overseas I think.'

CHAPTER 15

MID-MAY

MELBOURNE

On their arrival back at the office, Kate went up to her apartment to see Celia, who was sitting out on the balcony with both dogs lying on their beds beside her. Mitty gave her usual 'yip' of delight when she saw Kate, and made her way across the lounge as quickly as she could to greet her. Kate was pleased to see how quickly Mitty was regaining the use of her back legs now.

Kate cuddled the squirming little bundle, who was trying to climb up towards her neck. 'Everything okay Celia? Can I get you a drink or anything before I get changed?'

'No thanks Kate. The dogs and I have been dozing out here for the past half hour, so it's time I came inside. How was your meeting?'

'Interesting. I think we may have a group of influential ladies willing to help fund a refuge for women and their dogs. I also met the wife of the man who collapsed in front of me a few weeks ago – it turns out I did CPR on Sir Eric Smythe.'

'Do you mean one of the *Smythe Park* family?'

'Yes. I appear to have a definite gap in my knowledge of members of Melbourne high society, as Belinda had to explain his position in the Melbourne élite to me. Now, while I'm here, would you like to go up to my place near Coffs Harbour for a couple of weeks, before you think of going back home?'

'That would be wonderful Kate, but I can't keep imposing on your kindness.'

'I assure you, it is no imposition helping you in your recovery Celia.'

'What about Chas? Can he come too. He's never been in a plane before.'

'He can travel in a dog carrier at your feet. If he's given a mild sedative, he will be fine. I might take Mitty with me too, to keep Chas company.'

Later in the week, Kate set her GPS and quickly arrived at the South Yarra address that Lady Smythe had given her. She drove through the open wrought iron gates set in the high brick fence, and stared in awe at the beautiful white, double storied house set back from a raked gravel roundabout, surrounding a white marble pond and fountain centre piece.

Not long after Kate pulled up near the front steps, Lady Smythe came out of the front door and greeted her as she stood beside her car, admiring the surrounding garden and lawn. She took Kate's hands in hers 'Thank you so much for coming Kate. Eric is so looking forward to meeting you.'

'I'm looking forward to seeing him in much better health Lady Smythe.'

'Please call me Frances, my dear. When I'm at home with friends, I like to dispense with the formalities if possible.'

Just as they were about to enter the front door, a large Afghan hound, with a long, silky, cream coat, bounded around the corner of the house and up the steps. Sitting in front of Kate, with her elegant black face almost level with Kate's chest, she lifted her right paw.

'Meet Bella Kate. Once you shake her paw, she will remember you, then will be quite happy to go off and do her own thing.'

Kate shook Bella's offered paw. 'Hello Bella.' The big dog looked up at Kate's face and appeared to give a big grin, then went back down the steps, and off around to the back of the house.

'What a gorgeous dog she is Frances. My little pup could quite easily sit on Bella's head.'

As they entered the spacious hall, Kate told Frances a little of Mitty's history. A nurse carrying a small rug came down the carpeted stairs. 'Excuse me Lady Frances, Sir Eric is in the conservatory.'

'Thank you, Mary.'

Frances led Kate and the nurse through the elegantly furnished sitting room to the conservatory, a spacious room bathed in sunlight. Sir Eric sat in a wheelchair near the bay window, looking out onto a large area of lawn. As the nurse placed the rug over Sir Eric's knees, Frances walked over to him. 'Kate Rayne is here to see you dear.'

A wide smile spread over the man's face as he looked at Kate. 'Welcome to our house Kate. I owe you a deep debt of gratitude for your swift and competent action when I collapsed. My surgeon informed me that if you hadn't kept going for as long and as efficiently as you did, my subsequent surgery would not have been as successful as it has been.'

'You don't owe me anything Sir Eric. I'm just happy to see you looking so much better than when we last met! I was, after all, doing what I'm trained to do.'

'You're a paramedic, I believe Kate? Yet I have also heard that you are the instigator and major investor in *Windfall Holdings*.' When he saw Kate sit back in her chair and blush, he smiled. 'Forgive me for prying Kate, but your name has come up a number of times lately amongst my associates, many speculating on the source of such a substantial amount of money.'

'But how...?' Sir Eric cut in 'Kate, in my line of work we quickly get to know when large amounts of money enter the local financial world, and who is involved. I know of your family history, being related through marriage to your Uncle Malcolm, and of your employment with the Ambulance Service, but neither of these earn the amount of money that I am alluding to. Do you mind telling me how you came by the funds to set up *Windfall Holdings*?'

Kate sat and stared at Sir Eric for a moment, wondering what she should tell him. 'I won it Sir Eric. I don't usually buy Tattslotto tickets, but like many others, I bought one for the Super Jackpot early this year, and amazingly, I had the only winning ticket.'

'From memory, that was quite a considerable amount of money. Again, do you mind telling me how much you actually won?'

'Three hundred million dollars Sir Eric, but only my father, sister and aunt know the full amount. Others, like Uncle Malcolm and Aunt Jane, only know that I won a few million on Tattslotto. Could I please ask you and Lady Frances to keep the total amount to yourselves?'

'Oh, my dear, of course we will, won't we Eric? You must be concerned about being pestered by all and sundry, looking for handouts.'

'Thank you for your understanding Frances. I want my money to go to those who need it, not to those who think they should have it. I was very happy with my lifestyle before the win, and have little desire to allow it to change too much. I don't want to waste all that money on the high life, buying expensive things that I don't need.' Kate stopped speaking, looking aghast. 'Oh, I'm so sorry. That must sound awfully tactless, sitting here in your beautiful house.'

Sir Eric smiled. 'Don't be Kate. I admire your candour. Fran and I have always lived with affluence, and know how it can influence one's lifestyle for better and for worse.'

'I have invested two thirds of the money in *Windfall Holdings* Sir Eric, and plan to use it by assisting non–government funded bodies that rely mainly on public support to help people and animals in need.'

'Kate, Fran and I have spent some time this week discussing your colleague's proposal to her group, about helping women who want to leave their abusive partner, but can't bear to leave their pet, or pets, behind if they go to a women's shelter. We moved to this property in South Yarra eight years ago, not long after we returned to Australia, following a number of years of living in France, where our three adult children still live with their families. My two elder sisters remained at our family home, *Smythe Park* in Elsternwick, and lived there until their deaths last year. Both were quite elderly and died within two months of each other. The mansion has been unoccupied since then, and I have been trying to decide what to do with it. Now, I think I have a possible answer to my dilemma.'

'Frances tapped Eric on the knee. 'Before you go on Eric, I think we could all do with a cup of tea.' She leant back and tugged on a tasselled bell cord hanging behind her chair. A middle-aged lady, in a white blouse and mid-calf black skirt, entered the conservatory. 'Could you please bring in the tea and scones now Sonia?'

'Certainly m'lady. The kettle has just boiled.'

A few minutes later, she pushed in a trolley with a silver tea pot and hot water jug, plus cups and saucers, a small milk jug, a small bowl of sugar and a large plate of scones, already spread with jam and cream. When everyone had been served with a cup of tea and a scone, Sonia took her leave and Eric leant forward and looked at Kate.

'Now Kate, I have a property that needs to be utilised, and your company is looking for a way to help women, who want to leave their abusive partner. What would you say if I was to give *Windfall Holdings* access to *Smythe Park,* for the purpose of it becoming a pet friendly abused women's refuge?'

Kate was speechless, and Frances came to her aid. 'That was a rather abrupt way of putting such a suggestion to the poor girl Eric. Remember, she is still pretty new to the cut and thrust of your world.'

'Yes, I'm sorry Kate. I think your plans are commendable, and I am willing to provide whatever assistance you feel I might be able to furnish.'

'Thank you Sir Eric, I would very much like to have your support.'

'Eric, why don't we meet again soon, after Kate has had time to think over your offer, and you can explain to her what you actually do, and maybe have your legal representatives present too?'

'I would appreciate learning as much as I can, if you have the time Sir Eric.'

'Thanks to you, my girl, I have a lot more time available to me. And I'm just plain Eric to my friends.'

'Thank you, Eric. *Windfall Holdings* doesn't have a legal representative yet. We are currently in the process of seeking an appropriate corporate lawyer.'

'My friend Pam Thompson has a son who is a corporate lawyer. He might know of someone available,' mused Frances out aloud.

'Your friend's son's name wouldn't by chance be Arthur, would it Frances?'

Frances looked at Kate in surprise. 'Why yes, it is Kate. How on earth did you know?'

'The man who stopped to help, when Eric collapsed, is a corporate lawyer called Arthur Thompson. In fact, he lives in the building where *Windfall Holdings* has its offices.'

'Good grief, it must be him. Pam told me that Arthur moved to an apartment in the city not long ago. I always pride myself on being a rational person, not given to seeking reasons for things happening, but there seem to be a lot of coincidences cropping up in our recent acquaintance. Both you and Arthur being present when Eric collapsed, your relationship to my brother Malcolm, you entering into a similar sphere as Eric, your desire to help those less fortunate like I do, and I'm sure there are other coincidences if we cared to look. We must be destined to work together!'

'Don't get so fanciful Fran, though I would like to help you Kate, if you would like me to be involved in some way in your business.'

'Thank you Eric. You have given me a lot to think about. Would you mind if I take a little time to digest all that we have spoken about?'

'By all means, my girl. While you're thinking things through, I will ask my legal eagles to check Arthur Thompson's bona fides.'

'Would you like to visit us again next week Kate?'

'I am taking a friend up to Woolgoolga early next week, to help her recover from a domestic violence incident, but I can fly back, to be here by the end of the week.'

'Why don't you join us for a light lunch on Friday next week then Kate? Sonia much prefers preparing meals for visitors to cooking what she terms our 'boring repasts!'

Two days later Kate and Celia were at Melbourne Airport, with Mitty in a dog carrier sling, secured across Kate's chest by a wide padded shoulder strap, and Celia carrying Chas in a soft sided pet carrier. Mitty had her head out and was happily observing all around her, while Chas was taking little notice of the hustle and bustle, thanks to a minimal dose of the sedative that the vet had prescribed. Kate paid for both dogs to travel with Celia and herself in business class, where there was ample room for Chas's carrier at Celia's feet. Mitty remained in her carrier strapped to Kate, and quickly snuggled down and went to sleep.

Donald met them at the airport, and it wasn't long before Celia was ensconced on the balcony, admiring the view, and the four dogs were getting to know one another on the back lawn. Hugo and Chloe were much more interested in Chas, while Mitty was happy to sit on Kate's lap to watch their antics. After a while she slid down to the ground, and went off to explore her new surroundings. Hugo and Chloe gave her a quick sniff, then left her alone, giving the impression she wasn't worth worrying about.

Later that morning, Kate took Mitty down to the beach for her first foray onto sand. She found it hard going in the soft sand, but once Kate put her on the harder, damp sand she happily scampered around, sniffing a wealth of new scents. All was well until a wave, almost at the end of its surge up the beach, reached Mitty, whose little legs weren't long enough to stop the water washing halfway up her side.

Mitty had quite enjoyed her swims in the hydra bath, but this water was nothing like that. It was salty, and began to drag her back down the beach, which terrified her. Kate quickly scooped her up, before she was carried too far, and decided that, until Mitty grew a bit more, the beach was not going to be her happy playground.

Three days later Kate and Mitty returned to Melbourne after Celia had assured her that she felt comfortable staying with Jessie and Donald, while she recovered from her injuries.

CHAPTER 16

Towards the end of her evening shift two days after her return to Melbourne, Kate and her colleague Brian were directed to a suspected child bashing in the Botanical Gardens near the Shrine of Remembrance. Driving down Birdwood Avenue they saw the blue flashing lights of a police van, and pulled up behind it. A young constable led them to a bench away from the road, where another officer was crouched beside a small figure huddled on the ground beside the bench.

The sergeant turned his head. 'Young boy's been bashed and cut. Right arm's bleeding badly. He's worried about his dog.'

Kate looked down at the battered face of a young boy, who looked to be only about eight or nine. His eyes were closed, and his breaths were short gasps. The police sergeant was pressing a pad against the boy's bloody right arm, while the boy held a brown bundle to his side with his left arm.

As Brian began to check the young lad for other injuries, Kate squatted down beside him. 'Hello. My name's Kate. We've come to help you.' Kate noticed a flickering of the boy's eyelids, but the swollen eyes didn't open. 'Can you tell me your name?'

'Jim,' was the mumbled reply

'Okay Jim, I can see that you have a cut arm and sore face. Do you hurt anywhere else?'

The boy became agitated and whispered. 'Toby's dead. They killed him!' As the boy sobbed, Kate noticed his arm tighten around the bundle, which she suddenly realised was a small brown and black dog.

'Brian, are you right with the lad for a moment? I think I should check his dog.'

'Go for it Kate. If you can take the dog, I will check his left side. I have the bleeding on his arm under control. His face and torso have taken a beating. I wouldn't be surprised if his ribs have been damaged. Obs are okay, so we should be able to move him soon.'

'Jim, can I have a look at Toby? Are you sure that he's dead?'

'They put a rope around his neck and hanged him! When I tried to stop them, they bashed me, and one cut me!'

Slowly Kate put her hand on the dog's chest and she thought she could detect some movement. Taking a stethoscope from her pack, she listened to the rasping, laboured breathing. 'Jim, Toby is still alive. Please let me try to help him.'

At first the boy wouldn't release his grip on the dog, but eventually allowed Kate to lift him away. Quickly she laid the dog on the ground and noticed a piece of rope tied around his neck. She grabbed some scissors from her pack and cut the rope, then listened to his chest again. The breathing was still laboured, so she pulled out an oxygen bottle and placed the disposable mask over the little dog's face.

'I'm giving Toby some oxygen Jim. How are you feeling?'

Again, just a mumbled reply 'My head and chest hurt.'

'He's taken a fair beating Kate. How's the dog?'

'Still alive. Okay to take them both?'

'Sure. See if you can get a name etc once we have him aboard. Thanks sergeant. Lucky for the boy that you arrived when you did. Has he said anything about who bashed him?'

'No, nothing. Please let us know if he talks to you. He seems to respond a bit to you Kate.'

While Brian and the constable went to collect the stretcher, Kate placed a blanket around Jim, and kept administering the oxygen until the little dog began to show more signs of life.

'I think he's feeling a bit better Jim. Where do you live?'

'Don't have a home!'

'Oh. Where did you sleep last night?'

'Here.'

'Jim, can you open your eyes a little bit or is it too hard?'

'Feels too sore!'

'Ok. Just lie there and keep Toby warm.'

Brian soon arrived with the stretcher, so Kate helped him place Jim on it, with Toby lying beside him under the blanket. Once the ambulance was on the way Jim tried to sit up. 'Where are you taking me? I can't leave Toby!'

Kate held his free hand. 'We are taking you to hospital Jim, and I will take Toby to a vet, then I will look after him until you go home.'

'Haven't got a home anymore!'

'Where did you live when you had a home Jim?'

The little boy began to sob. 'With Grandad. But he died.'

Kate decided to leave the questioning, and held the boy's hand until he calmed down. By then, Brian was backing the ambulance into the ambulance bay at the Royal Children's Hospital. While they were waiting for Jim to be admitted, Kate rang a nearby twenty-four-hour veterinary clinic and arranged to drop Toby off on their way back to base. She looked at the small boy lying on the stretcher. 'Jim, I will stay in touch with you, to let you know how Toby is. But I need to know your full name, or the hospital mightn't let me see you again.'

'Jim Ross.'

'Was your grandad's name Ross too?'

'Mm.'

'Where did your grandad live Jim?'

'Broadmeadows, behind a shop.'

Before Kate could glean any further information from Jim, he was taken into a cubicle where a doctor was waiting to treat him.

Kate told the receptionist the information she had gathered, and explained that she had the little boy's injured dog. 'If he gets upset about Toby, tell him that Kate will look after him. Here's my card in case you need to contact me.' Kate handed over her card, then she and Brian left.

On the way they dropped Toby off at the vets, after Kate explained what they had been told had happened to the dog, and Kate had assured them that she would pay all costs.

The next morning Kate rang the hospital, and was informed that Jim had been admitted with concussion, three broken ribs, plus bruising to his face and torso, related to being kicked and punched, and a slash to his forearm requiring twenty stitches. He was very concerned about his dog and was asking for Kate.

Before leaving to see Jim, Kate rang the vets to inquire about Toby. Thankfully he had survived the night, and she was asked if she could collect him before lunch. When Kate walked into the ward, she saw Jim lying in the end bed with his face still swollen and his eyes shut. However, when the nurse pulled the curtains around the bed, his eyes slightly opened, and he saw Kate sitting beside him.

'Toby!?'

'Toby is doing well Jim. He will have a sore neck for a while, but his breathing has improved. I'm going to collect him from the vets when I leave here, and then I will take him home with me.'

'Can't you bring him here?'

Sandra the nurse groaned. 'Sister would skin me alive if I let you have your dog here in the hospital Jim!'

'Sandra, are you on duty this afternoon?'

'Yes, I'm on until four this afternoon.'

'Could I send you some photos of Toby when I get him home?'

When Kate left Jim, she accompanied Sandra to the desk, and was given her mobile number. 'We still don't have any more details about Jim, other than those you gave yesterday Kate. The police are looking into it, but no word yet.'

Kate left the hospital and went to the vet clinic. Toby seemed to recognise her, giving a brief wag of his tail. His neck was bandaged, and Kate was given some medication and his collar before she carried him to her car. Once she had parked in her garage, she carried Toby into the lift and went up to her apartment. Mitty was down with Scott and George, so Kate let Toby wander around by himself, while she made herself a salad.

Sitting out on the balcony, she was pleased to see Toby come out and sit beside her chair. He seemed fascinated looking down at the cars on the street below and people walking in the gardens. Kate suddenly realised that she had never thought about how far dogs could see into the distance. Then she remembered Chief and Blucy, and how they looked around when they first entered a paddock, and seemed to know where the cattle were in the huge paddocks at *Glen Rayne*.

Kate took her plate and mug back into the kitchen and noticed Toby's collar on the bench. Picking it up, she looked more closely at the attached tag and saw 'Toby' written on one side and a phone number on the other. Kate rang the number and received a message 'This number is no longer connected.' Damn! She really thought she had found Jim's home. She then rang the office. 'Belinda, could you and Scott please come up to my apartment and bring George and Mitty with you? I need some sleuthing done.'

When Belinda, Scott and the two dogs entered her apartment, Kate quickly told them about Jim and Toby. While she was talking, Mitty looked at Toby sitting on her bed, then walked over, sniffed his nose, and lay beside him. George looked at Toby, then at Scott and didn't move until Scott patted his head. 'Off you go boy. Be nice.' George walked slowly over to Toby, sniffed him, then walked back to Scott.

Kate, Scott, and Belinda sat out on the balcony. 'I have a bit of a challenge on my hands, to find the family of Toby's young master, and I am hoping that you two might be able to help me. All I know is the boy says his name is Jim Ross. He lived with his grandfather, with the same surname, who I gather may have just died. They apparently lived in Broadmeadows behind a shop!'

Belinda leaned forward. 'Do you know if he went to school there Kate?'

'No, I don't Belinda, but he would be a primary school student. There's a phone number on Toby's collar but it's disconnected.' She handed the collar to Belinda. 'This isn't a Broadmeadows number Kate. I think it's a suburb closer to the city.'

Scott opened the laptop he'd brought up with him. 'What we need to do is check the local primary schools, the funeral parlours and telecom.'

After the three of them had spent the next hour on the phone they appeared to have narrowed the search down to one funeral parlour and two local primary schools. As Belinda had surmised, the phone number was for the Hawthorn region and had been disconnected for twelve months.

Belinda and Kate drove out to Broadmeadows, leaving Scott in the office to complete a project that he hoped to finalise before the end of the afternoon, as well as to watch over the three dogs, now all settled on George's fleece. Kate had taken some photos of Toby with the other two dogs and sent them to Sandra.

Before leaving the office, Kate rang the number that the sergeant had given her and asked if he had found out more about Jim. The answer being 'no', he quickly wrote a brief letter giving her permission to look for Jim Ross's details and emailed it to her.

While Belinda went to the funeral parlour, Kate visited the two schools that had guardedly indicated there were students by the name of Ross enrolled at their schools. Armed with the sergeant's letter, Kate drew a blank at the first Primary School she called on, but at the second she was more successful. After explaining everything to the headmaster and showing him the sergeant's letter and her paramedic's card, he pulled a file from his filing cabinet.

'Yes, we do have a boy enrolled at this school called James Ross who fits your description, Ms Rayne, although he wasn't a regular attendee during the six months of his enrolment, and we haven't seen him at all for the past two weeks. He lived with his grandfather, who sadly died a fortnight ago. No one has seen Jim since the funeral. Apparently he and his dog disappeared that night.'

'I think we might have found him Mr O'Neill. He appears to have been rough living in the Botanical Gardens; at least that's where he was found after he and Toby were set upon.'

'The poor little soul. He's not yet turned ten, and as far as I'm aware, his grandfather was his only living relative. What will happen to him now?'

'He'll need to stay in hospital for a few more days, but after that I have no idea Mr O'Neill. Wherever he goes, he will want to keep Toby with him. It sounds like he is the last connection he has to his family.'

Kate and Belinda met up at the carpark and compared notes. Belinda had discovered that one elderly man with the surname of Ross had been buried locally during the past month: Harold Ross.

'Looks like Harold Ross was Jim's grandfather Belinda. Let's go to the address Mr O'Neill gave me, to see if we can find any more information.

The flat was behind a family run grocery shop. When Kate showed the owner the police letter, and explained why they were seeking information about Harrold and Jim Ross, he removed a set of keys from his desk drawer and took Kate and Belinda through to the adjoining flat behind the store.

'My wife and I used to live here when we first opened the shop, but we moved to our new house nearly ten years ago, and old Harry moved in not long after he sold his property. His grandson and dog came to live with him about a year ago, after Harry's son and daughter in law were killed in an accident. Nice little lad Jim is. Sadly, he ran away with his dog after Harry's funeral.'

'Has anyone else moved into the flat Mr Watson?'

'No, my wife and I haven't had the time, or the heart to clean it out. We kept hoping that Jim would come home.'

The small flat was neat and tidy, although the bedroom that Kate assumed had been Harrys had an unmade bed and medicine bottles still on the bedside table.

'Harry had a heart attack and was taken to hospital the night before he died, and we took Jim and Toby to our place, where he stayed until the day of the funeral. I have no idea if he returned here, before he and his dog disappeared.'

In the other bedroom the bed had been made, and clothes were hung in the wardrobe. A bookcase held a number of books, many relating to adventures of various animals, and a Harry Potter book lay open on the bedside table. Kate decided to take that back for Jim, and she also picked up a couple of Asterix and Tintin cartoon books from the bookcase.

'Do you mind if I take these for Jim to read Mr Watson?'

'No, take what you want. Do you think Jim will come back for his things?'

'Do you mind leaving it as it is for a bit longer Mr Watson? I will ask Jim if there is anything he would like me to collect for him. I am willing to pay you the rent owed, and will also pay for the flat to be cleared and cleaned when Jim has been through his things.'

That night Kate visited Jim, after speaking to the ward sister to give her the details that she had found out that afternoon.

'He must have been close to starving, the poor little mite. He's scoffed down everything put in front of him, and looked longingly at the food given to those in the beds beside him!'

Kate was pleased to see Jim looking a bit brighter. The swelling on his face was receding, and his eyes were nearly fully open. He was thrilled to see the books that Kate handed him. 'I will be able to read again, now that my eyes will open.'

'Is there anything else I can bring you Jim? Mr Watson has given me the keys to your flat, so I can collect anything you need from there.'

Jim smiled at Kate. 'These books are great thanks Kate.' He pulled a photo of Toby out from under his pillow. 'Is Toby alright Kate? Why does he have that big bandage around his neck?'

'Toby is much better Jim. The vet told me that he will have a sore throat and neck for a few days, after what happened to him, but he will recover. The bandage is to support the muscles of his neck, and to cover the wound caused by the rope. He has to eat soft food for a while, and he now has a harness to wear when I take him outside, because he can't wear a collar.'

'Who are the other two dogs in the photos? I love the little black one.'

'That's my little Mitty. She is a Chihuahua puppy and, like Toby, she also had to have some very special care. She and Toby get on well together. George, the other dog, is Service Dog who lives with Scott, one of my staff. As you can see, the three dogs sleep together during the day on George's bed in Scott's office.'

'Can I come to see them Kate?'

'I hope so Jim, when you are ready to leave here. Has anyone spoken to you about where you will live Jim?'

Jim suddenly burst into tears. 'A lady with a lot of papers came in this morning and said that I was scum, and that she would send Toby to the pound to be killed. Then she hit me! I will run away again if Toby can't stay with me!'

Kate was horrified to hear what Jim was saying. Could that be true, or just the ramblings of a young child under medication?

'Don't get yourself into a tizz Jim. I will see if I can find out more about your options in the morning. Please try to settle down, and think happy thoughts of being with Toby. I will give him a cuddle and kiss goodnight for you, when I get home.'

As Kate stood up, Jim looked at her shyly. 'Could I have one too please?' Kate bent down and gave the young boy a gentle hug and a quick kiss on the top of his head. 'I will see you again in the morning Jim. Sleep tight, don't let the bed bugs bite!' As she walked away, she heard him reply softly 'If they do, hit them with a shoe. I do!' Kate didn't know whether to laugh or cry as she walked towards the door.

CHAPTER 17

MAY

MELBOURNE

The ward sister stopped Kate as she walked out of the ward. 'Could you spare me a minute please Ms Rayne?' She led Kate to her office, where she gestured for Kate to sit in the chair opposite her desk, then sat down behind her desk.

'We are quite concerned about young Jim Ross Ms Rayne.'

'Kate please Sister.'

'Right. Jim appears to only speak freely when you are with him Kate. We are lucky to get a muttered 'yes' or 'no' but he does do as we ask. However, this morning when a Marjorie Hurston from DHS visited him, he became quite distressed. The horrible woman didn't realise that there was a nurse behind the curtain with the patient next to Jim, when she told him that they had places for scum like him, and that his dog would be put down!

Before Nurse Grant could leave her patient, she heard a loud slap and Jim cry out. When she pulled the curtain back, Jim was holding his cheek and the woman was standing over the poor little boy. Nurse Grant grabbed her raised arm and pulled her way from the bed, then called for help from a doctor who had just entered the ward. Together they forced the woman from the ward where I met them, having been summons by the emergency alarm.

Doctor Stewart and I escorted her to the front door and told her she was no longer welcome in the hospital and that we would be reporting her actions. A report of the incident, plus a signed statement from Nurse Grant is being sent to DHS and also to the police. I don't know how people like her are allowed to work for organisations like the DHS. Certainly not the sort who should be dealing with a fragile young child like Jim. I wouldn't like her to speak to a child of mine at any time.'

'Toby told me that she said he was to be sent to a home and his dog would be killed before she slapped him. He has threatened to run away if he can't keep Toby.'

'That would explain his two unsuccessful attempts to get out of bed this morning.'

Kate was appalled. What indeed would become of the poor little lad when he was discharged from hospital?

'Will you be visiting Jim tomorrow morning Kate?'

'I plan to Sister, before my afternoon shift starts after lunch.'

'I understand that you are a paramedic.'

'Yes. My partner and I were the ones who brought Jim in last night.'

'Would it be possible for you to bring Jim's dog with you in the morning?'

Kate looked searchingly at the sister. 'If you bring Toby to the ambulance bay, at 10 am, I will have Jim brought down in a wheelchair, or if he's not up to sitting, on a stretcher.'

Kate was overwhelmed. 'I will certainly be there Sister. Thank you.'

The next morning after breakfast Kate rang Frances Smythe. After initial pleasantries had been exchanged, Kate told Frances about Jim and her concern about his future.

'Did you say that DHS lady's name was Marjorie Thurston Kate?'

'Yes, I did Fran. I hope she's....'

Frances interrupted. 'She's no friend of mine Kate. No way! I know of her, and can't believe that she has been employed by DHS, and especially being allowed to deal with young children! I will be reporting this incident to the secretary, who is a good friend of mine.'

'Thanks Fran. The ward sister would be happy to tell you firsthand what happened with Jim, and she said they would be reporting her too.'

'Ok, I will contact the hospital straight away. Now Kate, am I right in thinking you are developing a soft spot for this little lad?'

Kate laughed. 'I suppose I am a bit Fran. I just can't bear to think what his future will be, being so young and alone. Are there any other organisations other than DHS, dealing with housing young orphans that I could contact?'

'There are a few. I will see what I can find out for you. I have to be in the city the day after tomorrow. Would you be free to have a chat then?'

'Would you like to come up to my apartment for lunch Fran? Nothing fancy, because I don't have a Sonia!'

After giving Frances her address, Kate went out onto the balcony and stared out into the distance, noting a yacht sailing on the bay. What were her feelings for Jim? Did she really want to be involved with him when he was discharged from hospital? Did she just feel sorry for him or was there more?

The next morning, Kate and Toby were waiting at the ambulance bay when the doors opened, and the ward sister pushed a puzzled Jim out to meet them. Kate quickly placed the excited terrier onto the delighted boy's lap as he sat in the wheelchair.

Sister's 'Be careful of those stiches and your ribs Jim' went unheeded as the weeping boy buried his face into the fur on his dog's shoulder. When he finally looked up, he stammered 'Thank you so much!'

'I will come back for you in fifteen minutes Jim. You will find that long enough to sit up for the moment.' As the sister went back inside, Jim looked up at Kate, and smiled at her in a way that made her heart melt, and tears spring to her eyes.

Finally, Kate managed to say 'Let's go over to those seats, so that I can sit down too Jim. Are you warm enough?'

'Yes thanks. Why are you crying?'

'They are happy tears Jim, from seeing you and Toby together again, and both looking so much better.'

'My ribs still hurt if I take a big breath, and sitting up is a bit uncomfortable, but it's worth it to be outside with Toby and you.'

All too soon for Kate, a nurse arrived to take Jim back to the ward. 'Sister sent her apologies. She was called away by a doctor.'

'Can Toby come to see me tomorrow?'

'Could we make it the day after Jim? I have some work that needs to be done, and it will give you a chance to feel stronger and to be able to sit up in that wheelchair a bit straighter. Scott said that he would call in to see you in the morning if you like, and he can bring George, his service dog. Would you like that?'

'George was in the photos with Toby, wasn't he? I would love to see them.'

Kate stood up and gave him a quick kiss on the cheek. 'See you later alligator!'

Toby chuckled. 'In a while, crocodile! Bye Toby. Say hello to Mitty for me Kate.'

Kate had little time to worry about Jim during the hectic shift that afternoon and evening. By the time she arrived back home just before midnight, she thought she would sleep as soon as her head hit the pillow. However, this didn't eventuate, and she spent the night tossing and turning, trying to rationalise her thoughts and feelings for Jim. Eventually, just as dawn was breaking, she fell into a troubled sleep and didn't wake up until after eight, when Mitty sat on her chest and began to lick her face.

Kate rang Belinda and told her that she would work from 'home', made some breakfast then tried to concentrate on developing plans for setting up service dog training programs for regional prisons. Later in the morning she prepared lunch, then went down to meet Frances at Ben's. Travelling up in the lift, Kate stopped on the third floor to show Frances the *Windfall Holdings* offices and to introduce her to Belinda and Toby. Scott and George had gone to visit Jim. As they travelled up to the penthouse, Kate explained how *Windfall Holdings* administered the entire building, and that the sixth-floor apartments were reserved for her staff.

Frances was thrilled that Kate had relaxed enough to invite her up to her apartment. She understood how uncomfortable her new friend was at flaunting her wealth to strangers, though she felt that she and Eric were more friends than strangers now to Kate.

Since her second visit to lunch with Frances and Eric, Kate and Frances had met on a number of occasions in the city for coffee and had become friends. She had also met with Eric a couple of times, to start discussions on the development of *Smythe Park* as a women's refuge.

'This is a beautiful apartment Kate. What a magnificent view.'

'It is, isn't it Fran? I spend a lot of time on the balcony when I'm up here.'

Just then Mitty woke up and realised that there was a stranger in the lounge area. She stood at the doorway to Kate's bedroom, with her hackles up and gave a rather comical growl. Kate quickly picked her up and gave her little head a rub. 'My goodness Mitt, that was a ferocious growl! This is my friend Fran.'

Kate held Frances's hand out to Mitty, who sniffed then licked the offered hand. 'She's a cutey isn't she. I'm not so sure about her guard dog role though!'

After lunch, Frances took a number of folders from her bag and explained what she had been looking up. 'Jim is an orphan, with no known relative isn't he Kate?'

'As far as I know, yes, Fran.'

'I have had dealings with a couple of organisations working with children who have lost their parents or been removed from their families by the courts. They help organise foster care for children in need, and also help with adoption in certain cases. Have you thought of the possibility of fostering Jim for a while Kate? At least until he has recovered completely from his injuries.'

'It has crossed my mind Fran. Would it be possible do you think?

He wouldn't be stuck up here all the time; I have a house up at Woolgoolga, looked after by a middle-aged brother and sister, who would love a young lad around when we visited. Also, my father and sister run a 500-hectare cattle property in north Eastern Victoria that I am sure he and Toby would love to visit.'

'That sounds wonderful for holidays Kate, but what about his schooling?'

Kate stared at Frances. 'Oh gosh Fran. I haven't given his schooling a thought! I don't even know what grade he's in!'

'That's not the end of the world Kate. Let's just think about the here and now. How long do you think they will keep Jim in hospital? And in your medical opinion, how long he will need to convalesce before he can go out and about, and attend school?'

'I'm not sure how long they will keep him in hospital – I think the ward sister will fight to keep him as long as possible, if he's to be sent to a home. Broken ribs can take six to ten weeks to heal, depending on your state of health and level of activity. Sometimes it can be months. However, for a young lad like Jim, I would guess more like six to seven weeks.'

'If you feel it's what you want or need to do, why don't you apply to foster him until he's fit and well? I will help you with the application if you like. You may find, that knowing of your medical background the hospital might be happy to release Jim earlier into your care.'

'I can work from here a lot of the time, and Belinda and Scott would keep an eye on him when I do my ambulance shifts. I could organise a tutor for him to do some schooling up here too.'

'Hey, whoa there Kate. One step at a time. Let's see what's available, and then ask Jim what he wants.'

'Providing that he can stay with Toby, I think he would agree to almost anything!'

'Would you like me to visit him and have a chat?'

'At the moment, I appear to be the only person who he will talk to Fran. If you tell him that you and I are friends, and show him some photos of you with Toby, maybe he will speak to you.'

CHAPTER 18

LATE MAY

MELBOURNE

Later that afternoon a nurse took Fran to Jim's bedside. 'Lady Smythe has come to visit you Toby.' Jim stared suspiciously at Frances. 'Are you one of those ladies that's come to take me away?'

Frances was shocked to see how terrified the young boy looked. 'No Jim, I am a friend of Kate and I have come to visit you this afternoon because Kate has had to go out in the ambulance. Also, I have more photos of your beautiful Toby to give to you.'

Jim's face lit up and he held out his hand to accept the envelope that Frances had taken from her bag. He seemed to forget his visitor as he looked through the ten photos of his beloved dog. Some had George and Mitty with him, another had been taken when he was walking in a park with Kate, and two were of Toby, Kate, and the lady.

Jim looked back to Frances. 'Why are you called Lady? Kate is just Kate.'

Frances laughed. 'Because I am married to a man who is a knight Jim.'

'Is he a real live knight?'

'Yes, he is called Sir Eric Smythe, so I am called Lady Frances Smythe. But you can just call me Fran, like Kate does.'

'How is Toby's neck Fran? I thought those boys had killed him when they hung him up with the rope.'

'His neck is getting much better. He still has the bandage on to protect the cuts, like you do on your arm. Kate changes the bandage each morning, and she is feeding him soft food to make it easier to swallow. Have you ever had a sore throat Jim?'

Jim nodded. 'Yes, and Gramps fed me soup until it didn't hurt to swallow.'

'Well, that's a bit how Toby feels at the moment, but he is getting better every day. Would you like me to tell Toby how you are feeling Jim?'

'My chest still hurts when I sit up or if I laugh, but my face isn't as sore' and my arm isn't too sore now.'

'I will have to try not to tell you any funny stories then. Are you enjoying the food here?'

'The food is great. I'm not nearly as hungry as I was before Kate found me. Is she coming to see me in the morning, like she said she would Fran?'

'I'm sure she will try to. She is very fond of you Jim, and wants you to get better as quickly as possible.'

'I like her too. I wish I could go home with her, instead of with that awful lady. She would let me keep Toby too.'

Fran looked thoughtfully at the young boy before she replied. 'Jim, am I right in thinking that you don't have any relatives?'

'Do you mean cousins and aunts and uncles?'

'Yes Jim, that's what I mean.'

'Mum and Dad didn't have brothers or sisters, same as me. Mum's mum and dad died just after I started going to school, and Gramps told me that his Dora died when I was a baby. So now Gramps has gone to heaven, there is just Toby and me.'

'Where did you live before you went to stay with your grandad Jim?'

'Kooyong, near the tennis courts. Dad was going to teach me to be a great tennis player like Roger Federer!'

'Roger Federer is a wonderful tennis player, isn't he?'

'Mm.' Jim yawned. 'Sorry Fran, I feel a bit tired.'

'That's alright Jim, I need to get home for dinner. Would you like me to visit you again?'

'Yes please Fran. I like talking to you, like I do to Kate. Could you please bring me some grapes when you come?'

Fran laughed. 'What colour do you like?'

'Red please.'

As Fran stood up to leave, Jim clutched her hand. 'Fran, can you please ask Kate if she will let me live with her if I am a good boy?'

'Yes Jim, I will ask her. Now you snuggle down with those photos of Toby.'

That night Frances told Eric about Jim, and the issue with Marjorie Hurston. 'Have you been in touch with Susan at the DHS Fran?'

'Yes, she was terribly upset to hear what happened to Jim. The police have been in touch with them and are looking for that dreadful woman. Apparently she went straight back to the office, where she lodged an application to have Jim placed in a home renown for housing wayward children before anyone was aware of the incident at the hospital. Then she left, saying that she had another appointment to go to!'

Eric was enraged. 'Surely they can cancel that application?'

'Once lodged, it will take some time to remove from the system, so if Jim is released from hospital soon, he might well be sent there.'

'We will see about that!' Eric grabbed the phone and dialled a number. 'Ah, Tony, Eric Smythe here. Could I meet you in your chambers before court in the morning? Something urgent has come up and I'm hoping that you may be able to sort it out. Thanks pal, I will see you in the morning.'

Frances watched her husband with concern. 'Eric, please don't get too riled. Remember, you are meant to be taking things easier now.'

'I feel fine Fran. I'm just so angry at such a blatant miscarriage of justice. Will you please drive me to Tony's chambers in Williams Street in the morning Fran?'

'I will Eric, providing you let me see Judge Thomas with you. Remember, I have met Jim and know more of his story than you do.'

Straight after an early breakfast, Frances and Eric drove to the city and were escorted up to Judge Thomas's chambers. Over a cup of coffee, Frances explained Jim's situation, and the application lodged by Mrs Hurston, prior to her disappearance.

The judge leant forward and steepled his fingers under his chin. 'Not yet ten you said Fran. Far too young to be a homeless orphan, let alone to be threatened like that to be separated from the only thing left in his life that he loves.'

Eric shook his head slightly when he saw Frances was about to speak.

'I will have an injunction placed on the application lodged by that woman straight away. Hopefully the police will soon find her and throw the book at her! Sorry, I detest people who use their positions to the detriment of others. I will also recommend Jim be placed with Ms Kate Rayne, until a more suitable home is found. That young lady is getting quite a name for her endeavours to ease the load of those struggling to survive. I thoroughly approve of the way her company is setting up schemes to benefit both humans and animals; not just handing out cash to anyone who thinks that they need it.'

'We are both very fond of Kate Tony. She and I are currently working on a project together.'

'She certainly did a good job on you, old man.' Judge Thomas laughed as he stood up and gave Eric a gentle punch on the arm.

That morning, when Kate and Toby met with Jim, the nurse left them with instructions to enjoy the sunshine while it lasted and to be back in half an hour.

'Does that mean that you can take me out into the park Kate?'

'I think we have time sir. Are you warm enough?'

'Yes thanks. Come on Toby, let's go for a ride.'

When they were well away from Flemington Road, Kate put Toby down to let him run free for a while, and was pleased to see that he didn't go too far from Jim. She gave Jim some fruit & nut mix to nibble, and sat watching the joy on the little boy's face as he watched his dog scamper around. *How could people be so heartless to think of separating them?*

As she watched, Kates' phone rang, and she noted that the call was from Fran.

'Morning Fran, how are you and Eric this morning?'

'We are fine thanks Kate. Are you with Jim this morning?'

'Yes, we are out in the park. Jim is in his element watching Toby running around.'

'Eric and I are in the city at the moment. Could we meet you at hospital reception in say half an hour?'

'Sure Fran. Is there a problem?'

'Far from it Kate! I will explain when we meet. See you soon.'

Wondering what Fran had found out, Kate slowly wheeled Jim back to the ambulance bay, and didn't have long to wait before the nurse arrived to take him back to the ward. After leaving Toby happily gnawing at a shin bone in the back of her Escape, Kate went into reception to meet Fran and Eric. Once they had ordered coffee and found a table in the coffee shop, Fran looked at Kate.

'Have you heard when Jim is likely to be discharged Kate?'

'Not yet. Why Fran?'

'Eric and I have been in contact with a number of people who have the authority to make things happen. If Jim is happy to stay with you, and you are willing to look after him until he is fully recovered from his injuries, he can be discharged into your care tomorrow morning.'

Eric patted Kate's hand. 'You look a bit like a stunned mullet my dear!'

'I can't believe it. He asked me this morning if he could come to stay with me, and I told him that I would love him to if it could be arranged.'

'Eric has the paperwork for you to apply to be Jim's guardian. If, as he says, he has no living relations, there is the possibility of extending that to adoption at some later date, if you both desire it.'

112

Kate stared at her friends, then smiled. 'Oh, that is the most wonderful news. When can we tell Jim?'

Eric handed Kate some forms. 'Fill these in while we have our coffee Kate, and I will ensure that they are processed asap. Then we will go up and see this young man who I have been hearing so much about.'

Half an hour later Kate introduced Jim to Eric.

'Do you have armour to wear into battle Sir Eric?'

'He has put on a bit too much weight to wear armour these days Jim!' laughed Fran.

Eric frowned at his wife. 'No, I don't have armour Jim. We modern knights missed out on the fun of riding a horse while wearing armour. I just have a special medal presented to me by the Queen at Buckingham Palace.'

'Wow, can I see it sometime please Sir Eric?'

'Yes, you can my lad. Now, I think Kate wants to speak to you.'

'Jim, would you and Toby like to stay with me when you leave hospital?'

'Do you mean to live with you Kate?'

'Yes, that's what I mean Jim.' She stopped speaking as Jim lent over and gave her a hug and a big kiss on the cheek. 'There's some paperwork to get sorted, but yes, you can come to live with Mitty and me.'

Just then the ward sister stopped at Jim's bed. 'I gather Jim is happy with your proposition Kate. Providing the doctor agrees after his visit to you tomorrow morning Jim, Kate can take you home. You will still need the wheelchair for a few more days, and will need to rest up for a couple more weeks until your ribs have healed properly, so you will need to follow her instructions instead of mine!'

CHAPTER 19

———⟶✦⟵———

LATE MAY

MELBOURNE

The next morning when Kate and Jim drove into her garage, Scott and Toby were waiting for them, Kate having rung him just before she left the hospital carpark. When Scott pushed the wheelchair into the lift, Jim looked at all the buttons. 'This building is a lot bigger than where Mum, Dad and I lived. There were only four buttons, and I used to push number three to stop at our floor.'

'Well Jim, I live up on the top floor, so would you please push number twenty.'

Like everyone who first entered the penthouse apartment, Jim was transfixed by the view from the large panoramic plate glass windows. 'Wow, you can see the MCG from here. Can you see them playing footy Kate?'

'You can certainly see the lights at night Jim, but the players are a bit hard to see!'

Then he spotted Mitty who ran from the bedroom to greet Kate. 'She is tiny Kate! Will she let me hold her?'

'Yes, she will. Just remember that she is still a puppy and don't grip her too tightly.' Kate picked Mitty up and put her on Jim's lap, and placed his hand on her back. Mitty immediately tried to climb up Jim's chest to lick his chin. 'I think she likes me. Can I sit on the ground with her Kate, in case I drop her? Then Toby can be with us too.' Scott and Kate stood back and watched the young boy laughing with glee as he and the two dogs cuddled together on the lounge floor.

'That's the best medicine for him Kate, providing they don't get too boisterous.'

'You are spot on there Scott. Would you and Belinda like to come up for dinner tonight. I'm going to order up some pizzas per request from Jim.'

'Thanks Kate, that would be great. See you at six?'

Kate laughed 'I'm going to have to readjust my mealtimes, aren't I?'

When Jim and the dogs settled down, Kate took him on a tour of the penthouse, showing him his bedroom and ensuite. 'There is also a bathroom if you want a bath anytime Jim.'

'I think it is fantastic to have my own shower and toilet.'

'Later I will take you up onto the roof, where there is a garden and places to sit when it's a bit warmer. Now, let's have some lunch, then I think it would be a good idea for you to have a rest in your room.'

'How long am I going to feel so tired and sore Kate?'

'Your body took quite a pounding Jim, and broken ribs take their own time to heal. The best cure is rest. Anytime you feel you need to, just head off to your room. You don't have to ask permission, and I'm sure that Toby and Mitty will want to go with you.'

Two hours later, Jim and the dogs emerged from his room and joined Kate in the chairs near the window. Kate put down her book and to her surprise, Jim climbed onto her lap. 'Do you mind if I sit here for a bit Kate. It's so nice to snuggle up to someone again. I used to sit on Mum's lap when I came home from school.'

'Sure you can sit on my lap Jim. At least until you get too heavy! You have put on weight since Brian and I put you on the stretcher!'

'Is Brian your boyfriend?'

'No Jim, he and I work together when we are on duty in the ambulance.'

'What about Scott?'

'Scott and Belinda work for me, and their apartments are down on the sixth floor of this building.'

'Do you have a boyfriend?'

'Not at the moment, unless it's you?'

Jim giggled. 'Do you have a family?'

'Yes, I do. My father and younger sister Julie live on a large cattle property in north eastern Victoria, and Dad's sister, my aunt Margaret, looks after my grandparents in Lakes Entrance.'

'Does that mean that your dad will be my new grandad now Kate?'

Kate was startled for a moment. A nine-year old's reasoning and questions were certainly different from the world she had been inhabiting of late.

'Well, yes I guess he could if you want him to be. We will have to ask him.'

'Do I have to call you Mum now?'

Kate thought for a moment. 'No, you don't Jim. You will have special memories of your mother and father, and I don't want to take their place. My mother died when I was a bit younger than you are, and Aunt Margaret came to look after us. She never tried to take Mum's place, and she kept talking about her so that I wouldn't forget her. Does it worry you to remember your parents?'

'No. I hate remembering about when I heard that they were dead, but I love thinking about things that Mum, Dad and I did together.'

'You told Fran that you lived at Kooyong. Where did you go to school?'

'Scotch College Junior School.'

'What grade were you in when you left there?'

'Grade three, but I never finished cause of Mum and Dad's accident.'

'What grade did you go into at school in Broadmeadows?'

'They put me back into grade three, but I didn't like it there, so I skipped school most of the time, and helped Gramps when I could. I know that it was wrong, but the boys there were horrid and made fun of my uniform.'

'What do you like to do Jim? I've not had much to do with boys your age, so you will have to let me know what you need or would like to do.'

Jim gave her a cheeky grin. 'Do you mean anything?!'

Kate ruffled his hair. 'No, you little scamp, I don't mean anything! But I will do what I can.'

'When I was at Scotch, I use to love playing with my friends. We played cricket, footy and did a bit of aths. And Dad was teaching me to play tennis.'

'So, you like being active, which is going to be a problem for the next few weeks until your ribs have healed. What about reading?'

'I like reading books I can understand. The Harry Potter books are good, although I prefer to have them read to me.'

Do you like swimming Jim?

'I like to swim in a pool, but big surf scares me.'

'Me too. There's a lake on the property where I grew up, where Julie and I learnt to swim. There is also a pool downstairs, so we can swim there if you like. Now, I will try to explain a little about what I do. As you know, I am a paramedic and I do three shifts a week, usually afternoons and evenings. I also work here in this building in an office on the third floor with Scott and Belinda.

Windfall Holdings designs and funds programs for the homeless, helps animal shelters, and funds the training of guide dogs, and service dogs, as well as other projects in the pipeline.'

'Dad got Toby from an animal shelter not long before I went to live with Gramps.' Jim gave a little sigh and looked out of the window.

'Okay, what say we read for a bit, then we will order some pizzas. What sort do you like?'

'I like the hot one with everything on it best, then the seafood one.'

'What other types of food do you like?'

'I like seafood and steak best. Roast lamb is nice with crunchy potatoes. Gramps usually cooked some meat and vegetables for tea, then gave me a fresh piece of fruit to eat. He always cooked porridge for breakfast, but I would rather Weet–Bix and toast.'

'I think we will go grocery shopping tomorrow, and we will buy what we both like.'

That night Jim had a wonderful time. He got on well with both Scott and Belinda, who, after they had polished off the pizzas, sat down and played Monopoly with him, while Kate dealt with a problem that had arisen between a new animal shelter and a local council.

Jim was worn out by the time the game finished and was quite happy for Scott to put him to bed. When Kate went in to say goodnight, he hugged her. 'Can Scott and Belinda look after me when you are on duty Kate? They are great fun.'

'I will ask them for you.' She bent over and kissed his forehead. 'Good night Jim. Call me if you need me.'

'Can you please leave the lounge light on just for tonight Kate, in case I wake up and forget where I am?'

Jim was still sleeping peacefully when Kate wakened in the morning. She set the cereal and bowls out on the table, made herself a coffee and went out onto the balcony. It was a cold morning, but she loved the breeze on her face. Once Jim felt comfortable with his new surroundings and was happy to be on his own for short periods of time, Kate thought that she would go out running again. Deep in thought Kate didn't realise that Jim was awake until Mitty ran out to her, with Toby not far behind. Kate looked around and saw Jim standing in the lounge, wearing a t-shirt and his boxer shorts.

'Good morning Jim. Did you sleep well?'

'Like a log Kate. I have only just woken up. What do you want me to do?'

Kate stood up and walked inside, shutting the sliding door.

'Once you get used to our daily routine Jim, you won't have to ask what to do. This is your home now, and you are free to do what you like, providing you don't destroy it! And never climb on the balcony barrier!'

'No way, I'm scared of heights. I like looking out, but I can't look down.'

'Why don't you help yourself to breakfast, and I will take Toby and Mitty up to the garden. I will take you up later when you are dressed.'

When she and the dogs returned, Jim was munching a piece of toast and had made himself a hot drink of milo. 'Is it okay for me to use the electric jug and the toaster by myself Kate?'

'If you are used to using them Jim, sure. Just take care. Are you used to using an electric stove?'

'Yes. I used to do some of the cooking for Gramps when he was tired. He would watch me though – I never cooked by myself.'

'Would you like to go out to Broadmeadows this morning, to go through your things and bring back what you want? You certainly need some warm clothes and pyjamas. I will hunt up some cases and boxes while you finish your breakfast.'

Jim shuddered as they drove through Broadmeadows. 'I don't like this place at all Kate.'

'We will be as quick as we can.'

They quickly packed Jim's clothes into a case and his books were put in a box. 'Is there anything else you want to take Jim? Anything of your grandfather's?'

'I don't want to go into his room, but there is a photo of Mum and Dad with me, and another of Gramps on a motor bike wearing his medals. Those are in his bedside drawer. I don't want anything else.'

When Kate opened the bedside drawer, she noticed a small bundle of letters, with an unopened solicitor's envelope on top, plus a bankbook, wallet, and bank deposit box key with the medals. Placing the contents of the drawer and the two framed photographs into a shopping bag, she went back out to where Jim was waiting, and they carried the case and box of books out to the car

When they arrived home, Kate and Jim looked through his

clothes, and decided that he really needed some new, better fitting outfits. Together they went to Myers and bought some warm shirts, trousers, and a couple of woollen jumpers, plus under clothes, pyjamas, and a tracksuit. Later, Kate pushed Jim in his wheelchair, while he steered a trolley around the supermarket and pointed out the items that he liked. Kate was quite impressed with his sensible choices – she had been expecting a lad his age to choose more junk food.

Jim was happy to spend the afternoon in the office with Kate, sitting in the lounge chair reading, or having a snooze in the swag that Scott had brought down for him to lie in.

CHAPTER 20

GEELONG
LATE MAY

When she was back at her office desk Kate looked at the address on the solicitor's envelope, then ran a search and found the telephone number for the solicitor's office in Hamilton. After explaining why she had the letter that they had sent to Harold Ross in her possession, and that she was looking after his grandson James, they arranged to meet at the solicitor's Geelong office the next morning. Mr Stewart was unaware of Harry's death, so Kate gave him the name of the undertaker who had organised Harry's funeral.

Kate rang Frances to discuss her call to the solicitors. When she heard that Kate would have to go to Geelong for the meeting, she offered to stay with Jim while Kate was away. She had visited the young lad a few times in hospital and he was quite happy in her company. To make sure that he was happy with the plans she suggested that she and Eric could call in for a visit after work, if that suited Kate.

Jim was thrilled to hear that Fran and Eric would be visiting, as he considered Eric to be his own special knight. When they arrived with a bottle of wine, plus a small pack of orange juice for Jim, they all went out to sit on the balcony. Kate turned to Jim. 'Jim, tomorrow

I have to go to Geelong for an important meeting. Would you be happy if Fran came to spend the day with you?'

Jim looked at Fran, who winked at him and made him giggle. 'Yes Kate. I like Fran.' He turned to Eric 'I like you too Sir Eric. Can you come too?'

Eric chuckled. 'I am sorry Jim, I need to be in a meeting tomorrow morning. But what say I ask Sonia to pack us a surprise picnic, and I have lunch with you both?'

When Jim took Frances inside to show her his new bedroom and ensuite, Eric spoke quietly to Kate. 'Alec Stewart, Judge Thomas, and I went to school together Kate. He is a good solicitor, very meticulous in all his dealings. He will question you quite thoroughly about your involvement with Jim, and what your plans are for his future. Take as much ID as you have, and if you wish, use Judge Thomas and me as referees. He doesn't have to know of your financial situation, other than that you are well able to provide for Jim's upkeep.'

'Thank you Eric. As far as Mr Stewart is concerned I could be someone trying to cash in on a family tragedy.'

The next morning, Frances arrived while Kate and Jim were having breakfast, so Fran had a cup of coffee with Kate. She handed Kate an envelope addressed to Alec Stewart. 'Eric has written a note for you to give to Alec, Kate. He thinks that it might be more suitable to give him a written reference, rather than just giving his name.'

'Thanks Fran. I really do appreciate your joint support.'

When Kate left the apartment, Frances was sitting on the couch, with Mitty on her lap and Jim and Toby snuggled up beside her as she read an Asterix book to them.

When Kate entered the offices of Stewart and Stewart, Lawyers & Solicitors, a young lady wearing a dark suit and carrying a number of legal documents followed her into the reception area. Placing the documents on the front desk she turned to Kate and smiled.

'Ms Rayne I presume? I am Jean Stewart.'

Kate shook Jean's extended hand. 'Good morning Jean. Yes, I am Kate Rayne.'

'I am afraid my father is running late this morning Kate. There has been an accident on the Hamilton Highway the other side of Inverleigh, a bit over half an hour from Geelong, and the highway is blocked.'

'I hope your father wasn't involved Jean.'

'No, he is fine thank goodness, but is caught up in the traffic jam while they clear the highway. I am Dad's partner, and am fully aware of the reason for your appointment with Dad today. Would you like to come into my office and we can at least go through the preliminaries?'

When they were seated in the spacious office Jean pointed to a voice recorder on her desk. 'Would you mind if I record our meeting Kate, so that Dad can listen to what we speak about, if he is delayed for too long?'

'No that's fine Jean, I have nothing to hide.'

'Good. First of all, I should tell you that Dad and Harry Ross were old friends since their early school days, and Dad has been his solicitor since they were young men and Harry took over running the family property near Hamilton. I knew Ian at state school, but lost contact with him when he went to Scotch College. Dad was horrified to hear of Ian and Julie's death last year and even more so of Harry's recent demise, and is very worried about Jim, his young grandson.'

'When I left my apartment this morning, Jim was snuggled up with a friend of mine listening to her read him an Asterix book, dialects included! Perhaps it would help if I explain why Jim is living with me at the moment.'

Half an hour later Jean sat back and smiled at Kate. 'It sounds like young Jim has fallen on his feet finding you Kate. Losing his grandfather so soon after his parents at such a young age would have turned his world upside down. Thank goodness you and your partner were able to rescue him, and get him off the streets, and that you saved him from being sent to a home for wayward children.'

'Jim and I quickly developed a rapport while he was in The Children's Hospital, enhanced at first, I am sure, by my care for his dog Toby. He is a lovely young lad, desperately in need of a secure, loving home environment. I currently have temporary custody of him while he is recuperating from his injuries, and even after such a short time together, I have become very fond of him. If he wants me to, I will happily take on a more permanent custody agreement, for as long as he wishes.'

As Kate finished speaking, the office door opened and an older man asked 'Can I come in Jean?'

'Certainly Dad. Come in and meet Kate Rayne.'

Kate stood up and shook hands with Alec Stewart. 'I am sorry to be so late Kate. I'm sure Jean has explained the circumstances. Please be seated and continue your conversation with my daughter.'

'Kate has been explaining how she came to have custody of Jim Ross Dad. I have taped everything so you can listen to our earlier conversation later on. Suffice to say, both Kate and Jim are happy with their current situation at the moment.'

'That's a relief. I was so worried about Jim when you informed me of Harry's death. Thank you Kate for caring for the young lad in this obviously traumatic time, and also for your information re the hospital that Harry was taken to and the name of the undertaker who dealt with his burial. With this evidence of his death I can now apply for probate and deal with his estate.'

Kate handed the unopened letter and other contents of Harry's bedside drawer to Mr Stewart, plus the letter from Eric. 'These were in Harry's bedside drawer Mr Stewart, and this is a letter to you from Sir Eric Smythe.'

'Ah, yes, I gather you are responsible for keeping Eric upright and standing. Thank goodness you were the one to resuscitate him until your colleagues arrived. Please excuse me while I read this.'

'Would you like a coffee or cup of tea while we wait Kate?'

'A white tea, no sugar would be lovely thanks Jean.'

As Jean left the office, Mr Stewart looked over his glasses at Kate. 'Eric tells me that you have become good friends with Fran and himself, and that you are working with him on a couple of business projects.'

'Yes, they are a lovely couple, and have become wonderful

friends. Jim has claimed Eric as his own personal knight, and Fran is looking after Jim today while I am here in Geelong.'

'That was something I was going to discuss with you Kate. I'm assuming that you are a single working woman and I need to ask – how are you going to look after Jim while you're at work?'

'Yes, I am a paramedic with the Metropolitan Ambulance Service and am on duty three evenings a week, and the other days I work for *Windfall Holdings*. My office is in the same building as my apartment, so until Jim goes back to school, he spends the day either in my apartment or with me in the office. A couple of my staff happily look after Jim when I am on ambulance duty, and Fran and my housekeeper also help when needed. So, at no time is he left alone for any period of time.'

'It's quite a commitment that you are taking on Kate, both personally and financially.

'Yes, I realise that Mr Stewart, but it's something that I am prepared to undertake.'

As Jean came back into the office and placed cups of tea in front of Kate and her father, Mr Stewart held up the unopened letter from his office. 'This letter is the final report and our account for the sale of Harry Ross's property to his former manager, who has been leasing the property since Harry moved to Broadmeadows.

As you are now acting as Jim's legal guardian I can tell you that he is now a very rich young lad. His parent's estate is already in a trust account for him, and Harry received a monthly payment for Jim's upkeep. As his grandfather's sole beneficiary Jim will now be in receipt of the full payment for the family property near Hamilton.'

'Mr Stewart, I'm financially secure and prepared to personally provide for all of Jim's upkeep. Could his grandfather's assets be added to Jim's trust account, to accumulate over time, for him to access later in his life?'

'Rest assured Kate, if you are happy for us to remain as Jim's solicitors, we will do our best to preserve Jim's inheritance.'

'Would you like me to bring Jim to see you Mr Stewart, when he is well enough to undertake a relatively long car trip?'

'That would be wonderful, thank you Kate. And thankyou once again for taking care of my friend's grandson. I gather Eric in joining Fran and Jim for lunch today.'

Kate laughed. 'Yes, he was going to cajole Sonia to put together a picnic lunch for the three of them to have in the gardens opposite my apartment building. Then I gather the three of them are going to see Mary Poppins while I am driving back to the city!'

CHAPTER 21

————⟢⟣————

EARLY JUNE

MELBOURNE

W hile Jim was having a check-up at the hospital, Kate rang the office at the Scotch College Junior School and asked to speak to the Principal. She was surprised how unwilling the lady was to listen to her, and how quickly her request was refused. When the lady hung up, Kate rang Eric and explained what had happened.

Half an hour later Kate received a phone call from the principal himself, apologising profusely for the earlier mix up, and a meeting was arranged for later that afternoon. Before Kate set off for the meeting, a courier delivered an official letter from Judge Thomas addressed to the principal, plus a less formal, handwritten note to Kate.

> *Dear Ms Rayne,*
>
> *Sir Eric Smythe informs me that you have been refused an appointment with the Scotch College Junior School principal, regarding Jim Ross.*
>
> *I have spoken to the principal David Wilson to vouch for your good name and intentions for young Jim, so I expect you will hear from him soon. If you don't, please let me know.*

*I hope all is going well with your new charge, and that
you are coping with the great change he has brought to your
life. I would be interested in hearing of Jim's progress, if you
have the time Ms Rayne.*

*Regards
Anthony Thomas*

When Kate arrived at the school office she was immediately
ushered into the principal's office. The tall, dark haired young man
stood up immediately and walked around his desk to shake Kate's
hand.

'Ms Rayne, thank you for coming. My name is David Wilson.
I apologise for this morning's fiasco. The girl you spoke to is new,
and Jim Ross's name meant nothing to her.' He gestured to a chair
in front of his desk. 'Please be seated Ms Rayne.'

'Thank you, Mr Wilson.' She handed the judge's letter to him. 'I
was told to give you this letter before we discussed Jim.'

Mr Wilson looked at the official envelope with the Judge's name
and chamber's address embossed on the top left corner. He looked at
Kate and grimaced. 'I fear this will be a wrap on the knuckles from
our esteemed Judge.'

Seeing Kate's puzzled look, he smiled. 'Judge Thomas is one of
our Old Boys, who keeps a watchful eye over his old alma mater.
Please excuse me while I read his letter.'

Kate looked around the office with two walls covered by
bookcases full of books and a large window overlooking the school
ovals. She noticed Mr Wilson frown a couple of times, then he smiled
and put the letter on his desk.

'Judge Watson speaks very highly of you Ms Rayne, and I have
been instructed to help you in any way I can. He also says that you
rescued Jim Ross and now have temporary custody of him!'

'That's correct Mr Wilson. The main reason I wish to speak
to you is to find out more about Jim's earlier life. I don't want to
question him too much, and dredge up bad memories, when he is

just beginning to settle down. Do you know that Jim's grandfather died not long ago?'

'No. That's why I was puzzled why Jim should need rescuing, and is now in your charge.'

'Are you able to tell me anything about Jim's parents and his earlier life while he attended this school Mr Wilson? All I know is that his parents both died in an accident last year, and he went to live with his grandfather.'

Mr Wilson sat back in his chair. 'Ian and Julie Ross were both employed here at Scotch College; Ian was a senior school physical education teacher and the head rowing coach, while Julie worked in the bursar's office. They lived in an apartment in Kooyong. Julie returned to work when Jim started school here. Tragically they were both killed in an accident while on holidays in New Zealand last September. I was told that Jim was staying with his grandfather while they were away, and that he stayed with him after their funerals. No one here has seen him since.'

'I am afraid Jim took longer than expected to settle after his parents' sudden deaths Mr Wilson, and he didn't cope too well in Broadmeadows, especially when he wore his uniform. He missed a lot of school and preferred to help his grandfather. As I mentioned, Mr Ross died suddenly a few weeks ago, and Jim and his dog ran away after the funeral. They lived on the streets in the city, and slept in the gardens near the Shrine until some louts beat him up a month ago, injuring him quite severely.

I am a paramedic, and my partner and I were called to attend to an injured boy. Jim's dog had been injured as well, so I took him to a vet after we left Jim at the Royal Children's Hospital. For a while I was the only person that Jim would talk to, mainly about his dog. He was terrified of being separated from him, as an officious lady had threatened, so I offered to look after them both, and was granted temporary guardianship.'

David Wilson looked at Kate and smiled. 'That's some undertaking Ms Rayne.'

'Kate please Mr Wilson.'

129

'And my name's David. So, what are your plans for Jim, Kate? Are you intending for him to come back to us?'

'I haven't thought that far. I was just hoping to find out as much as I could about Jim's past, so I don't accidentally put my foot in it!'

'Where do you live? Would it be possible for Jim to resume his schooling with us? I am sure that we could cover some of the fees of the son of a former staff member and Old Boy.'

'I would need to discuss this with Jim first David. The fees wouldn't be an issue and, although I live in the city, Jim could be driven to and from school. He has spoken of how much he has missed his school friends, but if he came back here, wouldn't he be in a different level to those boys next year?'

'We would have to look into that of course, as well as finding out what Jim's wishes are. But he is a bright lad, and with some additional tutoring, he could possibly cope in grade five next year. We would certainly like to have Jim back, if he wants to return. Do you mind me asking what plans you have for him for the rest of the year Kate?'

'At the moment, he is still recovering from his injuries, and is slowly recovering his strength and confidence. I plan to take him up to Woolgoolga, just north of Coffs Harbour, to give him a chance to get some fresh air and sunshine while he and his dog play on the beach. I do however want him to start thinking positively about his education and have been wondering if it would be prudent to employ a tutor for him, until he is enrolled in school again.'

'Would you like me to look into this further for you Kate, while you speak to Jim? You are welcome to bring him to see me if he would like to come back to us.'

'Thank you, David but I don't want to impose further on your time.'

'Ian and I were good friends Kate, and I saw quite a lot of Jim out of school. Unfortunately, at the time of the accident, I was traveling in Europe, and didn't hear of the tragic news until after I had begun working at a Yorkshire school as a participant of the International Teacher Exchange Program. I was informed that Jim had left Scotch and was living with his grandfather. I only returned home a couple of weeks ago and I regret to say, I haven't given him much thought since my return. Now I would like to see if I can rectify that.'

'Well, thank you David, I accept your offer. I will speak to Jim this evening, and will let you know his response. Personally, I would love him to come back to Scotch to complete his education here. My father is a Scotch Old Boy and I went to PLC, following in Aunt Meg's footsteps, and thoroughly enjoyed my education there, but Julie rebelled, and left school early, rather than leave home.'

'You must be a person of some importance, to have the backing of Judge Thomas and Sir Eric Smythe Kate.'

Kate looked shocked, and David laughed. 'It's not often that someone in my position is told, in no uncertain terms, by two of Melbourne's most eminent men, to comply with a stranger's wishes!'

'Good grief David, I am sorry. I am a friend of the Smythe's, and I asked Sir Eric for advice on how best to contact you in relation to finding out about Jim's history.'

'Don't worry Kate. Sir Eric and Judge Thomas are good friends from their school days, and young Jim is lucky to have you and those two looking out for him.'

David stood up. 'It has been a pleasure meeting you Kate, but I'm afraid I have a meeting that I must attend in ten minutes. Rest assured, I will look into possible solutions to Jim's education, and will keep in touch with you.'

That night after dinner Jim helped Kate clear up, then they sat on the lounge as had become their habit, and Kate read a chapter of Harry Potter and the Philosopher's Stone out loud to Jim. When the chapter was finished Kate looked at the young boy, snuggled on her lap. 'How much of this can you read by yourself Jim?'

Jim grinned. 'Nearly all of it Kate, but I love sitting on your knee listening to you read it out aloud. You use so many different voices, and you make it sound like it is really happening.'

'Praise indeed, young sir, I thank you for your compliment! Seriously though Jim, if you can read this well, don't you miss learning the other things that you did in school?'

Jim thought for a moment before speaking. 'I do miss school and my friends Kate. But where could I go to school near here?'

'I was wondering if you would be happy to go back to Scotch College. Would it upset you too much to go back there when you parents won't be there?'

'They worked in the senior school, so I never saw them during school time, and I am sort of starting to get used to not having them around.'

'Do you remember Mr Wilson, the principal of the Junior School?'

'Oh yes, he and Dad were great mates, and they took me to the footy a few times. Who do you barrack for Kate? I barrack for Melbourne.'

'Um, will you still like me if I say Collingwood?'

'I will try!' Jim tried to look serious, but quickly started to giggle.

'Would you like to see Mr Wilson again, to talk about your future education. I would be happy to arrange for you to be driven to and from school each day, if you want to go back to Scotch.'

'Yes Kate, I would love to see Mr Wilson again. Thank you.'

CHAPTER 22

EARLY JUNE

WOOLGOOLGA

Jim gripped Kate's hand tightly as he looked out of the window as the plane took off from Melbourne Airport. 'Wow, we are really up in the air Kate. Look how small the trees are, and look at the tiny cows!'

All too soon, the view of the ground was obscured by clouds, so Jim copied Kate and opened his book. Toby was sleeping peacefully in his dog carrier, and Mitty as usual was lying happily in her carrier sling across Kate's chest. Jim gave Mitty's ears a gentle scratch, then turned to Kate. 'How long will we be flying for Kate?'

'It takes about an hour and a half to get to Sydney, where we have to wait for about an hour, then we travel in a smaller plane for just over an hour to get to Coffs Harbour.'

'Can we go and see Sydney Harbour Bridge while we are in Sydney?'

'There won't be time I'm afraid Jim. Sydney Airport isn't actually in Sydney, just nearby. The runway that we land on is in Botany Bay, the bay next to Sydney Harbour where the bridge is.' Seeing his disappointed face Kate added 'Would you like to spend a weekend in Sydney Jim? We could check out the bridge, the Opera House, Tooronga Park Zoo, and other places that you might be interested in?'

'That would be grouse Kate. Could we go out on the harbour on a ferry for my birthday?'

Kate looked at Jim in surprise, realising that she didn't know his birth date. 'When is your birthday Jim?'

'I will be ten on the eighth of September.'

'Goodness, that's not far away! Would you like to visit Sydney for your birthday?'

Jim's eyes shone. 'I would love to Kate. Can Toby come too?'

'Sorry Jim. I don't think he would be allowed to stay in the hotel. Only dogs like George, that have special permission, can stay with their owners. I'm sure that Scott would look after Toby and Mitty for us while we're away.'

'Why can they come with us on the plane today?'

'Because we will be staying in my house at Woolgoolga.'

'Oh. How come these seats are so big Kate? Dad took me on a big plane once, but we were near the back, not like we are here up the front. Dad kept complaining that his legs didn't fit. My legs don't reach the back of that seat. Look.' Jim stuck his legs straight out, but didn't touch the front seat.

Kate laughed. She was slowly coming to grips with Jim's quick switches of topics in his conversation. 'I paid a bit extra to make sure that we had room for Toby to stay with us, and not be shut in with the luggage.'

'Toby wouldn't like to be packed in with the suitcases.'

By the time their plane landed at Coffs Harbour, Kate was beginning to realise just how much her life was changing. Normally, she found the trip to Coffs quite relaxing and usually managed to sleep for some of the way. This time she felt exhausted from Jim's continuous chattering and questioning. However, she was becoming very fond of the lad, and was determined to change her rather set ways to accommodate his needs.

Donald met them at the airport, and quickly made friends with Toby. Mitty just gave his hand a lick, then she lay back in her sling. When Donald began to drive out of the airport carpark, with Jim sitting in the front passenger seat, Jim looked at him in surprise. 'How come I can't hear the engine Donald?'

'This car is what is called a hybrid Jim. It has an electric motor for when we are traveling at slower speeds, then when we are on the freeway it runs on petrol.' Donald pointed to a dial on the dashboard. 'Watch that dial there. You will see it change colour as it switches from one to the other.'

While Jim studiously watched the dial, Donald looked quickly in the mirror at Kate. 'So, have you brought me another fishing buddy Kate?'

Before Kate could answer, Jim turned to Donald. 'Do you go fishing Donald? I went to a lake with Dad a few times, and loved putting the worms on the hooks. I don't think they liked it much though!'

'I go out in a boat Jim. Would you like to come out with me in the morning, if Kate approves?'

Jim turned around to Kate and pleaded 'Please can I go Kate? Please?

'We will need to get you a properly fitted life jacket first.'

Donald winked at Jim. 'We go past just the place on the way home Kate.'

'Alright, let's stop and see what we can find for him.'

Half an hour later they were on their way again, with a life jacket for Jim and also an appropriate dog vest for Toby.

After a quick greeting to Jessie, Jim and Donald took the three bigger dogs out onto the back lawn to get to know each other. Mitty was content to sit on Jessie's knee, while she and Kate had a much-needed cup of tea.

'You look exhausted lass. Nine-year-old boys certainly keep you on your toes, don't they! Plus, you have had a lot on your plate since you were last up here.'

'Life has certainly done a 180° on me Jessie. Once I get used to it, I'm sure I will be fine. I am very fond of young Jim, and I am determined to do what is best for him.'

Jessie looked affectionately at Kate. 'Don't try to do everything at once Kate, or give in to him all the time. As you get to know each other better, you will learn each other's limits. Now, you just lie back and relax while you are up here, and let Donald and me keep young Jim occupied.'

When Donald, Jim and the dogs came inside, Jessie put lunch on the table, and they all sat down to eat. Jim, who was looking out at the sea suddenly exclaimed 'What was that big black thing that made that splash!?'

'That's a whale Jim. They are heading north to calve before they head back down to Antarctica later in the year.'

'Cows have calves. Oh, Donald, there are two more.'

'Baby whales are also called calves Jim. If you like, we can watch through binoculars once we have finished our lunch.'

Kate was intrigued to watch Donald and Jim settle into their chairs on the balcony, each with a pair of binoculars and a pad and pen to record their sightings, chatting away as they waited to see more whales.

'Donald would have loved to have children. You don't mind if he and Jim spend time together do you Kate?'

'No, not at all Jessie. He speaks a lot about his father, and I think he needs to have men who he can look up to in his life. He and Scott from my office, spend a lot of time together.'

An hour later Jim had nodded off to sleep, so Donald carried him into Kate's bedroom and laid him on the bed. Jim's bedroom was to be one of the lower guest rooms, but as he hadn't been down there Kate thought that it was wise to let him sleep on her bed, then wake up to see the familiar top balcony where Kate, Jessie, and Donald sat and discussed what had been going on since her last visit north.

'How is Greg getting on now Kate?'

'He tells me that he is back to his old self, though he is enjoying having Tom working with him and Julie. He has bought himself a boat like yours Donald, and is now regularly heading to Lakes Entrance to annoy the fish. I think Julie is smitten with their new worker, and according to Dad, the feelings appear to be mutual!'

'And what about you Kate? Any beaus on the horizon?'

'Sorry to disappoint you Jessie. Unless you count the new nine-year-old male in my life these days! My life has certainly become a lot more interesting since his arrival.'

'Is it ok if your pint-sized beau comes fishing with me in the morning Kate? We won't go too far out, or be out for too long. Would you like to come out with us?'

'Heavens, no thanks all the same Donald. I plan to sleep in, then luxuriate in bed for most of the morning. When you and Jim come back and clean your catch, would you mind keeping him occupied until lunchtime?'

'I would love to. He's a bonzer young lad. I'm sure we can find something to keep us busy. Any bans on ice creams etc?'

'No, just not too much. He has his own pocket money, so make it share and share alike. Also, although his ribs have healed, he can't do anything too rugged. No rugby tackles etc.'

When Jim woke up, Kate took him and Toby for a walk along the board walk to the headland, where they sat and watched more whales pass by. When they arrived back at the house, Kate showed Jim his bedroom. He was thrilled that it had its own balcony, and he sternly instructed Toby not to press his nose against the glass.

Kate slept in the next morning and was thrilled to be presented with a steaming hot cup of tea by Jessie, who had heard her stir. 'Would you like your breakfast in bed Kate?'

'No thanks Jessie. I always get crumbs in my bed, and I plan to return here as soon as I have eaten.'

Kate was back in bed, sound asleep when a jubilant Jim arrived back from his early morning fishing trip with Donald, who had woken him before dawn. They had tiptoed downstairs with Hugo and Toby, and walked down to where Donald kept his boat. Two hours later he had caught three schnapper, while Donald had two whiting and a flathead. Jessie met them before they entered the house, and cautioned them to keep quiet, to allow Kate to sleep in, so Donald and Jim cleaned their catch outside.

After presenting Jessie with the prepared fish, Donald, Jim, and the dogs, joined this time by Chloe, went down to the shopping area for a big breakfast. Sitting looking at the remains of their meal Jim sighed. 'That was a great breakfast Donald, but I couldn't eat that every morning.'

'Neither could I lad. Once every so often is enough for me. Shall we go and see if Kate is awake?'

'In a minute Donald. Can I ask you something first?'

'Sure Jim. What's bothering you?'

'You know that my mother and father died last year?' Donald nodded. 'Well, I think I want to love Kate like I loved my mum. Is that wrong?'

Donald thought for a bit. 'No son, I don't think that's wrong. Kate is very fond of you. In fact, I would say that she loves you too, but probably hasn't realised it yet. She would like to look after you until you are a lot older than you are now, and is working hard with the authorities to make that happen, if that's what you want.'

'Oh yes Donald. I want to live with Kate for ever. She and Toby are my family now. And you and Jessie can be too, if you would like to be.'

'Have you told Kate this Jim?'

'No, not yet.

'Well, I think she would like to know how you feel. Come on, let's go before they send out a search party for us.'

Kate was still lying in bed, reading a book, when they arrived back. When she saw Jim peep around her door she smiled and patted the bed. 'Good morning my darling, come and tell me about your morning's adventures.'

Jim sat on the side of the bed, then looked at Kate. 'Do you mind if I have a cuddle?'

"No, of course not.' Kate held out her arms and Jim snuggled up beside her.

'I love you Kate. I want you to be my new mother.'

Kate held him tightly and began to cry.'

'Pease don't cry. I didn't mean to make you sad. Or are they happy tears, like when I was in hospital?'

Kate wiped her eyes. 'Just like then my love. I love you too, and would be honoured to be your second mother.'

'Kate, can I call you Mum? I won't ever forget my first mother, but I need you to be my mum from now on.'

Jim snuggled even closer, gave a sigh, then went to sleep.

Kate looked down at the sleeping boy, and felt as though her heart would burst with the love that she felt for him. Wow! She was more determined than ever to secure a safe future for her boy. Kate went back to sleep hugging Jim and didn't wake up until Jessie let Mitty into the room. She soon woke both sleepers by climbing up her little set of dog steps and jumping on both of them.

Jim looked lovingly at Kate. 'Did you mean what you said Kate?'

'Yes, my love I most certainly did. You will just need to give me time to adjust to my new title.'

When they went into the lounge Jim held Kate's hand and proudly announced 'Kate is my new mum now.' Kate blushed and Jessie and Donald smiled.

'How about you and your new mum cook those fish for us Jim, while Jessie and I prepare a salad?'

During the next week Kate and Jim learnt a lot more about each other. While Kate didn't divulge the extent of her wealth, Jim knew that she had a lot of money, but was determined to still work hard. He didn't know what he wanted to do when he grew up, but he told Kate that he wanted to learn as much as he could, to help him make up his mind when he was older. He went out fishing with Donald each morning and now called him Uncle Don and Jessie Aunty Jess.

As Donald confided to Kate 'Jim is desperate to have a family around him. I love my new role as an uncle. I never really knew Karl, and I don't think I would have liked the older boy if I had. Do you think Jim would be able to stay on with Jess and me for a bit longer, when you go back to Melbourne?'

'Unfortunately we have to go back on Sunday Donald, as we have a meeting with the school principal on Monday, but I will check with the powers that be to see if you can both be added to his list of carers. Scott and Belinda have been approved to look after him if I have to be away when he's at home. He might like to holiday at *Glen Rayne* at some stage, so I will have Dad and Julie added as well.'

CHAPTER 23

———◆———

MID-JUNE
MELBOURNE

The following Monday morning Kate drove Jim to the Scotch College Junior School in Hawthorn. As they walked through the gates Jim sighed. 'I never thought I would ever return here Mum.'

'Are you sure that it's what you want Jim?'

'Oh yes. I loved coming to school here. I had the best two friends before I had to leave.'

David Wilson met them at reception. Jim ran to him and hugged him around the waist. 'Hello Uncle Dave! Oh sorry. Mr Wilson, sir.'

Jim looked back to Kate. 'Mum, you and Mr Wilson have met before, haven't you?'

He was oblivious to the principal's quizzical look at Kate, and her embarrassed blush as David turned towards his office. 'Please come into my office.'

When they were seated, Jim looked at Kate and then David. 'I call Kate Mum now Mr Wilson. She is going to be my second mother.'

'Thanks for making that clear for me Jim. Now, the reason that you are here this morning is for us to assess your level of schooling. Do you understand what I mean?'

'Yes sir. What I should have learnt this year, and what I need to learn to catch up what I missed by skipping school.'

'I wouldn't have put it quite that way Jim, but yes, that's pretty much it. Are you prepared to sit a couple of little tests and answer some questions?'

Jim looked hesitantly at Kate then back to Mr Wilson. 'Do you remember Mrs Douglas Jim?'

'Yes sir. She was my teacher last year.'

'Would you be happy to talk to her to find out what you need to learn to catch up? Your new mum can sit in with you if you like.'

'Yes sir. Thank you.'

'Right, do you remember where the library is from this office?' Jim nodded. 'Good. Well, you take Kate to the library, and Mrs Douglas will be with you shortly.'

For the next hour and a half, Kate sat and watched Jim chat and answer questions with a middle-aged woman, who he obviously felt comfortable with. If Mrs Douglas felt his concentration was wandering, she changed the activity, or they would go for a short walk before undertaking a different task. Kate was most impressed, and thought of how many boring meetings she had attended that could have been made much more interesting, with similar observation of the participants' concentration levels. Finally, Mrs Douglas clapped Jim on the shoulder. 'That's enough young man, you did very well. I just need to put my notes in better order before I give them to Mr Wilson, otherwise he might fail me!'

Jim was laughing as he left the library, to find himself facing two young boys of about his age. 'Ross, Ross, you're back!' The two boys grabbed him and danced him around the corridor until they heard a loud 'ahem'!

'Oh, sorry Mrs Douglas, but it's Ross. Jim Ross. He's come back!'

'Thank you, Colin, I have been speaking with Jim and Ms Rayne.' Mrs Douglas glanced at Kate with a raised eyebrow. Kate nodded. 'We are hoping that Jim will be able to return to school here soon. Now, why don't you two scallywags take Jim out to the playground, while I talk to Ms Rayne. I will call you when you need to come in. Please come into my office Ms Rayne.'

'I would prefer Kate please Mrs Douglas.'

'Right Kate. Those two lads were Jim's best friends before his parent's tragic accident. They were inseparable, and were known as the 'three amigos'. All three were in the school choir and sang like angels, though at times they acted more like little devils! Colin Jones and Bradley Howard have been like lost souls since Jim left. They have done their work, but haven't had the 'joie de vivre' that they had before Jim's abrupt departure last year. As one of my colleagues put it 'They both seem to have lost their mojo!' They'll both pass grade four this year, but only just.'

'Both boys certainly looked happy to see him, and he them.'

'They did, didn't they? Mr Wilson was right to send the boys to see him. Jim's education hasn't suffered too much from his time away from school Kate. As I am sure you have noticed, he is a bright lad, and he guided those other two along with him in his quest to learn. With tuition mainly in maths and science this year I feel that Jim could manage grade five next year. If necessary, we could give him, and his friends, some extra tuition next year.'

'That's wonderful news Mrs Douglas. I will assist in any way I can to help Jim achieve what he wants to do.'

'Where do you live Kate?'

'In an apartment in Spring Street, opposite the Treasury Gardens.'

'Would that be near Ben's Coffee Shop by any chance?'

'Why yes. His shop is on the ground floor of my apartment block!'

'Ben is my nephew, and he has a younger brother Riley, who has completed his teacher training, but has been unwell this year, so couldn't take up his placement out in a country primary school. If you are interested, I could ask Riley if he might be available to give Jim the extra tuition he needs.'

'I am certainly interested Mrs Douglas. My office is in the same building where I live, and my colleagues and I usually have at least one coffee a day from Bens.'

'Very well, I need to get this report to Mr Wilson. First though, I had better get those three boys back inside. Do you mind waiting in the corridor for a moment?'

Mrs Douglas went to the door and called 'Come inside please boys. Now Bradley, not next year! Let Jim up this minute Colin Jones!'

Kate was shocked when three very bedraggled boys walked in with their arms around each other's shoulders. Jim's shirt was hanging out and was covered in wood chips, while Colin and Bradley looked particularly dishevelled.

'Your mothers are going to have a fit when they see you two, and I can see from the look on Ms Rayne's face that you won't miss out Jim!'

Colin stepped forward. 'We are awfully sorry Mrs Douglas, but we were so excited to see Jim again, we sort of got a bit carried away. It won't happen again, I promise.'

'I should think not. Go and clean yourselves up as best you can and report back to me in ten minutes. Kate, come with me and I will get you a coffee, before I see Mr Wilson.'

Kate sat in the staff common room and drank her coffee. She was amazed at the change in Jim when he was with Colin and Bradley. She could see what Mrs Douglas had meant about the boys' exuberance when together, and could imagine them actively enjoying each day together. How did their teachers cope? Finally, Kate and Jim left the school, delighted with David's offer of a place for Jim in grade five next year. Before she started the car, Kate looked at Jim, then began to laugh. 'You have no idea how scruffy you look Jim.'

'You're not too cross with me, are you Mum? I just couldn't help it; it was so good to see Colin and Brad again. I've missed them so, so much, and they said they've felt the same.'

'No Jim. I'm shocked but not too cross. I had no idea that you three were such good friends. If I had, I would have tried to get you together again sooner. By the way, how are your ribs after that bout of rough housing?'

'It hurt a bit when we were rolling on the ground, but when I told them about my ribs, we stopped being silly.'

'Good. Let's go home and get some lunch.'

'Could we please go to Macca's to celebrate Mum?'

'Okay, just this once. We won't be making a habit of it, will we?'

'Only when we have something to celebrate.' Jim suggested hopefully.

The next day, Ben arrived in Kate's office with his brother Riley. 'Our Aunt Mary said that she spoke to you yesterday Kate, and mentioned that Riley might be able to help Jim improve in some subjects.'

'Yes, she did Ben.' Kate walked around her desk and shook hands with Ben's brother. 'Hello Riley, I'm Kate Rayne, and the chap at the desk around the corner is Scott.'

Scott came out and shook hands with the young men. 'Can I come down for a coffee Ben, and we will leave these two to chat, if that's okay with you Riley?'

'Sure Scott.'

'Did Aunt Mary tell you why I couldn't take up my school placement this year Kate?'

'She just said that you had been unwell.'

'I had a bad case of glandular fever at the end of last year that lasted for a number of months, and it has left me with a type of chronic fatigue syndrome. Until that clears up, I can't get a posting in a school.'

'Do you think you would be able to tutor Jim for a few hours a week Riley?'

'Yes, I think so. I am quite capable of doing most things, providing I don't try to overdo it. It's just that I can't cope with the consistent day to day pressure of working with groups of students. And rest assured, what I have is not infectious. It's a complication I developed from suffering glandular fever. Aunt Mary told me that she would arrange for the appropriate work sheets and textbooks to be available for Jim to work with.'

'Jim told me last night that he can't wait to be back at school with his best friends Riley.'

The next morning, before Kate went down to the office, she received a phone call from the principal. 'Good morning Kate, David speaking. Sorry to ring so early, but a few things have come up relating to Jim's return to school. Nothing to worry about, but there are a few things that I need to discuss with you. I have a meeting in the city at lunch time, and I remember that you said you live in the city. Would it be possible to meet somewhere for a chat?'

'Good morning David. I will meet you wherever you wish, or if you would like to, you could come to my office in Spring Street. Jim will be upstairs, if you need to speak to him.'

'That would suit me fine Kate. Mrs Douglas informed me that you work for *Windfall Holdings* in the building where her nephew Ben has his coffee shop, and that his brother Riley is going to be Jim's tutor.'

'Yes, that's correct. My office is on the third floor. What time would you like to meet?'

'Would ten o'clock suit?'

'Fine David. Do you want to see Jim too?'

'Not at first, if you don't mind. See you at ten.'

Kate looked at her phone when he rang off and wondered what he wanted to talk about. She turned as Jim came into the kitchen with a towel wrapped around his waist. 'Sorry Mum, I can't find my clean jocks.'

'Check the laundry basket that Mrs Nash brought up earlier. I have a meeting this morning Jim. Are you happy to stay up here with Mrs Nash?'

'I like Mrs Nash, she's great fun. We chat about all sorts of things while she's working.'

'When she leaves, you can come down to the office, or would you prefer to stay up here until lunchtime?'

'I would like to stay up here and work on my Meccano truck for a while Mum.'

Kate had taken Jim to Hearn's Hobbies in Flinders Street, where

145

he had spent a blissful hour looking through the vast array of hobby material on view. Eventually, they left the shop with a Meccano set, like the one that Jim's parents had given him for his eighth birthday. Sadly, that along with most of his possessions, had been left behind when he went to live with his grandfather.

Just before ten David entered Belinda's office, and was surprised to see Kate sitting on the edge of the desk, looking at a sheet of figures. Kate looked up in surprise. 'Goodness, is it ten o'clock already? Good morning David. This is Belinda Turner, one of my colleagues. Belinda, David Wilson, Principal of the Scotch College Junior School. Come into my office David. Would you like a coffee sent up from Ben's?'

'A flat white would be wonderful thanks.'

'Do you mind Belinda? Get one for yourself and Scott as well. I will have my usual latte thanks.'

Kate led David into her office where Scott was putting a folder on her desk. 'Ah, Scott. This is David Wilson, David, Scott Mansfield, another of my colleagues.' After the two men shook hands Scott left the office and George trotted out after him.

'An service dog, is he?'

'Yes, Scott has PSTD, though you wouldn't know it now.' Kate led David to the lounge chairs near the window. David gazed out over the gardens. 'I don't think I could concentrate on my work if I had a view like this Kate!'

'It's even more spectacular from higher up! So, what's come to light regarding Jim's schooling?'

'The other day we discussed the possibility of Jim's reenrolment next year. Would you consider letting him come back straight away?'

Kate looked at David in surprise. 'He hasn't even started his tutorial sessions yet.'

'Yes, I know, but yesterday Colin told Mr Sullivan, the choir master, that Jim was coming back next year. Jim was an integral member of the soprano section of the choir before he left, and Mr Sullivan has begged me to ask you if Jim could be enrolled now, so that he can sing in the end of year concert.'

'But he's not ready to go back into classes yet David.'

'Mrs Douglas and I thought that it might be an idea to give Colin and Bradley extra tuition with Jim. If he was enrolled as a student right away, we could set up a tutorial area for them, and the school would employ Riley Johnson to be their tutor. I am sure that both Colin's and Bradley's parents would agree to their boys having additional tuition as, like their teachers, they have become quite concerned about their sons' lack of progress this year.'

'Jim will leap at the idea, if it meant that he could be with Colin and Bradley again.'

'There would also be choir practice after school, three days a week to be considered.'

'I am happy to have him driven to and from school whenever he needs to be there. I don't like the idea of a lad his age travelling alone on public transport.'

'A lot of our boys do, but I agree with you Kate.'

Belinda tapped on the door and entered carrying two cups of coffee. 'Thanks Belinda. Jim might be down soon. I left him engrossed in building whatever he's creating with his Meccano set, and Mitty was busy trying to steal any wheels she could find!'

Kate saw David's puzzled look. 'Mitty is my Chihuahua puppy. She and Jim's dog Toby are keeping him company in our apartment upstairs.'

'You actually live on site?'

'Yes, although there are a few floors between this office and my apartment. Do you want to speak to Jim now?'

'I think that would be a good idea.'

Kate picked up her phone. 'Hi Jim, can you please come down to my office. Mr Wilson is here and would like to speak to you. Leave Toby and Mitty in the apartment; just make sure that the balcony door is shut. See you in a minute.'

Not long after, Jim walked into the office and smiled at David.

'Can I still call you Uncle Dave when we're not at school, sir?'

David gave Jim a gentle hug. 'Sure you can Jim. How are you after your rough and tumble with your mates the other day?'

'A bit sore, but it was so good to see them again. And they haven't forgotten me at all!'

'Kate and I have been discussing your return to school. Come and sit beside me, and I will explain what we have talking about.'

Kate sat back and listened as David told Jim of their discussion. She was impressed by the way he interacted with him, not talking down to him, but imparting the information in a manner a nine-year-old could easily follow. It was clear that he cared for the boy, and it was obvious that Jim liked him too.

Jim's eyes were glowing when he turned to Kate. 'Can I really start back at school next week Mum? Can I pleeese?'

'Yes Jim, you...' Kates's words were cut off when Jim flung his arms around her neck and hugged her tightly. She looked over his head at David, who smiled and gave a thumbs up sign!

David stood up. 'I will leave you two to work out transport etc. I had better get to my meeting. When I return to school, I will get the enrolment forms organised and a timetable sorted for you Jim. Do you still have your uniform?'

Jim shook his head. 'Only some of it.'

'That's okay, I will see you Monday morning. Just wear what you are wearing today and we will see what we have in the swap shop.'

Kate walked with David to the lift. 'I look forward to seeing you and young Jim on Monday morning Kate.'

Kate stood staring at the lift door after David left, holding her hand to her chest. Her heart was pounding in a way she had never experienced before. Surely David's presence in her office hadn't caused such a reaction, although she found him to be extremely alluring.

Riley was thrilled with the news that he was to be employed by the school to tutor Jim and his two friends. He was sure that he could cope, and was assured he would be assisted if necessary. Kate also employed Riley to drive Jim to and from school. She had already decided to buy herself another Rav4, so set aside the Escape for Riley's use.

CHAPTER 24

MID-JUNE

MELBOURNE

Riley drove Kate and Jim to Scotch College on Monday morning, where they were met by David and Mrs Douglas. While she took Jim and Riley to the room allocated for Riley to use, Kate was ushered into David's office. There she was met by Annette Jones and Carol Howard, Colin's, and Bradley's mothers. 'I will leave you three to have a chat, and to look at these copies of our proposed program for your three boys, while I attend morning assembly. Jim, Colin, and Bradley will spend this morning with Mr Johnson once assembly is over. How long can you stay Kate?'

'I have the whole day available if necessary. Scott and Belinda are covering for me.'

'Good. We will go through uniform requirements etc at lunch time. Well, must be off. See you all later.'

After the usual introductions and some informal chatter, Kate felt quite at ease with the other two women, who were obviously good friends. After the first introductions Annette smiled at Kate. 'I couldn't believe it when Collin told me that Jim was back. I was so surprised and pleased, I forgot to mention his scruffy appearance!'

'I was the same Annette. Brad was actually crying when he told me. Both our boys have been so different since Jim left Kate; we were wondering if we might have to get help for them.'

Annabelle nodded. 'We had no idea that boys so young could form such a strong bond of friendship. It was as though they had lost a part of themselves. Unfortunately, with Mr Wilson overseas, no one was sure where Jim had gone to.

'Jim told me that he missed his friends terribly, and hated going to a different school. So much so, I gather he missed more days than he attended.'

'Poor little mite. And having to deal with the loss of his parents as well.'

'I hope you don't mind Kate but Mr Wilson told Annette and me that you have taken on caring for Jim. We met with him last Friday, and discussed how best to get the three boys together again.'

Kate had noticed both Annette and Carol called David Mr Wilson, so decided that she would try to do the same when with them.

'No, I don't mind who knows. I have applied to be Jim's guardian. He wants me to adopt him, but unfortunately that decision isn't mine alone to make. I would do it tomorrow, but official procedure has to be followed.'

'Look Kate, Carol and I have the morning free. Would you like to come for a drink at a café that we often meet at in Glenferrie Road? Much more comfortable that the principal's office!'

Twenty minutes later they were seated in a pleasant café, with an assortment of French pastries and cakes to choose from. There, they spent the next couple of hours chatting about their boys, their families, interests, and many other things going on in the world. They also went through the proposed tutoring program that David had given them.

Aware of Riley's health issues, and Jim's lack of recent school time, David had planned that for the first week, he was to attend only on the three days when choir practice was held after school. Jim was to have the morning sessions alone with Riley, then Colin and Bradley would join them for the afternoon sessions. Over the next couple of weeks this would be monitored, to see if the tutoring of all three boys could be extended to all five days of the week until the end of the year.

'Our boys' teachers are happy for them to have additional tutoring each afternoon. I hate to admit it, but I think our little dears have become rather disruptive in class this year, without Jim setting them a better example.'

'You are so right Carol. Last night Colin surprised Sam and me when he told us that he couldn't wait to get to school in the morning. This year, it has been a real effort to get him to school on time.'

Kate swallowed a piece of cheesecake and laughed 'Well, here's hoping having the boys together again will benefit everyone!'

'Mr Sullivan, the choir master, says that he is willing to have the 'three amigos' together again, if it means he has the three of them singing like they used to.'

After discussing the possibilities of the boys getting together at the weekend, the three women walked back to the school, where Kate and David went through the uniform items Jim would need.

'It would probably be better to wait until the new year to buy his full uniform Kate, as he is likely to put on a growth spurt now that he is being well fed, and is obviously enjoying his new home life. Providing he has some sports gear, and possibly a new shirt and school jumper, he should be fine for the rest of this year.'

Kate was pleased with the morning. She had enjoyed her time with Carol and Annette, and felt that she would like to get to know them both better. She had seen Riley and Jim briefly at lunch time, and both of them seemed happy with how the morning had proceeded. Hopefully, the afternoon would progress accordingly! She would have to be careful in her meetings with David though, as she was becoming quite attracted to him!

As there was choir practice after school, Riley was going to have a rest at his aunt's place nearby, then drop the boys off at their homes when he brought Jim home. Scott had offered Riley a bed for the nights that he would be late back, to save him having to travel further to go home to Ben's.

Kate travelled back home by tram, and called in at the office before going up to her apartment. Mitty was thrilled to see her, welcoming her with little yips of delight as she raced around the office. Finally, she lay on Kate's lap while she told Scott and Belinda of the morning's events.

At six thirty that evening, Jim burst into the apartment, raced over to Kate, and grabbed her around the waist. 'Oh Mum, I have had the groustest day! We learnt all sorts of things, and played during lesson breaks and Mr Sullivan says that I can still sing okay!'

Kate looked into the shining eyes looking up to her, then hugged Jim to her. 'I'm so pleased you had a good day darling. Go and give your hands and face a quick wash, then we will have tea and you can tell me all about your day.'

'Mr Johnson, that's what we have to call Riley in school, like I have to call Uncle Dave Mr Wilson at school. Anyway, Mr Johnson is a beaut teacher. He makes everything so easy to understand and remember. I didn't have to help Colin or Brad once. And choir practice was good too, once I did a few scales to warm up. I haven't felt like singing since last year, but tonight was good. Mr Sullivan had us singing stuff that I knew, so it wasn't too hard.' Jim gave a big yawn.

'Time for your shower, then bed young man. I will come in when you are in bed.'

After a very brief shower, Jim climbed into bed and Kate went in to say goodnight. 'Do you want me to wake you up in the morning to go swimming Jim, or would you rather sleep in?'

'No, I want to keep swimming with Scott. I can do six laps non-stop now, and he is teaching me to do breaststroke.'

Kate lent down and kissed Jim on the cheek. 'Goodnight my darling boy. I'm so pleased that you had a good day today.

'Good night Mum. Love you.' Jim was asleep before Kate had switched the light off.

The next morning Kate went for a run, while Belinda took George and Toby for a walk, and Scott and a weary Jim went swimming. Mitty received her daily exercise running around the pool as Jim and Scott swam laps. She had fallen in once, and now kept her distance from the edge, until Scott and Jim climbed out of the pool.

Jim was quite content to stay up in the apartment for most of the day, reading and resting. That night, he hunted out his sports gear. 'We have PE after lunch tomorrow, so Mr Johnson said we could go to that period.'

'I will probably be gone before you arrive back tomorrow night Jim, but Scott will stay with you until I arrive home.'

'That's okay Mum. Don't worry, I'm happy to have Belinda and Scott look after me. I know that you have to go on duty some nights. If you didn't, you wouldn't have found me, and who knows what would have happened to Toby and me.'

'Well, I'm certainly glad I found you.'

After the first week, Jim went to school every day, and the other two boys happily joined him in the tutorials each afternoon. Riley thoroughly enjoyed working with the boys, and found to his surprise that he was feeling much better and less fatigued by the end of each day. Having his aunt's place nearby was handy if he felt tired, but he rarely used it by the end of the second week. Access to a bed in Scott's apartment was a great help too.

With Jim at school, Kate was able to concentrate more on her *Windfall Holdings* projects. She hadn't realised how much of her time had revolved around Jim during the past month, and she recognised how much Scott and Belinda had shouldered the extra work, happily working beyond their initial responsibilities. Each morning they gave a brief account of who they had contacted, or were researching prior to contact, and Kate informed them of visits that she had undertaken, to interview potential recipients of grants from *Windfall Holdings*.

Kate decided to speak with Geoff when he came in to work, about changing their positions to research managers, with an appropriate increase to their salaries.

CHAPTER 25

LATE JUNE - JULY

MELBOURNE

Much of Kate's time in late June was taken up with the plans to develop a women's refuge at *Smythe Park*. She and Belinda had met several times with Sir Eric during the month, and Frances had taken them on a tour of the mansion and gardens. Both women were absolutely staggered at the size of the mansion and the beautiful reception rooms. Despite their shabby appearance, both women could envisage how they could be renovated. The mansion had thirty rooms, including a large kitchen, dining room, several reception rooms, a ballroom and twelve bedrooms, with attached dressing rooms. The original indoor bathrooms and toilets, added before the first world war, had been modernised, but it was decided to investigate the possibility of changing the dressing rooms into ensuites for each bedroom. Eric was willing to organise builders and painters to deal with the renovations that Kate and Frances felt would be needed to house possibly ten women and their pets. These would initially be limited to dogs and cats.

The garden was beautifully maintained by an elderly gardener and his middle-aged son. Frances told them that the older man had been working for the Smythe family for the past sixty years, since he was employed as a fourteen-year-old to help his father. Eric had continued to pay their wages when his sisters died.

When Kate and Belinda arrived back at the office, Kate had a phone call from Julie. 'Hi Sis, how are you coping with parenthood!?'

'Fine thanks Jules. How soon before we hear wedding bells for you and Tom?'

'I'm going to be as noncommittal as you, big sister!'

'Touché! Seriously though, how are things going at *Glen Rayne*?'

'Fine. Dad is as fit as a fiddle, enjoying his fishing trips to the Lakes. Would you believe, he took Chief and Bluey out in his boat last week?'

'No way! I hope they were good sailors!'

'Everyone seemed quite happy when they came home, and we all had a good feed of whiting that night. What I'm ringing for Kate is to ask if you can put Dad and me up for a couple of days next week? We are coming to Melbourne on Thursday for the Stud Sale at the showgrounds the next day.'

Kate sat back in her chair and thought for a moment. 'You would both be most welcome Jules.'

'Great, thanks Kate. Dad and I are really looking forward to meeting this new young love in your life! Do you think he will want to call me Aunty Julie?'

'I don't know Jules, but he has asked if Dad will be his new grandad.'

'Dad will be tickled pink to hear that.'

Later that afternoon Greg rang Kate. 'Can you find room for Margaret as well as Julie and me please Kate? Yesterday Mum and Dad moved into a Bairnsdale aged care home, as Dad now needs more specialised care, and Margaret is coming back to live at *Glen Rayne*. Your sister has moved into the cottage with Tom, though she cooks most meals for the three of us each night, and still does some of the housework. Margaret is happy to take over running the house like she used to.'

'So, I wasn't far off when I asked about wedding bells?'

'I wouldn't mention it to Jules just yet Kate, but it wouldn't surprise me the way things are at the moment. I would be happy to have Tom as a son in law.'

'Okay. It will be lovely to have Aunt Meg to stay as well. Jim will just have to clean up the spare bedroom that he has been using for his train set. Do you think you could stay on for the weekend?'

'I will consult your aunt and sister Kate, but I think a longer break would be good.'

Kate had her ambulance roster changed, so that she was home when Greg, Julie and Margaret arrived just before lunch on Thursday. Greg and Julie dropped Margaret and their luggage off at the office, then went straight to the showgrounds to settle their cattle, and to get them ready for the stud sale the next day.

When Kate took Margaret up to the penthouse, they carried their cups of tea out onto the balcony. Margaret looked searchingly at her niece. 'You are looking well Kate. Motherhood clearly suits you.'

'It has been rather exhausting Aunt Meg, but I am learning to live with a lively, nearly ten-year-old boy. Our time together up at Woolgoolga helped tremendously, and Scott and Belinda have been marvellous supports. Now that Jim is at school, life has settled down to some extent.'

'I can't wait to meet this young lad of yours. He sounds rather special.'

'Oh, he is Aunt Meg. I love him so much. What's more, the feeling is mutual. I cried when he asked me if he could call me Mum.'

Margaret hugged her niece tightly. 'All the money in the world can't buy that feeling, can it my darling?'

Just then Mr Nash came down from the garden, where he, Mitty and Toby had been working in the vegetable garden. 'Sorry Kate, I had hoped to be finished before your visitors arrived, but Mitty decided to remove the tomato plants behind me, so I had to replant them.'

Mitty ran over to Margaret to sniff her shoes. 'Oh, she's adorable Kate. Can I pick her up?'

Kate laughed. 'She would love you to. Just be careful that she doesn't jump from your arms when the others come in.'

Toby sat next to Margaret. 'This is Toby, Jim's dog. Much better behaved than young Mitty.'

Kate and Margaret spent a leisurely afternoon swapping news. Kate was sad to hear of her grandparents move to a nursing home, but Margaret reassured her. 'Dad needs specialist nursing now Kate, more than Mum and I can give him. At least they are still living together. Also, it now means that I can go back to *Glen Rayne* with a clear conscience, to keep an eye on your father, and to keep him company now that your sister is spending most of her spare time with Tom.'

'I gather that Jules and Tom are an item now, but she's a bit touchy talking about it.'

'Give her time love. She'll let us know when she's ready.'

Just then the front door opened, and Greg and Julie came in. Julie hugged her sister, and Greg gave Kate a quick kiss on the cheek. 'Lovely to see you again lass. I see that you are accumulating dogs here too!'

'Can't help myself Dad, though Toby is Jim's dog.'

Julie looked around the apartment. 'What time does Jim get home from school? I'm looking forward to meeting him.'

'He should be home in about an hour. Time for us to have a cuppa and catch up on family news.'

Kate had just placed the leg of lamb in the oven, when they heard running footsteps and the door burst open. Jim entered the room, then stopped, and looked at Kate. She went to him and put her arm around his shoulder. 'Come and meet your new family Jim.'

Jim looked shyly at the three strangers standing in front of him.

'This is Aunt Meg Jim.' Margaret stepped forward. 'It's lovely to meet you Jim. Can new aunts kiss nearly ten year old boys?'

Jim looked at Margaret, then stepped forward. 'Yes, please Aunt Meg.' He smiled when she bent down and kissed him on the cheek, then he kissed her on the cheek too.

'This is my sister Julie.'

Jim looked at Kate 'Is she the one you call Jules on the phone Mum?' Jim turned back to Julie. 'Can I call you Aunty Jules please?'

'You most certainly can Jim. Come and give me a hug.'

Greg watched Kate while she introduced Jim to his new aunts, and couldn't believe the radiance he saw on her face. Then Jim turned to him. 'You're Mum's dad, aren't you? Does that mean you are now my grandad?'

'Yes, I think it does son. I would be pleased to have you as my grandson.' He held out his hand to shake hands with Jim, then Jim gave him a big hug. He turned to Kate. 'I have never had this many relations before Mum. It's great.'

'I'm pleased it makes you happy Jim. Now, how about getting changed and helping to me get dinner ready.'

Jim looked at the oven. 'Oh ripper. We're having roast lamb. My favourite!'

The next morning, Greg and Julie left early for the show grounds, while Kate, Jim, Scott, and Belinda followed their normal morning pre breakfast activities. Margaret had a sleep in, then prepared breakfast for Kate and Jim.

When Jim left for school with Riley, Kate took Margaret out to *Smythe Park* to show her the beautiful mansion, and she explained the plans to run it as a women's refuge for those with small pets. Margaret was amazed at the concept. 'Aren't you and the Smythe's worried about this beautiful place being damaged Kate?'

'No Aunt Meg, not at all. The majority of abused women are not the ones at fault. Most are housewives, used to keeping house and looking after their families. We will employ a cook and a housekeeper, but the guests staying here will come fully aware that they will be expected to assist in all areas of running the house and maintaining the gardens.'

'Amazing Kate! When do you expect it to be open?'

'Hopefully before the end of the year.'

Kate called in at the office when they returned later in the afternoon, and spent some time discussing their projects with Scott and Belinda, then she took Toby and Mitty up to the apartment and began to prepare dinner. Jim had choir practice, so wouldn't be home until six thirty, and she had no idea what time Greg and Julie would be back. Julie had rung to say that the sale was going well, but didn't know when they would be finished.

Greg and Julie were ecstatic when they arrived back, not long before Jim. Three of their bulls had topped the sale, one of them setting a record price for his age. 'Jules and I have both agreed that some of that money will go to Beyond Blue, and the Black Dog Institute Kate.'

During the weekend Kate took the family out to the Healesville Sanctuary. Jim was thrilled to be allowed to pat a dingo that a keeper was leading through the sanctuary, and was spellbound watching the eagles flying freely above his head, as they soared from one end of the open flight area to the other. One eagle went out of sight for a short time, then swooped back over the trees and landed on his trainer's arm. Other birds were included in the display, but it was the majestic wedge- tailed eagle that captured his imagination.

CHAPTER 26

JULY

MELBOURNE

A couple of days after her family went home Kate received a phone call from David. After briefly discussing Jim's progress at school David said hesitantly 'Kate, I have been given two tickets to the Australian Ballet in Melbourne next Friday night and I wondered if you might like to accompany me to the performance.'

Kate was lost for words for a moment then replied 'That would be wonderful, thank you David.'

'Great, I will call this evening to give you all the details. Thanks Kate.'

When he rang off Kate sat back in her chair and stared out of the window thinking of her developing feelings for David. She'd had a couple of close relationships since leaving school but none of them had caused the feeling of deep affection that she was quickly developing for David despite only having met him on a handful of occasions. Could one really fall in love that quickly?

It soon became apparent that her feelings for David were reciprocated, as following their attendance at the ballet they contrived to meet as often as their busy work schedules would allow and spent a great deal of time talking on the phone when they were apart. Often

Jim accompanied them on weekend outings but he was astute enough to leave them alone together at times as when they took him to the zoo and he asked to join a group being taken through the butterfly enclosure. Kate and David sat on a bench near the lion enclosure drinking coffee, having promised Jim that they would remain there until his return.

'Have you heard any more about your application to become Jim's full-time carer Kate?'

'No, nothing yet David.'

'Judge Thomas rang me last night, to tell me that he has heard that one of Mrs Hurston's cronies has been spreading rumours that you are out partying most nights, leaving Jim alone.'

'What?' Kate turned so quickly the coffee flew out of her cup, just missing David. 'How could she? Yes, I work three ambulance shifts a week from 1pm – 8 pm, but Jim is never left alone David. Scott or Belinda are always with him, and he likes being with them. And they are with him on the infrequent evenings you and I have been out together.

David looked compassionately at Kate. 'I have a feeling that this rumour, no matter how false, could put a spoke in your wheel Kate. Would you consider giving up being a paramedic?'

Kate was horrified at the idea, and sat looking blindly towards the lions.

'I love my job, and I am a skilled paramedic David; but I love Jim more. If giving up my job would help to secure his future with me, I'd resign tomorrow.'

As she began to cry, and fumbled for her handkerchief, David put his arm around her shoulder and handed her his handkerchief. As she cried on his shoulder, she was comforted when his arm tightened around her. When she sat back, she gave him a weak smile. 'I'm sorry David. I don't usually cry on men's shoulders.'

'Don't be sorry Kate. You can cry on my shoulder anytime, although I hope you don't have need to do it too often! But can you afford to give up your job?'

Kate considered how much she should tell David. She was

thoroughly enjoying his company, and hoped that their relationship might develop further. 'I would miss my paramedic life David, but I don't rely on that salary for my income. *Windfall Holdings* covers my needs quite well. Jim definitely comes first, and it will be nice to spend more evenings with him. And with you when we get the chance.'

David put his arm around her shoulder again 'Do you mind Kate?'

Kate snuggled against him. 'I don't mind at all David.' He leant over and kissed her gently on the lips, and raised an eyebrow.

Kate smiled 'I don't mind even more!'

David and Kate spent several minutes embraced in a long lingering kiss, until reluctantly David let her go. 'I hear footsteps approaching, so I'm afraid we will have to desist for a while.' He kissed her on the nose, then sat back, just as Jim ran towards them.

'The butterflies were beautiful Mum. Some even sat on me! Can I have an ice-cream now please?' While David took the excited boy to the kiosk Kate went to the washroom to wash her face in cold water. She didn't want Jim to see that she had been crying, and it also gave her a chance to regain her composure after David's show of affection.

Worried about the possibility of her ambulance shifts jeopardising Jim's future Kate spoke to Mr Brown, her supervisor. He was most sympathetic, when she explained her dilemma with her night shifts. Loathe to lose an experienced paramedic like Kate, he agreed to change her shifts to three midweek shifts from 8.30am – 4.30pm. starting Tuesday the following week.

Much as she wished to hear David's voice, Kate knew that she mustn't ring him during school hours. She knew that she wouldn't be able to concentrate on her work, if he rang her in the middle of her shift. She did however text him the information regarding her shift change, for him to pass on to Judge Thomas.

CHAPTER 27

———————⟞⟩◉⟨⟞———————

EARLY AUGUST

MELBOURNE

A month after their first night out together Kate received a text from David. 'Can we pls meet at Cook's Cottage 5pm tonight? XX'

Kate was waiting outside Captain Cook's Cottage when David walked up behind her, wrapped his arms around her and kissed her on the neck. She turned and they eagerly embraced, holding each other tightly, then after a long kiss they drew apart, conscious of other people nearby.

'My car is parked in Clarendon St, darling. Let's go.' David placed his arm around Kate, and she held him around the waist as they walked slowly through the park.

'I miss you so much when we are apart Kate. I sometimes feel like a lovesick schoolboy. Don't laugh! I do actually know what that felt like. I will tell you all about my unrequited love for Sarah Smith one day.'

'You are never far from my thoughts either David. I must admit, I have never felt so attracted to someone as I'm to you.'

David hugged her closer. 'Is it just an attraction or something stronger?'

Kate stopped and looked at David. 'I began to fall in love with you the first day we met in your office darling. I just can't believe how much I love you now, even after such a short time!'

'Oh, my darling, I don't know if men are meant to admit to it, but I feel exactly the same. I didn't know what hit me when you walked into my office that day. You have no idea how relieved I am to hear you say you love me too. I love you so very, very much.' He leant down and kissed her as they approached his car.

David opened the passenger door and handed Kate into the front seat, kissing her quickly as she sat down, then went around to sit in the driver's seat. Kate looked nervously at David 'Before we go any further David, there is something important that I must tell you.'

David looked shocked 'Don't tell me that you are already m…' 'No, I'm definitely not married! When I told you that I work for *Windfall Holdings,* I wasn't being totally honest. Yes, I do get paid an income, but in actual fact, I am the CEO, and I own the company!'

David stared at her in amazement, then took her right hand and kissed it. 'Don't look so worried Kate. I still love you, no matter whether you own a company or not. But now some things are making more sense. What I mean is, I didn't really take in fully a couple of things that you have said. Like Jim's fees not being a problem, you living in the same building as your office. And now I remember Jim's address is at level 20. When I was in the lift to your office the other day, I noticed 20 was the top floor. So, do you and Jim live in the penthouse?'

Kate looked troubled as she nodded. 'Would it bother you to know that I am a woman of considerable wealth David?'

'Do you mean, would I be upset if the love of my life, who I desperately wish to marry, is wealthier than me, then the answer is a definite no!' He leant over and kissed her, then chuckled. 'I will just have to learn to love your money, as well as you!'

Kate giggled and snuggled against David's shoulder. 'Should I take that as an involuntary proposal of marriage Mr Wilson?'

David sat back looking a bit surprised. 'Well, yes I guess it was Kate. A very clumsy version of one I'm afraid. I know that we have only known each other for a few weeks, and I can't get down on one knee sitting here in my car but, Kate Rayne will you please do me the honour of becoming my wife? And may I please add 'As quickly as possible?'

Kate sat up and smiled at David. 'I would be honoured to become your wife David. And I agree whole heartedly with your add-on!'

They spent more time relishing a long, passionate deep kiss, then sat back and gazed at each other. 'Kate, there is nothing I would like better than to make passionate love to you here and now, but would you mind if we take things more slowly until we marry?'

Kate looked perplexed. 'Is there a problem David?'

'Oh no Kate, nothing like that! I take my position as the principal of the Junior School very seriously. Word of our engagement will spread like wildfire, and although I know it sounds prudish, I want to be able to honestly dispel any of the rumour mongers' attempts to taint your name with the assumption that we are having an affair. Also, I need to know that I am setting a good example to the boys.'

'I could easily succumb to you ravishing me here and now my love, but I understand. And there is also Jim to think of.'

'I don't think he will mind us getting married, do you? As a married couple we might be able to adopt him, not just be his guardians.'

'That would be wonderful. How soon could we get married?'

'How about we go to dinner and make plans? I think much better on a full stomach!'

David parked his car in the apartment carpark, and after Kate had changed into more suitable attire and organised for Scott to keep Jim company they caught a taxi to the Eureka Tower at Southbank, to allow David to celebrate their engagement without having to worry about driving home later in the evening. They agreed that Kate would drive his car to the school the next morning.

David had booked a table at Eureka 89, a restaurant atop the Eureka Tower, and he and Kate were soon seated next to a window with a magnificent view of the city lights. During the evening, the happy couple enjoyed a sumptuous meal, and each other's company. Before the dessert was served, David stood up then knelt on one knee beside Kate, holding her left hand. 'I know that I jumped the gun this afternoon my love, but may I formally ask will you please marry me?'

'I haven't changed my mind David, so my answer is still an unequivocal yes!'

David slowly placed a ring made from twisted grass on the ring finger of her left hand. 'We will go shopping for your engagement ring tomorrow, my darling.'

The maître d'hôtel, alert to what was occurring, quickly produced a bottle of champagne, opened it with a flourish, then poured two glasses for the happy couple. 'Congratulations Madam, Sir. Please accept this champagne on the house.'

Following dessert, they sat drinking the champagne, and began to make plans for their soon to be shared future. 'Would you like to be married in the Littlejohn Memorial Chapel at Scotch College Kate?'

'I would love to sweetheart. Mum and Dad were married there in 1987.'

'I will speak to the Chaplain tomorrow, to see how soon we can be married in the Chapel. It is a pretty popular venue, so we might have to look elsewhere to be married sooner rather than later.'

'Don't forget it's Jim's birthday on the 8th September. We can't use that date.'

'I doubt the Chapel would be available that soon my love, or that we can legally marry that quickly. How long do you want to wait? I gather ladies need time to prepare for their wedding.'

'I would marry you in my tracksuit tomorrow, if it was a tossup between waiting to get a dress or marrying you sooner!'

'Now, that I would like to see! Maybe I should try for an earlier date somewhere else!'

'Tempting as that sounds David, I would like my family to be present at our wedding, so we will need to give them a little bit of leeway. What about your father? Do you think he would be able to come over?'

'Don't hold your breath, but I will ring and ask him tomorrow. Hopefully, I will have some news about the Chapel when you return

166

my car in the morning. With any luck I will be able to free up my day tomorrow, and we can go ring hunting. Then we will announce our engagement to all and sundry!'

Much later that evening the taxi dropped Kate off in Spring Street, then took David to his flat near the school.

Kate went for a short run the next morning, and returned to the apartment as Jim came up from his swim. 'I did ten laps this morning Mum!' he shouted, discarding his bathers as he ran to the shower.

Kate sat at the breakfast bench while he ate his Weet-Bix. 'Jim, would you like David to live with us?'

'Do you mean Uncle David?'

'Yes, he has asked me to marry him and I have said yes.'

Jim turned to look at Kate. 'So that would make him my new dad instead of my uncle?'

'If you like.'

Jim threw himself into Kates arms, nearly knocking her off her bar stool. 'I would love to have both you and Uncle Dave as my new parents. Oh, wait till I tell them at school!'

'Hold on Jim. Can we please keep this our secret for a day or so, until we announce our engagement? I wanted to ask you first, before we told anyone else.'

'Okay Mum, I won't even tell Colin or Brad, but I won't be able to stop being excited. What if they ask me why I'm so excited?'

'Just tell them that you will tell them why as soon as you can. David will tell you when that will be.'

Jim scraped his plate clean, then jumped off his stool and hugged Toby. 'Did you hear that Toby. We' are going to have a new dad as well as a mum soon.'

CHAPTER 28

Kate parked David's car in his school car park at ten thirty, and went in to reception to return his keys. The receptionist looked up as she approached the window. 'Mr Wilson would like to see you please Ms Rayne.' She pressed a button on the intercom. 'Ms Rayne is here to see you Mr Wilson.'

David's office door opened, and he winked at Kate. 'Please come in Ms Rayne. I have that information we were discussing yesterday.'

When he had ushered Kate into his office and closed the door, he swept her into his arms and kissed her firmly on the mouth. 'I can hardly wait for the time I can kiss you openly in front of others, my love.' Kate agreed and sat down. 'Jim is beside himself with excitement at the thought of you becoming his new dad.'

'I don't want him to think that I'm taking Ian's place Kate.'

'I love the reasoning of a nine-year-old boy David. When Jim asked if he could call me Mum, he told me that he wouldn't ever forget his first mother, but that he needed me to be his new mum. He told me this morning that he would love to have both you and me as his new parents. He told Toby that they were going to have both a mum and a dad soon!'

'Wow. I love that little scamp so much. Having him become part of my new family is just icing on the cake.'

David sat down facing Kate. 'Darling, I spoke to the school Chaplain first thing this morning. We are required to lodge a Notice of Intended Marriage a month before the wedding. Would you believe, there's been a rare cancellation for two o'clock on Saturday 22nd September which would mean that we would just comply with that requirement! Would that be too soon for you my love?'

Kate gasped and sat back in her chair. 'Goodness David. I honestly hadn't expected to be married quite that quickly!' She gazed at him for a moment, then laughed. 'That will be wonderful darling. I might just have to wear that tracksuit after all!'

'We need to confirm the date and go to see the Chaplin this afternoon, to complete the paperwork.' David walked around his desk and hugged Kate. He gave her another long kiss, then reluctantly went back to his chair. Having the desk between them helped him to both think more clearly, and to keep his desires at bay.

'I also spoke to Judge Thomas this morning Kate, and he rang me back about half an hour ago. I hope you don't mind, but I told him of our imminent engagement announcement, and he used that information to put a rocket under the people dragging the chain over your application for Jim's care. The document granting you full guardianship for Jim will be sent to your office by courier tomorrow morning. If you don't have it by midday, please let him know immediately. He also told me that we could apply to adopt Jim, if he wishes, once we're married.'

'So, I didn't need to change my shift times after all!'

'Please leave them as they are now Kate; then both Jim and I can see more of you when we are not at school.'

'You don't mind if I keep working?'

'Not so long as you keep safe. Or until Jim's new little brother or sister arrives!'

'I think we had better leave to look for that ring now my love, before our resolve crumbles. That rug is starting to look awfully enticing!'

David took the rest of the day off, and he and Kate went into the city, where they bought an elegant, but unassuming yellow gold, ruby, and diamond engagement ring. The solitary ruby was surrounded by twelve smaller diamonds, and sat reasonably flat in its setting. They also chose two plain gold wedding rings.

While they had lunch at a restaurant overlooking the Yarra, David held Kate's left hand and examined her new ring. 'I love the ring you chose Kate.'

'I didn't want anything too pretentious. I fell in love with this ring the moment I saw it, and I can wear it under my surgical gloves when I'm at work.'

'You said that you are a wealthy woman Kate, but you don't flaunt your wealth for all to see, do you?'

'Darling, only my family know the extent of my wealth, and now that you are the most important person in my life, I need to tell you as well.'

Kate quietly told David of her Tattslotto win, and waited for him to absorb the information she had just disclosed.

David sat staring at the river for what seemed like hours to her, but it was really just for a couple of minutes, then he turned to face her, smiled then kissed her hand. 'My adorable Kate, what you have just divulged is certainly a shock, but it makes no difference to my feelings for you, nor to my desire to spend the rest of my life with you.'

'I promised myself not to let my wealth influence my life too much David. Sure, there have had to be some changes. I now have access to a lot more ready cash, live in an extremely luxurious penthouse and have bought a lovely house in Woolgoolga, but I want to live my life as I wish, not showing off to all and sundry the extent of my fortune. I choose to keep working, not for the money, but because I want to use my skills to help others. That is the reason *Windfall Holdings* was established, to use my money to help both humans and animals in need.'

'Kate, I admire your values, and would like to think that I hold principles akin to yours. I want very much for us to live our lives

170

together, much as we do now. Well, with one crucial exception obviously! I plan to remain principal at the Junior School for as long as they will have me, although I will have to change my current accommodation!'

'Do you realise that neither of us have seen each other's apartments yet David. Nor have we discussed where we will live following our wedding.'

'I don't think my one bedroomed flat could aspire to be called an apartment Kate. You and I could live there after our wedding, but it isn't large enough to include Jim as well.'

'Would it be too far for you to travel to work from Spring Street?'

'No sweetheart, I don't think so. It takes less than twenty minutes most of the time.'

'Do we have time for me to show you the penthouse before we see the Chaplain?'

'So long as we don't linger!'

Like others before him, David was astounded at the luxuriance of the apartment, and the spectacular view from the large panoramic window.

'You get used to the furnishings David, but never the view. I must tell you; the penthouse was fitted out before I came to live here!'

They had a quick tour through the apartment, stopping briefly to look at what would soon become their bedroom, then they went back to Scotch College to see the Chaplain. He was delighted to meet Kate. 'David told me that your father and mother were married here Kate. I am sure he will be thrilled to hear that you are planning to follow in his footsteps.'

'Yes, I'm sure he will be. I plan to ring him to tell him after dinner tonight.'

The Chaplain raised an eyebrow at David. 'You are having a short engagement David. Tongues will wag.'

'We want to try to set a good example for Jim by not living together until after our wedding Bill, so the shorter the engagement the better! Another reason for accepting the earliest date possible, is because we've been advised that we can apply to adopt young Jim, once we are married.'

'Great to hear David. Now, let's get that form signed and dated so you can be married on the 22nd September.'

After leaving the Chaplain's office, Kate and David went back to his office where he and Kate announced their engagement to his staff. Kate proudly displayed her ring, and David explained that they were applying to adopt Jim once they were married.

Kate rang Greg that night. 'Dad, David and I announced our engagement today, and we're getting married in the Littlejohn Chapel at two o'clock on Saturday 22nd September.'

'Congratulations sweetheart. I thought that you two would make a great couple, but may I ask, why the haste?'

'We love each other dearly Dad, and a recent cancellation meant that there was a vacancy at the Chapel that day, which suits David and me down to the ground. I know we're being old fashioned, but we are not moving in together, for Jim's sake. We have also found out that we can apply to adopt him as soon as we are a married couple.'

Kate heard Julie squeal when she realised what her sister and father were talking about. 'You're a fast worker Sis. You've only known the guy a month, if that!'

'We are soul mates Jules, and love each other passionately, plus the Chapel is unexpectedly available on September 22nd, so why wait?'

'What will you get to wear in such a short time?'

'I'm sure there are dresses to be bought in the shops Jules. Or, as I told David, I would happily wear my tracksuit!'

'Don't even think it, you terror. Can I be your bridesmaid?'

'Stop jumping the gun Jules, and give me a chance to ask you if you would be my bridesmaid. Will you?'

'Yes please. That means that I will have to come to the city soon to get my dress!'

'Can Dad and Tom hold the fort for you if you come this weekend, so we can go shopping on Monday?'

'Sure. Hold on, Dad is calling something from his room.' She paused. 'He wants to know if you would like to wear Mum's wedding dress if it fits you Kate. I had no idea he had it packed away in his room. I wonder how he kept it away from Vitriolic Velma!'

'Please tell him that I would love to try it on Jules, and would be thrilled to wear Mum's dress if it fits me. Bring it with you when you come.'

CHAPTER 29

AUGUST

MELBOURNE

The next morning Scott and Belinda were thrilled to hear the news of the engagement, and they offered to help Kate in any way they could. Knowing that their organisational skills way surpassed hers, she willingly gave them carte blanche to organise the wedding. She provided them with a list of people who she wished to invite, and promised to get a list from David as soon as possible.

Mid-morning Carol rang Kate. 'Congratulations on your engagement Kate. You and Mr Wilson certainly caught us all by surprise, although Annette and I had noticed that you were both getting on rather well and we hoped for both your sakes that something might eventuate in time. But you could have knocked me down with a feather when Brad came home last night, and told me that you and his principal were officially engaged. Word is going around that you are having a very short engagement, and are being married in four weeks!'

Kate laughed. 'Settle down Carol, Brad is right. David and I are engaged, and will be married in four weeks. Apart from the fact that we both dearly love each other, there is a vacancy on the 22nd October at the school Chapel, and the earlier we are married, the sooner we can apply to adopt Jim. It's nothing more shocking or wicked than that, I assure you. I know that tongues will be wagging, and many mistaken assumptions will be made, but could I please ask you and Annette to try to dispel the rumours you might hear. I couldn't bear to think of David's good standing at the school being harmed by malicious gossip.'

'We will certainly try Kate. Is there any chance that we three could meet for a quick lunch today?'

'Yes, if it would be possible for you and Annette to meet me in the city Carol. I have a fair bit of work to catch up on before the weekend.'

Carol rang off, after a meeting time and venue had been arranged, leaving Kate a couple of hours to work through her emails and numerous invitations to visit organisations seeking assistance from *Windfall Holdings*. Many she passed on to Scott and Belinda, but there were a couple that she put aside to look into later that afternoon.

She was ecstatic when a courier arrived with the official notification that she had been appointed James Ross's guardian, for as long as was deemed necessary, this appointment to commence immediately. She immediately texted David 'Letter delivered. Permission granted for legal guardianship! XXOO'

'Fantastic. Love you!!!'

Kate walked to Southbank, where she met Carol and Annette, who were sitting at an outside table overlooking the Yarra River. A drinks waiter appeared, and took their order, leaving menus for the three women to peruse. Annette smiled at Kate. 'You are a dark horse Kate! But you and Mr Wilson have Sam and my heartfelt congratulations on your engagement. Carol told me why you are forgoing a longer engagement, and we have already had great fun scuppering some of the amazing rumours being spread. By the end of the weekend, I am sure that Mr Wilson will once again be held in the high esteem he has enjoyed, and you will be the envy of most of the junior school mothers!'

'Hold out your hand and show us your ring Kate.'

'Oh, that's beautiful. I love the setting, and the way it flashes in the sunlight.' Carol turned Kate's hand, and watched the ruby and diamonds twinkle.

'I love the setting too, especially as it will allow me to keep my ring on under my gloves when I'm on duty.'

'Won't you give up your ambulance work after you're wedding Kate?'

'No, I intend to keep working for as long as I can Annette. David and Jim will be at school all day, so I will work during those hours. Please don't be offended, but I'm not used to the social lifestyle that you two enjoy. I love meeting up with you like this, but I would feel that I was wasting the skills that I have developed over the years, if I stopped work once David and I are married.'

'We are not offended Kate. Annette and I were both married soon after we left school, so we didn't have careers to give up, and we both married men who expected us to stay at home to entertain and look after the children when they came. Mr Wilson, sorry Kate, we should call him David to you now; I can't see him having those expectations of you, not that he couldn't afford to.'

'Yes, well let's order, as I have a job to get back to this afternoon!'

They all laughed and ordered lunch. 'Obviously we haven't sorted out invitations yet, but you two and your husbands are definitely invited to attend our wedding. Colin and Brad as well, if that's okay?'

'Thank you Kate. I'm sure both boys would love to go.' Carol cocked an eyebrow at Annette who nodded. 'Annette's mother loves looking after both of our broods when Annette, Sam, Mark and I go out together.'

David spent that evening in the apartment with Jim and Kate. After one quiet growl when a strange man entered her kingdom, Mitty decided that she liked David, and was quite happy to sit on his knee for a while, then she went back to her bed, where she could watch everyone in the living area.

They enjoyed a dinner of grilled steak, boiled chat potatoes and salad, then Jim and David spent some time playing in Jim's room with his Meccano. After they both said goodnight to Jim, Kate and David sat out on the balcony and discussed their forthcoming wedding.

Kate told David of her lunch with Carol and Annette, and of the latter's comment on scotching the rumour mill. David laughed and pulled his chair closer to Kate so that he could put his arm around her shoulders. 'As the wife of the Junior School Principal, my love, you will have to be stoic, and tolerate the mothers of my young charges. Some think an unmarried man is fair game, and flirt inexcusably, while others, with adolescent daughters, dream of marrying them off to me! These will be the women with the more malicious tongues now that their schemes have been foiled.

Have you heard when Julie is arriving? I'd love to see your mother's dress, but I gather that's a big no-no. Thank goodness I don't have to wait much longer to see it, or for other things that I am longing for!'

'Please David, I am finding it as hard to wait as you are. We really must try to think of other things. Goodness knows, there is plenty to get ready before our wedding day. What are we doing for our honeymoon?'

David's eyes twinkled. 'Sweetheart, I thought we weren't going to think along those lines!'

He ducked the cushion Kate threw at him. 'Careful love, you don't want that to go over the barrier!'

'I meant, where will we go for our honeymoon, and for how long, you goose.'

David chewed his lip. 'I'm sorry sweetheart. Last term is awfully busy for me, so we can't be away for too long.'

'I am sure we wouldn't have to be away for too long, for you to satisfy your desire to have your wicked way with me!'

I will have to go now if we don't quickly change the topic.'

'Okay. How about we book a hotel room for Saturday and Sunday night, and if you are in a fit state, you can go back to work on Monday!'

'And what state do you think I will leave you in, my dear?'

Kate laughed. 'I have the feeling we both might be rather worn out by Monday morning!'

'What say we come back here Monday morning, after Jim has

gone to school, and come back to earth slowly, then I will return to school on Tuesday!'

'That sounds a wonderful plan my love. And I will go back to tending the sick and injured.'

'When should I move my gear over here Kate?'

'What sort of gear are you referring to?'

'Clothes, sports gear, personal stuff. I don't own any furniture or kitchen utensils, as the flat is rented fully furnished.'

'If you pack a case with what you will need for a few days after our wedding, Scott could collect it while we are away. Then I could help you pack up the rest after school later during the week. What are you doing tomorrow my love?'

I'm afraid I will be working all day Kate. I know that it's Saturday, but I have been somewhat distracted this week, and need to catch up on quite a lot of work. It's much easier to do that when I have the place to myself. What are you planning to do?

'Jim is spending tomorrow with the Howards. They are planning to take the boys up to Eildon to catch some trout! So, I too will catch up with some work, before Jules arrives for lunch on Sunday. Would you like to come here for dinner Sunday night? Actually, why don't you bring over some of your things that you won't be needing in the next three weeks, and you can start claiming your dressing room. I will clear my things out tomorrow.'

'I can't believe that this place has his and her dressing rooms, plus a double shower, which I am sure we will both enjoy immensely!' When David placed his hand on Kate's thigh she rapidly removed it. 'It is time for you to go my love, or you will have to endure a solitary cold shower!'

CHAPTER 30

—⟫●⟪—

EARLY SEPTEMBER

MELBOURNE

When Kate returned from dropping Jim off at the Howard's on Saturday morning, she rang the Langham Hotel to book one of their luxury one bedroomed suites situated near the upper floor from Saturday 22nd September, to depart on the morning of Monday 24th September. When she revealed that the room was for her honeymoon, and she was unsure what time Saturday evening she and her husband would arrive, the receptionist assured her that they would be welcomed at whatever time they arrived.

Kate sat looking at her phone after the call ended, having just realised that she had spoken of David as her husband for the first time, and it felt so right.

Carol and Mark rang Kate before they arrived back in Spring Street at six o'clock to drop Jim off, to allow her time to meet them at Ben's. 'Sorry we can't stay longer Kate. By the time we drop Colin off, we will be running late to collect our girls from their grandmother's. Don't forget your fish Jim.'

'Thank you Mr and Mrs Howard. I had a great day. See you guys on Monday.'

'See you Monday Ross.'

Jim spent the evening regaling Kate with his day's adventures. The highlight of the trip to Eildon was his visit to the trout farm, where he had caught his fish. 'Shall we cook it for lunch tomorrow Jim, when Julie arrives?'

'Oh, I'd forgotten that Aunty Jules is coming to stay. Yes, let's cook it for her.'

It wasn't long before Jim was asleep in bed, so Kate went out to sit on the balcony. It was a beautiful September night, the lights below twinkling brightly. She sipped her wine, and wondered what it would be like having David living with her and Jim, once they were married. In addition to sharing her bed with him, they would all have to make considerable adjustments to their present lives.

Julie arrived just after midday the next day, and collapsed onto the lounge. 'I swear the Melbourne traffic gets worse every time I come here Sis!'

Kate handed her sister a cold glass of beer. 'Here Jules, wrap yourself around this and see if it relaxes you.'

'The way I feel at the moment, it could take the whole bottle!'

Julie just managed to put her glass down when Jim charged into the room and flung his arms around her. 'I have been waiting all morning for you to arrive Aunty Jules.'

Julie gave him a kiss on the cheek. 'Well young man, I have been driving all morning to see you! How have you been?'

'I went fishing yesterday, and caught a big fish for our lunch today, didn't I Mum?'

'Yes, my love you did. Now, how about you let Aunty Jules finish her drink, and you set the table.'

An hour later Julie put her knife and fork down on her plate. 'That was a beautiful fish Jim. Did it fight much when you caught it?'

'It took a while to reel in, but I remembered what Uncle Don told me about taking my time, and letting the fish tire itself, then reeling in the slack before it tried to swim off again.'

'I can see that you and Dad are going to be great mates Jim. He loves his fishing. Not quite as much as his cattle, but close.'

'Right Jim, what are you planning to do this afternoon, while your aunt and I catch up on news?'

'Is it okay if I go down to see Scott and George?'

'Ring Scott first and ask him. If it's okay with him, off you go.'

Soon after Jim and Toby had disappeared, Kate and Julie sat out on the balcony. 'Jim has cleaned up the spare room Jules. He's so looking forward to David coming to live here, he says that he won't use it for a playroom after you go, so it will be ready for him. I don't think he has realised yet that David won't be sleeping in the spare room!'

'That will be interesting. It's awfully hard to work out how children think at times isn't it?'

'Tell me about it! I love Jim dearly, but sometimes I struggle to keep up with his mercurial decision making.'

'Dad is so pleased that you and David are getting married in the Little John Chapel Kate. He rarely spoke about Mum when we were younger, but lately he has been reminiscing a lot about his beloved Jean.'

'I wonder if his run in with Velma has anything to do with that?'

'Who knows. So, tell me Sis, how are you and David managing your lives of self-restraint?'

'It's not easy Jules, but we have coped so far. Thank goodness we are having such a short engagement!'

'Your honeymoon should be interesting!'

Both young women laughed. 'Tom and I aren't going to bother with a honeymoon when we get married, seeing we have essentially been living together for nearly four months.'

'Are you seriously thinking of tying the knot Jules?'

'Yes Kate. Your comment about why should you wait to marry when you and David are soul mates, and love each other profoundly, has persuaded Tom and me that we are ready too. Plus, I reckon if you feel you love and trust David well enough after only a month, to share your money with him, I love and trust Tom enough to share my portion of *Glen Rayne* with him.'

'Well, good for you Jules. David was pretty shocked when I told him the extent of my win, but we both share the same principles and values, and are determined not to let it affect our lives together.'

An hour later Julie stared at her sister in amazement. 'Oh Kate, you look absolutely gorgeous! Mum's dress fits you to a T!'

Kate was wearing her mother's white satin A line dress, with a V-neckline and a keyhole back, covered by a fine long sleeve appliqued lace bodice with a high neck collar. It fitted her perfectly, and with moderate heels would be just the right length.

'Dad has often mentioned how much you remind him of Mum now that you are older Kate. He will be blown away when he sees you in her dress.'

Kate looked worried. 'Do you think it will upset him, if I wear it?'

'I don't think so. It was his idea for you to wear it if you wanted to.'

'Oh, I want to very much Jules. It feels so comfortable, and could have been made for me. How about you take a photo, and send it to Dad to see what he thinks?'

Julie handed a small oblong box to her sister. 'Before I do, try these on.'

Kate opened the box, and took out an exquisite pearl necklace. 'This is Aunt Meg's necklace. Mum wore it on her wedding day, and Aunt Meg has offered it for you to wear as well.'

Kate was quite overcome with emotion as Julie carefully placed the pearls around her neck and did up the clasp. For a moment she truly felt that her mother was in the room, smiling at her. Julie took a couple of photos of Kate, and sent them to Greg, then helped her remove the dress and pearls. By the time they had carefully repacked the dress, Julie's phone rang.

'Hi Dad' Julie listened for a moment then handed the phone to Kate.

'Hello Dad, thanks for sending Mum's wedding dress for me to try on. As you can see, it fits me beautifully, and I would love to wear it for my wedding.'

'Kate, you look just as divine in that dress as your mother did on our wedding day.'

'It won't upset you if I wear it?'

'Oh no Kate, not at all. It was my idea to offer you the dress, and although I must admit, I did a double take when I first saw those photos, because you look so like your mother, I will be thrilled to walk you into the Chapel on your wedding day. In a way, it will feel as though Jean is there with us.'

'Thank you so much dad. Love you.'

When the dress and pearls were put away in Kate's bedroom, she and Julie sat out on the balcony. 'What style and colour dress do you want to wear Jules?'

'My choice would be to wear a burgundy colour Kate, nothing too flashy so I can wear it again sometime. Though, who else are you having in your bridal party? They might have other ideas.'

'You will be my only bridesmaid Jules, and David is having one of his school friends as best man. We are going to ask Jim if he would like to be a page to carry the rings down the aisle in front of Dad and me.'

'So, tomorrow I need to buy a dress and shoes, while you will be looking for some white shoes. What else do we need to think of?'

'David is organising the hiring of the men's gear. He will get ties to match your dress. I wonder if they would have a similar suit to fit Jim?'

'What about flowers and bouquets?'

'Belinda and Scott have become my wedding planners and are organising everything, with army precision!'

David arrived at five o'clock, and after he had deposited two suitcases inside the front door, he greeted both Kate and Julie with a chaste kiss on the cheek and he hugged Jim.

'Don't tell me your good intentions have got up and gone David!'

Oh, ye of little faith Julie! As this is soon to be my home, I am just bringing over some of my non-school gear, to make the final clean up after our wedding a bit easier. Jim, do you want to come down to help me with the rest?'

Ten minutes later they arrived back, Jim carrying a small case and David a large cake. 'Gaspare sends this Italian Cream Cake with his best wishes for our engagement Kate. He has also invited us down for a meal tonight.'

Gaspare greeted them at the door of his restaurant, and led them to a window table, where three glasses of champagne and a glass of Jim's favourite soft drink had just been poured. Gaspare kissed Kate's hand and shook hands with David.

'Congratulations on your engagement Kate and David. Please accept this meal, as my family's gift to you. The cake is for your dessert, to eat at your leisure. It will keep well in the fridge, if you decide to eat it later. Welcome also Miss Rayne and Jim. Please be seated.'

He held out Julie's chair while David held Kate's. Kate was pleased to see Jim wait until both she and Julie were seated, before he sat down at the same time as David. After a delicious meal comprising of a variety of dishes, David left to drive home. 'Goodnight my love, Jim and Julie. Good luck with your shopping tomorrow ladies. I will see you at school tomorrow Jim.'

As they walked to the lift Jim turned to Kate 'Can we have some cake before I go to bed Mum?'

'How in the world could you eat any more Jim?'

'Just a little piece please Mum? It looks so nice.'

Kate looked at Julie, who was trying not to laugh. 'Maybe Aunty Jules will have some with you.'

'Sorry Sis, I couldn't eat another thing. How about we have some for breakfast Jim?'

By the time the lift reached the penthouse, Jim had decided that maybe he had eaten enough, and cake before school sounded a much better idea. He quickly brushed his teeth and jumped into bed, kissed Kate and Julie goodnight, then turned over and went straight to sleep. The next morning, after a cake-based breakfast, Jim happily went down to meet Riley, and Kate and Julie took Mitty and Toby down to the office, before walking down Collins Street, stopping to look at dress and shoe shops as they went.

By mid-morning Julie had her dress and shoes, and Kate a pair of comfortable white shoes that they both agreed would suit their mother's dress. After a fortifying latte, they walked back to the apartment. When they put their purchases in the spare room Julie looked at her watch. 'Do you mind if I head off home now Sis? I will stop for some lunch on the way.'

'I don't mind Jules. If you leave now, you will miss a lot of the traffic. Give my love to Dad and Tom.'

That night, after dinner and some more cake, Jim sat on the lounge with Kate. 'Mum, you know how the choir is practising for the concert at the end of term?'

'Yes sweetheart. I am really looking forward to it.'

'Well, Colin, Brad and I will be singing Pie Jesu, all by ourselves.'

'Goodness Jim, what an honour! Mr Sullivan must think the three of you sing well.'

'Well, yes I suppose he does. But Mum, this morning he asked me if I thought you and Uncle David might like us to sing it at your wedding. Would you?'

Jim looked expectantly at Kate. 'Oh my darling, what a wonderful idea. Would you like to do it?'

'Yes, I really would Mum. It would really make me feel that I am part of your wedding.'

Kate hugged Jim to her. 'Darling, whether you, Colin and Brad sing or not, you will be a very important person at our wedding.'

'A big boy at school said that you won't love me after the wedding Mum, because you will love Uncle David instead.'

Kate was horrified. 'Oh, Jim that was a really dreadful, untruthful thing for him to say. I love you dearly, and always will.'

'But you will have Uncle David to love after the wedding.'

Kate sat Jim on her lap. 'Love is an extraordinary concept my darling boy. The amount of love you have grows, to allow you to share it with others when you need to. You loved Toby before you met me, didn't you?'

'Oh yes, I've always loved Toby.'

'Well, do you love Toby any less, now that you love me too?'

'Gosh, no Mum, I love him just as much as I ever did, and I love you to bits.'

'Good. Well, I certainly don't love you any less now that I love David as well. In fact, I think I love you more now than I did when you first came to live here with me. Having David living with us will just mean that there will be two of us to love and care for you, not just me. Nor will I have less love for you or David, if one day you have a little brother or sister.'

Jim looked up at Kate. 'I really love you Mum, and I love Uncle Dave too. Do I have to wait till the wedding to call him Dad?'

'I think when you are at school you should keep calling him Mr Wilson or Sir, but here you can call him Dad whenever you like, and see how it feels.'

'Mr Sullivan would like to speak to you or Dad tomorrow about us singing.'

Jim went to his room softly humming Pie Jesu.

Kate rang David, and told him of her recent conversation with Jim. They both agreed that it would be wonderful to have the boys sing at their wedding. 'I will speak to Mr Sullivan tomorrow Kate, to work out the details for the trio's performance. I have a good idea who has been giving Jim grief, but I am pretty sure the other two amigos will look out for him. I would prefer not to interfere if possible, but will keep an eye on things. The boy in question is leaving Scotch at the end of the year, thank goodness.

You start your day shift at eight thirty in the morning, don't you? I will bring Jim home after choir practice and give Riley an early night. Love you sweetheart. Sleep tight.'

'I spend each night dreaming of you my darling.'

CHAPTER 31

EARLY SEPTEMBER

MELBOURNE & SYDNEY

When Frances and Eric arrived home from France, Francis rang Kate as soon as she'd opened the wedding invitation. 'Hello Kate, Eric and I have just arrived home to find an invitation to your wedding! What in the world is going on? Don't tell me the David Wilson you are marrying, is the principal at the Scotch Junior School?

'Yes Fran, we...' Fran interrupted. 'But you've only known him for a bit over a month Kate! What have you been up to while Eric and I've been away?'

'We fell in love Fran, pure and simple. Cupid's little arrows struck us both at the same time, at the zoo would you believe?'

'You are kidding me Kate!'

'No, we were watching the lions at the time!'

'Oh, Kate my dear. Please forgive my appalling manners. I should be congratulating you on your engagement, not interrogating you. Do you think we could possibly blame my inexcusable conduct on jet lag?'

Kate laughed. 'Fran, please don't upset yourself. I can imagine what a shock it must have been for you to open the invitation on your arrival home, after all those hours travelling. I am on duty tomorrow and Thursday. Could we meet up on Friday sometime? I'd love to see you, to hear about your trip and your granddaughter's wedding. And I will fill you in on what's been happening while you've been away. David has spoken to Judge Thomas, so no doubt he will chat to Eric sometime soon. Get a good night's sleep tonight Fran, and call if you wish after 5pm tomorrow, when I should be off duty.'

Frances and Eric visited Kate and Jim at the penthouse on Friday night, and stayed for dinner when David arrived. They spent a congenial evening, discussing the impending wedding, and also listening to Fran and Eric's account of their trip to France, and their granddaughter's wedding. Eric had brought back a small statuette of a knight on horseback, both in full armour, for Jim. He also had his medal from the Queen, to show to the excited boy.

A week later Jim woke up earlier than normal on the morning of his birthday. He ran into Kate's bedroom and jumped onto her bed. 'Wake up Mum. It's my birthday! I am a big boy now. I am ten years old!'

Kate sat up, rubbing her eyes, then she held out her arms to Jim. 'Happy birthday my darling. Is a ten-year-old boy too old for a hug and a kiss?'

Jim flew into her arms and hugged her tightly. 'Never Mum! I love you hugging and kissing me!' After a moment he added 'Well, maybe not so much when we are out with other people.'

Kate laughed. 'I will try to remember that.'

'Thanks Mum. When do we fly to Sydney?'

'Not for a few hours yet, love.' Kate looked out of her bedroom window at the lights twinkling in the dark. 'The sun hasn't risen yet, and you are going to school for the morning, remember, so that you can see your friends before we leave.'

'Oh yes, I forgot. Can I get into bed with you, while we wait for it to get light? Before Kate could reply Jim snuggled down beside her under the doona and promptly fell asleep, and she thought that it wouldn't be long before she woke up with David cuddled up to her when she woke up. To take her mind off such fancies, she turned her thoughts to the day ahead.

She had booked a suite in a luxury hotel at The Rocks, near Circular Quay for Friday and Saturday nights, as well as return airline tickets to Sydney for Friday afternoon, returning to Melbourne late Sunday afternoon. Jim was going to school as usual, to spend his birthday morning with his friends, then she would collect him from school, and they would go to the airport, where they were due to fly to Sydney at one o'clock.

When he left for school with Riley, Kate packed two cabin bags for their weekend away, then went down to the office to go through some financial details with Geoff. The company's new corporate lawyer, Jacinta Hawkins, was in her office next to Geoff's, so Kate went in to greet her. 'Good morning Jacinta, how are you settling in?'

Jacinta stood up. 'Good morning Ms Rayne. I am beginning to develop a better understanding of the company's set up and ideals. Geoff has been a great help explaining everything, and I have spoken to the lawyer who initially worked with him at the start.'

'That's good to hear. Have you been in touch with Sir Eric Smythe's lawyers yet?'

'Yes, we have had a number of meetings regarding 'Smythe Park', and have reached an amicable agreement for you and Sir Eric Smythe to scrutinise.'

'Thank you, Jacinta.'

Jacinta had been working for the company for a couple of weeks, after she had been recommended by the lawyer who had helped Kate and Geoff set up *Windfall Holdings*. Initially, Kate and Eric had speculated if Arthur Thompson might become their corporate lawyer, but before Scott could contact him, he had moved out of his apartment and disappeared.

Fran had spoken to her friend Pam Thompson and discovered that Arthur had been sent, at short notice, to work at his firm's New York office. Kate was happy to employ Jacinta and, like Geoff, had told her that she was free to take on private cases, providing they didn't interrupt or conflict with her work for *Windfall Holdings*.

Leaving Mitty and Toby in the office for Scott to look after for the weekend, Kate went back to her apartment, collected their cases, and drove to Scotch College. While Jim was called to reception, Kate and David had a quick farewell kiss in his office, then went out to reception to meet Jim. David walked out to the car with them, and gave Jim a hug and a new tablet with some games and books already downloaded onto it. 'Happy birthday Jim. Have a great time in Sydney, and please look after your mum for me. See you Sunday night.' After a chaste kiss with Kate, he stepped back and waved as they drove away.

At the airport, Kate and Jim went up to the Qantas Lounge, where he took great delight in choosing food from the variety of dishes on offer, while they waited for their flight to be called.

Jim was quite relaxed when the plane took off, having been on a plane twice before! He played with his new tablet for a while, and happily ate the lunch provided. When they landed in Sydney, Kate and Jim went to the airport train station, and caught a train to Circular Quay Station. From there, they walked the short distance to the Shangri-La Hotel, where she had booked a suite for two nights.

The views from their suite were spectacular. They were up high enough to be looking down on the Opera House and Sydney Harbour Bridge, and out over the harbour towards the Heads. After spending half an hour checking their suite, and Kate pointing out the various landmarks from their windows, they set off for a walk around Circular Quay towards the Opera House. Jim was more interested in the harbour bridge than the Opera House, but dutifully followed Kate as she walked around the beautiful white masterpiece.

As they retraced their steps to return to the hotel, Kate pointed to a ferry terminal at Circular Quay. 'That's where we will catch the ferry to Taronga Zoo in the morning Jim. Are you looking forward to visiting there tomorrow?'

'You bet Mum. Colin and Brad want me to take them back a souvenir if that's okay.'

Kate bought two tickets for the morning ferry, then they continued walking back to the hotel, until Jim spotted a McDonalds.

'Can we please have my birthday tea here Mum? This is a celebration isn't it?'

To Kate's amazement he managed to devour a full Maccas meal and a milkshake, while she nibbled on some of his chips, hoping that he wouldn't be ill during the night! Although it was still relatively early in the evening, by the time they reached the hotel, Jim was feeling quite tired and was happy to curl up on Kate's lap to watch the sun setting from their room, then he went to bed much earlier than normal.

'Goodnight Mum. I have had a beaut birthday. Thank you.'

Kate ordered room service, and enjoyed a splendid but lonely meal, looking out at the lights reflecting on the harbour, wishing that David could be sharing the meal with her. She sent him a photo of the view 'Missing you terribly darling. Jim asleep after great birthday. Love & kisses xxoo ∞

The next morning Kate woke up early and watched the sunrise until Jim stirred. 'Good morning my dearest ten-year-old. Did you sleep well?'

Jim stretched, then came over and gave Kate a big kiss. 'Yes, I did Mum. Can I lie beside you, and watch the view changing?' Kate moved over and Jim snuggled up beside her.

'Mum, Colin says that when Uncle Dave becomes my dad, and comes to live with us, he will sleep in your bed with you. Is that true?'

Kate looked at Jim in surprise. 'Well yes Jim, we will sleep together as man and wife.'

'So, will you be trying to make me a brother or sister then?'

'Would you like a brother or sister?'

'Oh yes please Mum.'

'Well then, I guess we will just have to try to, as you put it, 'make you a brother or sister!'

'I'd like that. Brad says that when you shut your bedroom door, I shouldn't go into your room, cause that's when you will be trying. Can we climb the bridge while we are here Mum?'

Kate closed her eyes, thankful for Jim's habit of instantaneously switching topics. 'If it's fine I will try to get tickets for Sunday morning.'

She reflected that so much was going to change in a couple of weeks. Sharing her life with David would be different and exciting for them both, but they would also have to be aware of Jim's presence in their new life, and not allow him to feel excluded by their need for each other.

Following a light breakfast in the dining room, Kate and Jim walked back to the ferry terminal and boarded the Taronga Zoo ferry, for the short trip to the zoo. He was delighted to see a large cruise ship sailing under the bridge on its way to berth at Circular Quay.

They spent a wonderful day exploring the numerous trails, to look at all varieties of animals, including the big cats, reptiles, elephants, koalas, birds, and giraffes. Jim burst into fits of giggles when the giraffe wrapped her tongue around his hand when he held out some celery for her. Kate kept an eye on him, but was transfixed by the stunning views of the harbour from where she stood. They both enjoyed the seal walk and seal show, and again Jim was enthralled by the free flight bird show.

When they finally caught the ferry back to Circular Quay, they were both worn out, although Jim perked up when he saw some grey Naval ships berthed at Garden Island. 'Are they real, fair dinkum Navy ships Mum? Ones that go to war?'

'Yes, they are definitely real Jim, but we hope they don't have to fight in a war.'

'Well, what do they have those guns for?'

'Oh my love, I am too tired to think of an answer to that question.'

'That's okay Mum. I think I might be too tired to listen if you did!' Both were laughing as they left the ferry and made their way back to their hotel.

Early the next morning, Kate and Jim walked to Climb Base, the area where the Sydney Harbour Bridge climb commenced. There, they were kitted out in blue and grey overalls and full harnesses, and locked their personal belongings in a locker, before they were briefed on the climb and clipped to the safety cable.

For the next three hours their guide led their group of fourteen up ladders, catwalks, and the outer arch of the bridge to the top of the arch. Their tour guide took group and individual photos, with the magnificent panorama of the harbour and Opera House behind them. From there, they crossed to the arch on the Darling Harbour side for their decent to Climb Base.

Thankfully it was a beautiful, clear sunny day, with just a slight breeze that helped to keep the climbers from overheating. Kate considered herself to be quite fit, but she had to admit that she enjoyed the frequent stops their guide made to take photos and provide commentary on the bridge and the Sydney landmarks and history.

Jim had a marvellous time, walking next to Kate, pointing out features he recognised, questioning her on others that took his fancy. On their return to the hotel, they had a quick lunch, then caught the train back to the airport, in time to catch their mid-afternoon flight home to Melbourne. Both Kate and Jim slept for most of the flight.

David was at the penthouse when they arrived home, and had prepared a light meal for them, aware that Kate would probably be exhausted, after the strenuous weekend that she and Jim had embarked on. While Jim went down to regale Scott about his weekend, David and Kate sat together on the balcony, after a long, loving embrace.

'Do you realise sweetheart, that this time next week we will be on our honeymoon, with no constraints to our desires whatsoever?'

'I hope I don't feel as exhausted then, as I do at the moment my love.'

'We'll pace ourselves and savour the experience. We will have the rest of our lives together to take pleasure in each other's company.'

'Mm..' was Kate's response as she fell asleep against his chest. David held her lovingly, until Jim and the two dogs arrived back.

David left soon after dinner, leaving Kate and Jim to retire to bed. After his shower, Jim went straight to bed and hugged Kate when she went in to say goodnight. 'Thank you for taking me to Sydney Mum. I have had the most best birthday ever. We had fun, didn't we?'

'Yes, my love, we did. You should ask Mrs Douglas if you can write about the things we did.'

'When are Grandad, Aunty Jules and Aunt Meg coming to stay for the wedding Mum?'

'They will be arriving on Friday Jim. Now, cuddle down and have a lovely sleep.'

Kate had a quick shower and was almost asleep when she fell into bed. Her alarm woke her, to allow her to get breakfast for Jim and see him off to school, then she returned to bed and slept until lunch time. Keeping up with an energetic ten-year-old was certainly an arduous undertaking!

The fortnight before the wedding seemed fly past. Kate's mid-week ambulance shifts seemed busier than normal, and she had plenty to keep her busy on the other week days. Apart from helping to plan her wedding Scott and Belinda were still busy keeping in touch with the many organisations that *Windfall Holdings* was supporting. They kept her informed of the improvements to facilities and support made possible by the contributions from *Windfall Holdings* and she was determined to make as many personal visits as possible before the end of the year.

David managed to spend some evenings with them, leaving when Jim went to bed. He was working late many nights to try to free up some time for them to be together as a family. Kate arranged for a cleaning company to clean David's flat on the Friday before the wedding, after it was decided that David would stay overnight with Frances and Eric. Much to Riley's delight, he had been employed as a fulltime Junior School teacher for the following year and was to move into David's old flat, once it had been cleaned.

Kate and David had chosen a simple but elegant invitation that Belinda addressed according to the lists that David and Kate had provided. Of the fifty guests invited, David's guests were mainly his colleagues and their spouses, as he had no family members to invite.

Although his father had congratulated him when he rang, he had refused to travel from Hong Kong to his wedding.

Kate's guests, on the other hand, were her family members, colleagues, and friends she had made since moving to Melbourne. A reception centre, on the bank of the Yarra River a couple of kilometres from the school had been booked, and would provide the wedding cake that Kate and David chose. Kate's and Julie's bouquets, and the men's buttonholes, had been ordered, while two white Rolls Royce bridal cars and drivers were hired and a photographer booked.

Greg, Margaret and Julie planned to arrive the day before the wedding, while Tom was driving to the city the morning of the wedding, then driving back with Julie the next day, as he didn't want to be away from *Glen Rayne* for too long. Greg and Margaret were staying to look after Jim, until Kate and David returned from their brief honeymoon on the following Monday.

CHAPTER 32

———⟫●⟪———

MID-SEPTEMBER

MELBOURNE

To Jim's delight, Greg, Julie and Margaret, Jessie and Donald had all arrived by the time he came home from school on Friday afternoon. After greeting everyone he turned to Kate. 'The teachers had a party for Dad this afternoon, and I was allowed to be with him. There were plenty of cakes and yummy biscuits to eat. Then Sir Eric arrived just after school finished, and took Dad to stay at his and Fran's house.'

Greg chuckled. 'Protecting him from his friends' ill intentions no doubt! Now, what say we take Kate out, to mark her last dinner as a single woman?'

The next day, which thankfully was forecast to be a pleasant, warm day, Kate went for her usual pre breakfast run, while Jim and Scott swam their laps. After breakfast she and Julie left for their appointment with a bridal hair and makeup stylist in the city, then returned to the penthouse to join Margaret and relax before a light lunch. Scott and Greg kept Jim occupied during the morning, then took Tom under their wing when he arrived in time for an early lunch, before the men changed into their suits.

Margaret assisted both girls to dress, and was left speechless when she looked at 'her two girls', who she had brought up, standing together near the panoramic window in the penthouse. Kate looked exquisite, wearing her mother's wedding dress and her pearl necklace, while Julie, who she rarely saw out of jeans or moleskins, looked stunning in a burgundy form hugging, floor length silk dress.

Jim, who was downstairs with Greg was, at Mr Sullivan's request, wearing his new grey school shirt, school tie and shorts, as this was what the boys would be wearing at the end of term concert.

At one fifteen Julie, Margaret and Jim met in the foyer of the apartment building, while Greg went up to escort Kate down to the waiting cars. When he walked into the penthouse and saw Kate he stopped and stared at her, then straightened his shoulders, and walked over and held her hand. 'Are you alright Dad?'

'Oh, Katie my love, you look just as gorgeous as your mother did in that dress, and you are so like her these days, I forgot for a moment that it was you, and not my beloved Jean standing there! I think this afternoon is going to have some déjà vu moments for me, regardless of the dress you wear.'

He held out his arm to her. 'Are you ready my darling girl?'

Together they went down to meet the others in the foyer, then went outside to where the two white Rolls Royce bridal cars were parked at the front door. Greg handed Kate into the back seat of the front car before carefully sitting beside her, while the other driver assisted Margaret and Julie into the back of the second car, then sat Jim in the front with him.

The journey to Scotch College seemed to take no time at all, and soon they were turning off Glenferrie Road to pass through the open school gates to make their way to the Littlejohn Chapel. The bridal car stopped along Monash Drive for a few minutes, to allow the passengers in the second car to get out and walk up to the front door of the Chapel to wait for the bride. When the bridal car stopped at the Chapel steps, Kate was amazed at the number of steps that she would have to climb. 'Thank goodness it's not raining Dad!'

'You will be fine Lass. It's dry and not windy. Your mother told me that a gust of wind hit her when she was nearly at the top of these steps. Luckily, her father had a good grip on her arm, or she might have taken off like Mary Poppins!'

Kate was still laughing when they approached the front door with a beautiful stained-glass window above it. Julie stepped forward to meet them. 'You are not getting hysterical are you Sis!? I don't have a paper bag for you to blow in.'

'I'm fine Jules. It was just something that Dad said to me. How is Jim?'

'Oh, he's fine. Mr Sullivan took him inside, and he is keeping an eagle eye on his 'three amigos'!

Julie handed Kate her bouquet and gave her sister a quick kiss on the cheek before she lowered her veil. 'Off you two go, and remember Dad, it is Kate your daughter on your arm, not Mum!'

As the organist played the first notes of Wagner's Bridal Chorus, Greg and Kate stepped into the Chapel, and slowly walked down the aisle past the smiling guests, and a beaming Jim and his two friends standing with Mr Sullivan near the front. David and Alistair, his best man, turned to watch Greg and Kate's progress, and he gazed in adoration as she approached him.

When they stopped by David's left side, Greg gently lifted Kate's veil back and gave her a soft kiss on the cheek before stepping away. Kate handed her bouquet to Julie and turned to David, and they both smiled lovingly at each other. Their attention was gained by the Chaplain when he invited the guests to be seated, then the ceremony began. Kate was aware of David's close proximity throughout the service, and was relieved when they said their vows, exchanged rings, and were declared man and wife. Following a quick kiss, they sat together near the alter for the remainder of the service.

At the end of the prayers, Mr Sullivan led the three young boys to the front of the Chapel, then stood facing them, a little to the side. As he lifted his right hand, the organist played the introductory notes, then the three young treble voices began to soar throughout the Chapel. Soon there weren't many dry eyes, and David handed Kate his handkerchief, after quickly wiping his own eyes. When the last note faded away, there was unexpected, spontaneous applause in the Chapel, and Mr Sullivan quietly instructed the boys to bow, then sit down.

As the Chaplain stepped forward to lead Kate and David out to sign their marriage certificate, he stopped and whispered in David's ear. David nodded and the Chaplain went over to Jim. 'Will you come with us please Jim?'

He led the puzzled boy over to Kate and David, then they walked together into the registry with Jim between them, holding their hands. After Julie and Alistair had witnessed Kate and David's signatures, the Chaplain handed the pen to Jim. 'As you are not yet eighteen Jim, you can't be an official witness, but you can still sign here to bear witness to your new parent's wedding.' He pointed to a space under the other two signatures, and Jim signed his name, then gave both Kate and David a big kiss.

The Trumpet Voluntary was played as Kate and David walked back down the aisle, with Jim, grinning widely, clinging to Kate's left arm. They paused outside the door at the top of the steps, looking out over the immaculate oval, where a game of football was in progress, and waited for their guests to exit the Chapel. Some photos were taken of the bridal party on the steps of the Chapel, but the professional photos were scheduled to be taken in the garden before the reception.

Kate hugged Colin and Brad when they shyly approached her. 'That was the most magnificent rendition of Pie Jesu I have ever heard boys. Your parents will be very proud of you, as I am of Jim. Thank you so much for making our wedding so memorable.'

The formal photographs, in which Margaret and Jim were included, were taken within the reception centre garden. Margaret was thrilled to be included. 'You have been our mother for most of our lives Aunt Meg, so this is my way of formally recognising your selflessness, and the love you have given us.'

When the wedding party joined their guests inside the reception centre they made their way to the Bridal Table, where Margaret was ushered to the mother of the bride seat beside David. The 'three amigos' were also seated at the Bridal Table next to Julie. Following the meal and the speeches, Kate and David cut the three tier wedding cake, then David led Kate onto the dance floor to complete the Bridal Waltz, before their guests joined them for a foxtrot. Kate danced with her father, then with Jim and the other two boys, while David danced with Margaret, Julie, and Frances.

Midway through the evening Kate, David and Julie quietly left the reception room, to go to an area set aside for the bride and groom to change out of their wedding clothes into more casual attire. While Julie packed the wedding clothes and her Aunt Meg's pearls into a case, Kate and David returned to the reception room to say goodbye to Kate's family and their guests.

Both of them hugged and kissed Jim before they left in the waiting taxi. 'We will be home waiting for you when you get back from school on Monday Jim, then we will start our life together as a family.'

When they reached the Langham Hotel, after signing in as Mr & Mrs Wilson a bellboy led them up to their room, and opened the door with a flourish. As David passed him a tip, the lad held up a Do Not Disturb sign with a smile. 'I will leave this outside the door for you Sir.'

As the door closed behind him, David walked over to Kate and took her hand. 'Come with me my darling wife. We will appreciate the view later on. Much, much later on!'

CHAPTER 33

───·>●<·───

MID-SEPTEMBER
MELBOURNE

The next morning Kate and David sat out on the balcony of their hotel room, enjoying a very late breakfast in the morning sunshine. 'Well Mrs Wilson, is that a smile of contentment I see?'

'It most certainly is Mr Wilson, and you too have a smile like a Cheshire cat!'

'Mm. And to think that I baulked at the thought of marriage for so long!'

'You were just waiting for the right person to come into your life, like I was!'

'You have no idea how ecstatic I am that we finally found each other. Shall we go inside to make up for all those years of waiting?'

Later that afternoon, after returning from a pleasant stroll along Southbank, the happy couple were once again sitting out on the balcony, looking out over the river and City. 'You love your views don't you my love? I am sure your favourite place in the penthouse is the balcony.'

Kate laughed. 'I think our bedroom will be from now on, because while we are in bed we still get to see a wonderful view through the windows!'

David chortled. 'Fat chance!'

'I don't like living in the city much David. I hate the feeling of being closed in when I am surrounded by masses of people, and being out on the balcony or in a spacious room with a great view stops that claustrophobic feeling. Before I came to live here whenever I stayed in hotels or motels, I've usually had a view of the wall of the next door building, or my room was so close to the road, you'd swear the next truck was going to go through it! 'Two things that I have changed, since my big win, are travelling business or first class and staying in luxury hotels with great views.'

'I'm sure that, in time, I will be able to adjust to your choice on how best to utilise your money to give us a comfortable life my love.'

'It is our money from now on, remember darling.'

Although David now knew the full extent of Kate's wealth, he had no great desire to have access to it, nor to be involved in the running of *Windfall Holdings*, but to appease Kate he did agree for a joint account containing three million dollars to be opened in their names.

Kate and David left the Langham after breakfast on Monday morning, having received a phone call from Greg informing them that Jim had gone to school, and he and Margaret were leaving to drive home to *Glen Rayne*. A courier collected their suitcase, to leave at Ben's then they leisurely walked across Princes Bridge, stopped at Hearn's Hobbies to buy Jim a new carriage for his train set, then they visited the bank to their joint account. After having a coffee near the Town Hall they caught a tram up to Spring Street and walked down to their apartment block, collected their suitcase, and took the lift straight up to the penthouse.

When Kate opened the penthouse door, David kicked their cases into the apartment then swept Kate into his arms and carried her over the threshold. After pushing the door shut behind him he carried his laughing wife into their bedroom.

By the time Jim rushed in after school, Kate had a leg of lamb roasting in the oven and David had prepared the vegetables. 'Mum and Dad, you are back!' David and Kate hugged the excited boy, until he stopped sobbing. 'I'm crying like you did Mum, cause I'm so happy that you are both back home with me now.'

'We are a family now Jim, here for each other.' David handed him the wrapped package. 'This is your mother's and my wedding present for you.'

'Thank you Mum and Dad. Oh, I love calling you both that!' He ran off to his room to open his present. His whoop of delight made Kate and David laugh.

After dinner, Jim told his new parents about his time with Greg and Margaret. 'When you both left on Saturday night we stayed dancing for a while, until Grandad said that his legs were getting tired. He, Aunt Meg, and I came home in a taxi, and they stayed here with me while Aunty Jules and Tom stayed down stairs in one of the flats on Scott's floor, when they came home later.

After Aunty Jules and Tom left to drive home in the morning, Grandad and Aunt Meg took Colin, Brad, and me to Luna Park. Boy, did we have fun! We went on all the rides, and Grandad and Aunt Meg came on some of the less scary ones with us. You should have heard Aunt Meg scream when we were on the Ghost Train!'

Kate and David were in fits of laughter, listening as Jim entertained them describing their exploits on the numerous rides, until it was time for bed. 'We need an early night tonight Jim. Even though you and I are on holidays your mum is on duty at 8.30 as well.'

Before going to bed, David and Kate sat out on the balcony, sipping some champagne they had found left in the fridge. 'I must say, dealing with boys of Jim's age everyday hasn't prepared me in any way for living with one. I'm going to need your help my darling, to get this parenting business right.'

'I'm only just getting used to parenthood myself David.'

'We have not discussed it before sweetheart, but have you thought how many more children you would like to have?'

Kate snuggled up against David. 'I think two, plus Jim would suit me fine. What about you?'

'Three total sounds fine to me.'

'Do you mind if we hold off having a baby until after Jim's

adoption is approved David? I want him to have no doubt that he is one of our family, before any babies arrive to divert our attention from him.'

She laughed when David frowned. 'Don't worry darling, I will stay on the Pill until we're ready to increase our family, so we can still 'keep trying', as Jim so charmingly puts it, to make his new little sibling!'

'Phew! I don't think I could survive another spell of abstinence, especially after the past weekend!'

Kate was wearing her paramedic uniform when they all sat down for breakfast. Jim swallowed his glass of milk and wiped his mouth. 'Do you ever drive the ambulance Mum, or do you always sit in the back, like you did when you saved Toby and me?

'I sometimes drive the ambulance Jim. We tend to take it in turns, especially when we are going to a call out.'

'With the lights and sirens going?'

'Yes, but only if we need to when it is an emergency, and we have to get somewhere quickly.'

'Did you have them going when you took me to hospital?'

'Yes, my love we did. We had to get you to hospital as quickly as possible, as you were a very sick boy, and Toby was pretty sick too.'

Jim turned to David. 'Do you know that Mum saved Toby and me, Dad?'

'Yes, I know. She is a pretty clever mum isn't she? I am awfully pleased she saved you, so that you can now be our son.'

'Will I get into trouble if I forget and call you Dad at school Dad?'

No, I'm sure the teachers will understand, and most of the boys as well. But you must remember that while you are at school, I will have to treat you as I do all the other boys, not as my son.'

CHAPTER 34

———◦)》●《(◦———

LATE SEPTEMBER – DECEMBER
MOUNT BULLER & MELBOURNE

Following her first shift after the wedding, Kate's supervisor offered her a week's leave until the end of the school holidays. When she returned home, David and Jim had just returned from the movies where they had watched Harry Potter and the Deathly Hallows. When they had washed up after dinner, Jim went into the spare room where his train set had again been set up and David and Kate relaxed on the lounge, it being too wet and windy on the balcony. After David sat back after giving Kate a loving kiss he asked 'Can you ski Kate?'

'Yes I can David, though I haven't been up to the snow for a while now. Growing up at Hinnomunjie, we were pretty close to the snow fields.'

'As the ski season appears to be longer this year and you have some leave, would you like to spend the next few days of our holiday up at Mount Buller?'

'I would love to David, but isn't it a bit late to book accommodation?'

'Andrew Hardy, friend of mine has two rooms booked in a chalet up there for the holidays, but they had to return to Melbourne yesterday because his mother in law broke her hip a couple of days ago, and they need to look after his father in law. Andrew emailed me at lunch time to offer us the rooms. If we could go tomorrow they are ours for the next five days.'

Jim was ecstatic when Kate and David told him of their plans. 'We will have to buy some suitable ski wear in the morning before we drive to Mt Buller. Tonight we will pack what we will need in the chalet. We will also have to buy some chains for the Rav4.' David laughed and added 'I don't think my little Escort is suitable for family trips!'

The next morning, after saying goodbye to Belinda and Scott when they left Toby and Mitty in the office, the family spent a couple of hours kitting up, then set off on the almost four hour drive up to Mt Buller.

When they arrived at David's friend's chalet they discovered that they would have it to themselves as the other two couples had gone home that morning. The chalet had two rooms with double beds, and two rooms with single bunk beds, open plan lounge and kitchen, bathroom, toilet, and boot room. It was on Stirling Road not far from the square. After a quick meal at the Kooroora Hotel they were all ready for an early night.

After hiring their boots and skis David and Kate took Jim to the ski school to book lessons for Jim, then after arranging to meet him for lunch David and Kate bought their B-TAGs then spent some time on the easier green runs to regain their 'ski legs' then they moved onto the intermediate blue runs, neither feeling that they wanted to go on the more advanced black runs.

By the end of their stay on the mountain Jim was skiing well enough to tackle the shorter blue runs with Kate and David. All three of them were feeling quite weary on the drive home and Kate and David were happy to share the driving.

The next day Kate rang Mrs Hardy to thank her for the use of their chalet and to enquire after her mother's health. Katherine was relieved to tell her that her mother's hip operation had gone well and she was resting comfortably. Kate then arranged for flowers to be sent to the Hardy's house and also to Katherine's mother in St Vincent's Hospital.

As Andrew and his thirteen year old son were ardent Melbourne supporters like Jim, David arranged for four tickets to the next football match Melbourne played at the MCG, as a thankyou for their trip to Mt Buller.

Fourth term was a hectic time for both David and Jim. David drove Jim to school each day, while Riley drove him home in the afternoon if David had meetings to attend. Extra choir practises were scheduled towards the end of the term to prepare for the end of year concert. If they were both late on the same night the family often had dinner downstairs at Gaspare's.

On the night of the concert David and Kate sat at the front of the hall with the rest of the staff and their partners. The concert was an outstanding success, with the choir performing a wide repertoire of music, including classical and modern pieces and some carols. The three young boys sang Pie Jesu at the end of the performance, and they sang as well, if not better than at the wedding. This time Kate was prepared with her own handkerchief, and was bursting with pride when the three boys bowed and the audience applauded, until Mr Sullivan led the boys in a repeat performance, with the rest of the choir accompanying them.

Jim was beside himself with excitement when they finally arrived home, and it took Kate and David some time to calm him down enough to get to sleep. It was a very bleary eyed boy who dragged himself down to the car the next morning, to accompany David to school to spend the last day of term for the Junior School students with his friends. That night Jim went to bed early and quickly fell into an exhausted sleep. David and Kate had an early night too and lay cuddled together in bed, looking at the night lights twinkling through the window. David had four professional development days the following week, then he too would be on holidays until late January.

'Darling, would you like to spend Christmas at *Glen Rayne*? I would love to have Christmas with the family, then I thought we could fly up to Coffs Harbour before New Year's Day to spend some of January at our house at Woolgoolga. I know that Jessie and Donald would love to look after Jim for much of the time, allowing us to extend our honeymoon, this time with a different view!!!'

CHAPTER 35

LATE DECEMBER

HINNOMUNJIE

A couple of days after David finished at school he, Kate and Jim drove to *Glen Rayne*, to spend Christmas with Kate's family. Jim had spent the development days with Colin and Brad, sleeping overnight at both their homes, while Kate contacted all of the *Windfall Holdings'* affiliations, to inform them that the office would be closed over the festive season, and the first three weeks of January. She assured them all that she could be contacted in an emergency.

Scott and Belinda planned to spend Christmas and the New Year together on Norfolk Island. They had known each other since joining the army, and had met occasionally throughout the years, when their postings had allowed it. However, since they had been working together for *Windfall Holdings,* Kate had noticed their platonic friendship slowly developing into a more caring association, and she hoped that the holiday away together might develop their relationship further. George had all the paperwork and vaccinations required to travel to Norfolk Island and back to Australia, and as a service dog, he had been able to spend the ten day quarantine period at home with Scott.

While Kate and David shared the driving, Jim was happy to

sit in the back with Toby for much of the trip, to use the backseat entertainment system that Kate had agreed to have installed. Mitty happily slept on the knee of whoever was sitting in the front passenger seat.

They decided to travel north up the M31 to Glenrowan, where Jim had a great time learning about Ned Kelly, then on to Bright, where they stayed the night. After breakfast the next morning, they drove up to Dinner Plain, then to Omeo, where Kate showed David and Jim the primary school that she and Julie had attended, then finally they headed up the Benambra Road to *Glen Rayne*.

From habit, Kate stopped at the front gate to check the mailbox, then she slowly drove towards the house, to give David and Jim a chance to view the lake, homestead and the wide valley rising to the rugged, timbered ranges surrounding them. When Kate pulled up in front of the house Margaret hurried out to greet them, and had just stepped down from the veranda when Jim leapt out of the car and raced over to hug her. Embracing the excited boy, she looked over his head and smiled at Kate and David as they walked over to greet her.

'Welcome to *Glen Rayne,* my darlings. It is lovely to see you all again.' She bent down to pat Toby, who had walked over to greet her. 'Julie, Tom and Greg are moving bulls at the moment, so Toby will have time to have a wander around his new surroundings before Bluey, Chief and Brodie arrive back. Come inside and I will put the kettle on.'

When the adults reached the veranda, they turned to watch Jim and Toby dashing around the large yard. Mitty at first appeared to be intimidated by the strange, large open area, but after following Kate to the veranda steps, she turned and raced over to join Jim and Toby, as they paused near the shed. Margaret looked concerned. 'I wonder what she will do when the three working dogs turn up in the yard?'

Kate called 'Jim, if the others come home while we are inside, please hold Mitty until you introduce her to Chief, Bluey and Brodie, and see how they get on.'

Once inside, Margaret showed them to their rooms – Kate and David were in Kate's old room and Jim in Julie's. By the time their luggage was deposited in their rooms Jim, Toby and Mitty joined them in the kitchen, where Toby and Mitty made a beeline to the dogs' beds near the back door, and after circling a few times they lay down together.

'I expect the others back for lunch soon. Would you like a cup of tea while we wait? Margaret put the kettle on while Kate put out four mugs. Greg, Julie and Tom returned soon after and following a brief greeting, Toby and Mitty were introduced to Chief, Bluey and Brodie. Surprisingly, the greeting went very smoothly, and soon all five dogs were lying together on the blanket while the family ate lunch.

When everyone had finished eating, they all went out onto the front veranda while Tom and David went over to the shed, and emerged pushing a small red quadbike. Kate leant over to Jim. 'This is David's and my early Christmas present for you Jim. Tom is going to teach you how to use it correctly, so you can join Julie and the men when they go out around the property.'

Jim was beside himself with delight when he was shown the 110cc junior quadbike and helmet that Tom and Julie had collected from the Bairnsdale bike shop a few days before their arrival. However, before Jim was allowed to start it, Tom explained he would have to learn to use it correctly, emphasising that quad bikes were farm vehicles, to be ridden sensibly and not as playthings.

While Kate, Julie and Greg rode their horses over to the next valley to check the cattle, Tom spent the afternoon teaching both Jim and David how to correctly ride their quadbikes. Having never ridden one before, David was happy to join his son to learn the correct way to ride a quadbike. Before they were allowed to start their bikes, they learnt the names of the various parts of their vehicles, the controls and how to do basic maintenance i.e refuelling, tyre pressure, oil checks, brake checks. Once this was completed, Tom taught them how to ride correctly and safely, using the large seat to adjust their position, according to the terrain they were on

Once a course was set up, using empty plastic twenty litre drums, they both practised riding forward and in reverse, cornering and doing emergency stops. Finally, Tom announced that they were ready to go for a ride away from the yard, so making sure that the dogs were still shut away, Tom, David and Jim rode out of the yard and made their way around the lake. Careful to keep his speed at a pace to ensure that Jim had good control of his bike, but fast enough for him to enjoy the experience, Tom headed out on a track going up the valley, then turned off onto a track heading up through the bush to one of the higher paddocks. When they returned later in the afternoon and parked their bikes in the shed, Jim was ecstatic, and raced inside to regale everyone with his achievements. Both David and Tom were happy to sit back and relax while Jim kept his aunts, mother and grandfather entertained.

Needless to say, Jim was ready for bed earlier than usual that night. When his parents went in to say goodnight he hugged them tightly, and had tears in his eyes when he thanked them for his unexpected present.

The next few days were hectic, combining the usual farm work with the preparations for a larger family Christmas than usual. Jim had the chance to ride his bike each day, but he also went to Bairnsdale with Kate, Julie and Margaret to collect the turkey and to buy the provisions for Christmas dinner and for the rest of their stay.

Kate also took Jim to meet her grandparents, and to wish them a Happy Christmas. Although she was sad that they were now living in residential care, she was pleased to see how well and alert they both were. While she was at *Glen Rayne* she arranged with Greg and Margaret to pay the amount of her grandparents' bond for their new accommodation back into their bank account and to cover other costs that would occur in the future.

Phillip and Dianne were thrilled to meet Jim who, after some initial shyness, happily chatted with his new great grandparents. Finally wishing the happy couple the compliments of the season, and promising to introduce them to David on their way home, Kate drove back to *Glen Rayne* with the car packed with parcels and bags full of supplies, plus a list of other necessities that were to be delivered before Christmas day.

Tom took David and Jim to Omeo, where the local CFA were selling Christmas trees. After careful consideration, a tree was bought, tied to the tray of the ute and the trio returned triumphant with their purchase. Jim, David, and Kate then set to, festooning it with decorations retrieved from the top of the wardrobe in Margaret's bedroom. By dinner that night the tree looked magnificent, covered with decorations, tinsel, and some balloons as well as a new set of lights, twinkling in the dusk.

Christmas Day passed in a flurry of opening presents, eating far too much, and attending the church service at Omeo. The locals were thrilled to meet Kate's new husband and son who, with Kate's help, gallantly tried to remember who was who, but were relieved when Margaret and Greg rescued them to take them home. Kate had the feeling that people thought Jim was David's son, but didn't say anything to dissuade them, and just graciously accepted their congratulations.

On Boxing Day, everyone was happy to take things easy and David, Greg and Jim were keen to watch the first day's play of the Boxing Day cricket match between Australia and England at the MCG. A new TV antenna, Julie's present to Greg, ensured a much sharper picture than previously, so they were able to see each ball played. As Kate explained to David, 'I remember watching fielders run about and the batsmen run up and down the pitch, but I never actually saw a ball! This is a different game altogether!'

CHAPTER 36

———————⊰●⊱———————

END OF DECEMBER

The day before the Wilsons were due to drive home, Greg and Julie went to Bairnsdale for a meeting with their bank manager, so Tom and David took Jim on a long ride up into the ranges, stopping several times where gaps in the trees revealed spectacular views of the Victorian Alps. At one location the track ran parallel to a sheer cliff, looking over a wide grassed valley extending to rugged tree lined ranges on the other side.

Tom had just stopped to point out a mob of their cattle standing under trees bordering a wide river running through the valley, when Jim grabbed his sleeve, and pointed to what looked like a large colourful flag flapping in the breeze on the edge of the cliff, away to their right. 'What's that over there Tom?'

Shading his eyes, Tom looked carefully to where Jim was pointing. 'That looks awfully like the canopy of the paraglider we have seen flying around lately Jim. The pilot must be down the cliff!'

All three quickly started their bikes, and followed the track to where the colourful material was snagged on a rock back from the cliff edge. As they watched, some of the material began to rip. David turned to Tom. 'That's not going to hold for much longer. Jim, please stay away from the edge of the cliff. I am going to look over to see if I can spot the pilot.' David lay down at the cliff edge and looked down. 'There is a person sitting in what looks like a sling, in front of a small motor in a metal crate. It's about five feet below the edge Tom and the person isn't responding to my voice. How in the world can we stop him/her falling when the canopy rips further?'

'I should think our two quads would weigh more than a paraglider, especially if we sit on them David. Let's see what happens if we park across the lines.' Quickly the two men parked side by side between the edge of the cliff and the rock, with their back tyres on the lines attached to the fabric. 'Be ready to ride off if you feel your bike move David.'

'If we are stuck sitting here, how can we help the person below us?'

'We will just have to send Jim for help. I will write a list of things Kate will need to bring up, if we are to save that person.'

While Tom wrote a list in his note book, David sat on his bike with his arm around Jim, who was sitting on the seat in front of him. 'Jim, do you think you can ride down to the homestead by yourself to get Kate?' Jim turned around to face David. 'Yes, I can Dad. I know that this is an emergency, but I promise I will ride carefully and not go too fast.'

Tom handed Jim a page torn from his notebook. 'Take this to Kate Jim. It is a list of things that she needs to bring up in the ute. Tell her that my phone won't work up here, but the CB radio in the ute will connect with the house. Take care lad. Stay on the track that we came up on, and you will be home in about fifteen minutes.'

True to his word, Jim rode carefully down the track, staying well away from the cliff edge, and arrived in the yard feeling very proud of himself. He rode right up to the house and was met by both Kate and Margaret as he ran up the steps.

'Jim, what in the world are you …' 'Mum please listen to me. There is a person hurt up on the ridge, and Dad and Tom are trying to stop him falling down the cliff.' He thrust the paper to Kate 'This is a list of stuff that Tom needs.' Margaret looked over Kate's shoulder as she read the list

> blue rock–climbing bag
> red & green ropes in cottage bedroom

Kate's 1st Aid pack
Blow-up mattress in Margaret's wardrobe
Blankets

No phone coverages up here Kate. Will need to use winch on ute

'Jim and I will collect the climbing gear from the cottage Kate, while you get the other things. Come on Jim, I will need your help with the ropes.'

Kate went to Margaret's room to find the inflatable bed, pleased to note that it was a self-inflatable model, took the spare blankets from her room and left them on the veranda while she grabbed her first aid pack from the car. By the time she had checked the ute for fuel, thrown in an additional coil of rope and backed the ute over to the veranda, Margaret and Jim arrived with a large blue rucksack, a blue helmet and the two coils of climbing rope.

When everything was packed in the back of the ute, Margaret handed Kate some bottles of water that she had collected from the laundry. 'I will wait by the radio Kate, in case we need to call the ambulance. Take care, both of you.' She gave them both a quick kiss, then walked up onto the veranda to wave goodbye as Kate drove out of the yard.

'Ok my little man, which track do we take?' Jim pointed to a track to their left. 'That one Mum. See I hung my jumper on the branch, so I would know which one I came down.'

'What clever thinking Jim. Hop out and grab it, as it will be colder when we get up higher.' When Jim climbed back into the ute and did up his seat belt Kate drove carefully up the rough track. 'I am very proud of you darling, riding down this track by yourself.'

'I promised Dad and Tom I would be careful Mum. Tom told me the other day that my bike is a farm vehicle that will allow me to travel around the property, not a toy to show off on, so I have to take care of it, as well as myself.'

Kate was relieved to see the two men still sitting on their bikes when she turned the corner near the cliff. Quickly she parked the ute facing the cliff, so they could use the winch, then turned to Jim.

'Please don't go anywhere near the cliff darling. We might be a bit preoccupied for a while, so I need to know that you are back here near the ute.'

'I understand Mum. I will wait here unless you, Tom or Dad tell me to do something else.'

'Kate, is there any way you can tie the paraglider lines to the ute's bullbar? If you secure it, David and I can get off these bikes and see what can be done for that poor blighter down the cliff.'

Looking at the fabric snagged on the rock, Kate thought she could thread the extra rope she had brought up between the numerous lines and the canopy then tie it off to the bullbar, thereby ensuring the paraglider couldn't fall further when the men stepped away from their bikes. This done, she joined them at the cliff edge and lay down to survey the scene below.

The paraglider was resting on a small bush growing on the cliff face, and the pilot was slumped forward in the harness. Kate yelled 'Can you hear me down there?' She thought she could see a slight movement of one hand, but wasn't sure if it was voluntary or from the gentle movement of the paraglider.

'I will go down and hook the winch onto the frame above the pilot, if you and Kate can lower me down David.'

'Wouldn't it be better if I go down Tom? I am lighter, and you two should be able to lower me okay. Also I have had training in this sort of rescue, and I can do a quick assessment of the pilot, before you winch him up.'

David wasn't thrilled to think of his new wife undertaking such a risky procedure, but could understand the wisdom of her statement. Quickly Kate strapped on Julie's harness, and adjusted her helmet to fit snuggly, while David tied both the green and red ropes to the bulbar. Tom then attached the green rope to the figure 8 device on Kate's harness, to allow her to abseil down to the paraglider. The red rope was also attached to her harness as a belay rope, to stop her falling if her abseil failed, and also to tie herself off so she could free her hands to assess the patient.

'When you are ready we will lower the winch hook, and you can clip it onto the frame above the pilot Kate. Stand on the glider, and we will winch you both up together.'

Slowly Kate lowered herself over the edge of the cliff, while Tom and David controlled the red rope, and carefully lowered herself down to the pilot, then tied off her abseil rope to allow her the use of both hands to check the man sitting in front of her. 'I have tied myself off. Keep pressure on the red rope please.' She firmly squeezed the man's shoulder. 'Can you hear me? Can you feel that?' She detected a pulse in the man's neck and could see that he was breathing, but he was unconscious.

'He's out for the count. Send down the snap hook and I will do a more thorough assessment when we are on firmer ground.' She heard Tom's 'Watch your head', then saw the hook coming down towards her. 'That's enough!' She grabbed the hook and snapped it onto the middle of the top bar of the frame, behind the unconscious man. 'Ok, take it up slowly.' As the paraglider began to rise, Kate pushed her feet against the cliff wall, while holding the motor frame and turned the machine, so the man was facing away from the cliff, then she stood on the bottom of the frame as it slowly scraped up the smooth face of the cliff.

Before they reached the edge of the cliff, Tom signalled for the winch to stop. 'We will pull you up first Kate, then we can lower the machine down as it comes over the rim, while you keep an eye on your patient.'

Thankfully, Kate scrambled onto solid ground and stood up, then she saw that Jim was controlling the winch, diligently watching Tom's hand signals as the frame came up over the rim. The two men gently laid it on the ground, while Jim kept the winch going to drag the machine away from the cliff, stopping it when Tom held up his hand.

'Can we keep Jim here at *Glen Rayne* when you go home Kate? He is rapidly becoming my right hand man.' Tom walked over to Jim, ruffled his hair, and said quietly 'Well done mate.'

David and Kate unclipped the pilot's harness, and gently laid him on his back. Kate quickly ran her hands around his head and neck, then down his body and limbs, checking for bleeding and possible injuries. He was bleeding from a gash on his forehead, and there was a red stain on his right trouser leg. Kate put a pad over the head cut. 'Hold that please David. Don't press too hard.'

She quickly cut the bloody trouser leg, and revealed a deep gash on the man's calf, from which blood was steadily dripping. Pressing a pad over the wound, she used a pressure bandage to hold it in place. Further investigation showed that the man's other leg had a compound fracture below the knee and his right arm appeared to be fractured too. He had numerous abrasions and some less serious lacerations to his body that David dealt with while Kate placed a cervical collar around the man's neck, then immobilised his broken leg by bandaging his other leg to it. She supported his broken arm in a sling, then bandaged his forehead and checked his pulse and breathing again, before she sat back on her heels and looked at her husband. 'Thanks David. We need to get him down to the homestead as soon as possible. Do you know if Tom has managed to contact Aunt Meg to call for an ambulance?'

'All done my love, and our son has already inflated the bed, so we are ready to move your patient on your say so.' By the time the man was carefully placed on the mattress on the tray, he was showing signs of slowly regaining consciousness. A blanket was wrapped around him, and Kate sat on the other folded blanket, ready to steady him when needed.

David drove the ute, while Tom and Jim followed on the quad bikes. With a storm forecast for that night, Tom was reluctant to leave the bikes out in the elements overnight, so the three adults discussed the possibility of Jim riding one of the bikes home. Tom was sure that Jim could handle the bigger bike, as long as they went down the track together at a sensible speed. Kate proudly watched Jim carefully riding the big bike beside Tom, as they slowly followed the ute. When they reached the edge of the timber and the track was more even, David sped up a little, but Kate was pleased to see that the two bikes didn't try to keep up with them.

Jim was delighted to travel down with Tom, and listened carefully whenever he was given a directive. By the time they arrived back at the homestead, the man was being loaded into the ambulance, and Kate was explaining what had occurred up on the cliff. Jim parked the bike beside Tom's in the shed, then ran over to where he had left his bike near the house, and rode it carefully into the shed to park next to the other bikes.

Just as the ambulance left, two local police arrived to question the family about the rescue of the injured paraglider pilot, then Tom drove them up to the crash site. Tom explained where he and David had parked their bikes to await Kate's arrival with the ute and climbing gear.

'It was just as well you arrived when you did, and parked on the canopy lines Tom. By the looks of that canopy, the man would have ended up at the base of the cliff pretty quickly if you hadn't arrived when you did.' The policemen took photos of the area and the paraglider, then the three men loaded the frame and canopy onto the ute and they set off back to the homestead.

On the way down the policeman in the front seat turned to Tom. 'How far from the homestead are we Tom?'

'Close to four kilometres Stan. As you saw when we came up it's a pretty rugged bush track in places. David and I were worried sick, waiting for Kate to arrive, not knowing how Jim was coping with the ride down. I am going to make sure that we have a radio on the bikes when we come up here from now on. Mobile phones are only good when you have reception!'

Back down at the homestead the constable turned to Kate. 'I believe that you are a paramedic Mrs Wilson. Certainly a stroke of luck for the injured chap.'

'I basically did what any trained first aider would do Constable Grey, although my first aid pack is more comprehensively stocked than a basic first aid kit. However, in my professional opinion, that man owes his life to our son. He would have bled to death if Jim hadn't ridden down to the homestead to get me.'

The policemen looked at Jim with new respect. 'How old are you Jim?'

'I am ten Sir.'

'How long have you been riding a quad bike?'

'Mum and Dad gave me my bike a couple of days before Christmas, and Tom taught me how to ride it properly, otherwise I wouldn't have been able to ride it down to get Mum.'

'Well, he seems to have done a good job lad. Thank you all for what you did to save Lionel Croom's life. Before we leave, would you like to show us your bike Jim?'

When the policemen saw Jim's bike they smiled. 'That's a great bike. Do you like riding it?'

'I love it. It's much easier to ride than that big one.'

The constable turned to the adults standing near the shed door. 'I wish a lot more farmers would buy smaller quad bikes for their children to ride around their farms.'

The next morning, when the SUV was packed, Toby and Mitty had been separated from their new friends, and the family were saying their farewells, Jim looked beseechingly at Kate. 'Mum, can I come to *Glen Rayne* during school holidays to help Grandad, Tom and Julie? Oh, and I would help you in the house too Aunt Meg!'

'That might be possible Jim, though not necessarily every holiday.'

Before they left Bairnsdale, Kate called in on her grandparents to introduce David to them. During a very pleasant half hour sitting out in the garden, Kate and David told them about their wedding, and of Jim and his two friends' performance. Dianne looked at Jim. 'That is my favourite piece of music Jim. Could you possibly sing some of it for me?'

Jim looked at Kate and David who nodded. 'Alright Great Grandmother, I will try.' He cleared his throat, then confidently began to sing the two verses that he had sung at the wedding and concert. People in and near the garden stood in amazement, listening to his pitch perfect soprano performance, and tears streamed down Dianne's cheeks. Applause rang out when Jim stopped singing, and his cheeks began to redden. Then he grinned and bowed deeply, before giving Dianne a hug.

They drove back to Melbourne via Yarram stopping on the way

at the shelter that had initially rescued Mitty. The staff were thrilled to see her looking so fit and well. Tanya wiped her eyes as she held Mitty. 'I honestly didn't believe the she would survive the trip to Melbourne Kate, let alone recover so fully from the operations that she had to endure. You have done wonders with her, and she is now a normal healthy little pup.'

They then detoured to the coastal township of Inverloch, where they had fish and chips for a late lunch on the beach of the sparkling inlet. Once Jim and Toby returned from a long run along the beach, they set off for Melbourne, and were relieved to arrive home late in the afternoon. When Jim and Toby emerged from his bedroom after he had deposited his case and bag of Christmas presents, he flopped into a chair beside his parents on the balcony, gratefully accepting the glass of apple juice that Kate handed him.

'Thank you so much Mum and Dad. That was a truly wonderful Christmas and a great holiday. *Glen Rayne* is a fantastic place, and I just love my new family to bits.'

'That's great to hear Jim. I think they are pretty special too, and I just adore my new family!'

'I agree with you Jim, I'm loving having you and Kate as my brand-new family, as well as our new relations in East Gippsland.'

CHAPTER 37

DECEMBER - JANUARY

WOOLGOOLGA & SYDNEY

Two days after arriving home in Melbourne, Kate, David, and Jim repacked their cases, and caught a taxi to Melbourne Airport to fly up to Coffs Harbour. Colin and Brad were joining them after New Year's Day, to spend two weeks of their holidays with Jim at Woolgoolga.

David had never been to Woolgoolga, and was looking forward to seeing Kate's, no, their house up there, and longed to spend some time relaxing, hoping that Kate's assurance that Donald and Jessie would keep the boys occupied most of the time would come true.

The flight up to Sydney was uneventful, and certainly more comfortable that his previous flights in economy, and even with Toby and Mitty in the cabin with them, he had plenty of room to stretch his legs. He could see why Kate was prepared to pay extra for the business class seats and service, and was sure that he could easily become accustomed to the comfort. The seats on the smaller plane to Coffs Harbour were still bearable, as they had front row seats so he could still stretch his legs out for the hour's travel.

Donald was waiting for them at the airport, and quickly collected their luggage from the carrousel, before leading them out to the

SUV. Kate and David sat in the back with Toby and Mitty, while Jim sat in the front seat and informed Donald of all of his adventures over Christmas. Kate cuddled up against David, and every so often indicated points of interest on the twenty five kilometre journey north along the new freeway to Woolgoolga.

David fell in love with the house the moment he stepped inside, and could understand the appeal it had for Kate. He happily sat out on the balcony looking out to sea, and not long after he had finished his cup of tea, he fell asleep in his chair.

Quietly Kate, Jessie and Donald went to the kitchen, then Donald continued out to the backyard where Jim was playing with the dogs. 'Do you fancy a walk to the bait shop Jim, to see what they have for us to use in the morning? No need to go inside, I asked your Mum before I came out to see you. We will take the dogs with us.'

'David looks exhausted Kate.' Jessie and Kate were sitting at the kitchen bench quietly chatting.

'He is worn out Jessie. He was recovering from his stay in England and his flight home when we first met, then with our wedding, the end of the school year and living with an energetic ten year old, he hasn't had a chance to rest and unwind. I am hopeful that the stay up here will give him the chance to slow down and relax.'

'Donald and I would love to spend more time with Jim and his friends when they come up, if you would like a bit more time alone to relax together Kate. We can also easily make a barrier of pot plants on the top balcony, to block off your end of the balcony to give you more privacy in your bedroom.'

'What a wonderful idea Jessie. We will do that when David wakes up.'

'Kate, please don't take offence at what I am about to say. Why don't you and David fly down to Sydney tomorrow morning, book into that swish hotel you stayed in with Jim for two nights. You could watch the New Year's Eve fireworks from your room, then relax New Year's Day and the next night, before you collect the boys at the airport at lunchtime on the 2nd. Have an extension of your honeymoon maybe!'

'No offence taken Jessie. You and Aunt Meg could be clones! She suggested we try to get some time away together before school starts again. I think I will take you up on your offer, and try to book some seats and the hotel straight away.'

By the time David woke up, Kate had booked two seats on a mid-afternoon flight to Sydney, with two return seats on the flight that Brad and Colin were booked on, plus two nights in the same room in the hotel that she and Jim had stayed in at the Rocks for New Year's Eve and the following night.

Donald and Jim brought back their bait, as well as some pizzas for dinner, so they all had an early dinner, then sat out on the balcony listening to the waves on the rocks below and watching the starlit sky. Jim was happy to head to bed early, and after Kate and David went down to say goodnight to him and Toby, they too said good night to Jessie and Donald and retired for the night.

Donald and Jim, with Hugo and Toby, went out fishing early in the morning, while Jessie was pleased to potter around quietly downstairs with Mitty and Chloe keeping her company, allowing Kate and David to have a good sleep in, waking only when the two ravenous fishermen returned at nine o'clock. Jim was quite happy for Kate and David to leave him with Donald and Jessie for a couple of days, so that they could plan activities for the time that Brad and Colin would be staying.

David was rendered speechless when he walked into their hotel room situated near the top of the Shangri-La Hotel, with its 270° panoramic windows overlooking the harbour, Sydney Harbour Bridge, and the Opera House. Finally, he turned to Kate 'Your description of this room in no way prepared me for this amazing view darling. What in the world will it be like when the fireworks start?'

'I have no idea my love. We will just have to make sure that we sit up to watch. Now, what say we have a rest before dinner. The Altitude Restaurant is amazing too.' To Kate's surprise David fell asleep in her arms soon after they lay on the bed, but then she felt pleased that he was beginning to relax enough to sleep, and she was sure that it would be a very late night.

Kate and David went down to the Altitude Restaurant for a delightful meal, enhanced by the magical view of the 9.00pm fireworks display through the panoramic windows. When they finally returned to their room, they discovered a bottle of French champagne had been placed in an ice bucket, care of the hotel management, wishing them a Happy New Year.

Lying on their bed watching the fireworks at midnight was the most awesome and incredible experience, as at times they appeared to be right in the middle of some of the exploding pyrotechnics. Their view of the Harbour Bridge fireworks display was breath-taking, as was their lovemaking at the conclusion of the pyrotechnical spectacle.

After a leisurely breakfast, Kate and David caught the ferry to Manly, where they spent the day in the surf and lazing on the beach in the shade of a hired shade tent. Luckily Kate had packed their swimwear, as few shops were open on New Year's Day. David was a keen surfer, but he couldn't persuade Kate to join him when he hired a board and paddled out to join a group of surfers waiting for the right wave to carry them back to the beach. Kate was quite happy to hire a boogie board, and catch the smaller waves closer to shore. When she had had enough she went back to their shade tent, and lay on a beach lounge watching David surfing.

As Kate had confided in Jessie, she was concerned about David's fatigue, and at first she was worried that he was over exerting himself out in the surf, then she suddenly realised that it was probably the best thing for him. Tiring yes, but he was relaxing out there, much more than if he was compelled to rest in bed. She decided to suggest that he buy himself a board when they returned to Woolgoolga.

This led her to think more about Colin and Brad's visit. Did they enjoy surfing? She knew that, like her, Jim didn't like big surf, and after the fun that she'd had with the boogie board, she thought she might buy a couple for their use at Woolgoolga. Maybe she would buy a couple more for the boys, that could be used later by other visitors.

Jessie, Donald, and Kate had earlier discussed the boys' visit, and Jessie had enquired about their sleeping arrangements. She felt sure that the three boys would prefer to sleep in the one room if possible, so she and Donald, with Kates' approval, had replaced the large bed in the spare guest room with three king size single beds. Jim was thrilled with this arrangement, although, until his friends arrived he and Toby still occupied the other room, which had been designated as his room.

Kate went to sleep in the shade tent, and was awakened by David dripping water over her at he leant over to kiss her. 'Wake up sleepy head! You are missing all the fun.' He grabbed his towel and wiped some of the water off himself, then sat on the other lounge beside Kate. 'Oh, my love, that was the first time that I have surfed for well over twelve months, and it was awesome! I feel a new man!'

'I didn't realise that you are a surfer darling. I guess there are still a number of things that we have yet to find out about each other.'

David leant over and kissed Kate again. 'And what fun we will have finding them! Ian and I spent a lot of our youth surfing, and we still went out whenever we could after he married Julie, although she wasn't the keenest surfer, and stopped altogether when she had Jim. While we were both teaching at Scotch, we often went to local Victorian beaches for a late afternoon's surfing. In fact, the last time I rode a wave, was the weekend before I flew out to England, when Ian and I went to Bell's Beach for a day's surfing.'

'I am afraid I won't be much of a surfing companion for you sweetheart. I don't cope well with big surf, though I had a ball earlier on that boogie board!'

Unfortunately, I gather that Jim isn't too keen on heavy surf either, though I wonder if he would have a go on a boogie board. Maybe we could get the three boys to give it a try.'

'Well, there are some great surf beaches for you to check out around Woolgoolga. Why don't you buy yourself a board and a wetsuit when we are back in Woolgoolga? The boys and I can deal with the waves closer in, while you go out and tame the bigger stuff!'

'Sounds a great idea. Now, what say we find somewhere nearby to get some lunch. That exercise has whetted my appetite.'

Mid-afternoon Kate and David returned their hired gear, and

unhurriedly walked arm in arm to the wharf, to catch the ferry back to Circular Key. Cuddled together up near the front of the cabin, they took little notice of the scenery as the ferry crossed the harbour, although when they neared the Harbour Bridge they both sat up and watched as the ferry passed under it.

On their return to the hotel, they both had a long hot shower, then lay on their bed until it was time for dinner. The view from the restaurant windows minus the early fireworks display was quite different, the colourful city lights twinkling in the night air creating a stunning vista of the panorama below them.

That night, they derived pleasure in taking their time to arouse each other, and revelled in fully gratifying each other's desires. Eventually, utterly spent, they both slept, and didn't wake up until just before nine o'clock, when a cruise ship passing under the bridge sounded its horn.

David leaned over and kissed Kate on her lips. 'Good morning my darling. Last night was a truly sublime experience that I never want to forget.'

Kate dreamily looked at David. 'We certainly make beautiful music together, don't we my love!'

'What say we play it again now!'

'Much as I would love to sweetheart, we have to get up, pack, have a quick breakfast, then make our way out to the airport to meet Brad and Colin at noon.' Kate kissed David, then quickly rolled out of his reach, and raced for the bathroom.

CHAPTER 38

WOOLGOOLGA

JANUARY

Kate and David were waiting near the arrivals gate when Colin and Brad emerged with the other passengers. Following some initial awkwardness in greeting their school principal and his wife, Kate hugged each boy. 'Welcome to Sydney lads. You can call David Sir if you'd prefer, but I insist on Kate. I am still getting used to being called Mrs Wilson, and might unintentionally ignore you, if you call me that while we' are here on holidays.'

Each boy had a cabin bag and a backpack with them. 'Do you have any luggage booked through or are you traveling with what you have with you Brad?'

'Just what we have with us, Sir.'

'Great, we have a bit over an hour 'till our flight to Coffs, so let's go to the Qantas Lounge for a quick bite to eat.'

Like Jim had the first time Kate took him to the Qantas Lounge, Brad and Colin took great delight in choosing food from the variety of dishes on offer. Noting that Kate and David had only chosen a cup of tea and a croissant, Colin looked sheepish. 'Sorry Kate, Brad and I were so excited at the thought of flying to Sydney by ourselves, we couldn't eat breakfast, and the tiny biscuit that they gave us on the plane just made us hungrier.'

'The food is here for eating Colin. Just don't eat too much and make yourselves sick.'

When their flight was called, they walked to Gate 1, where their tickets were scanned, then they walked down the stairs to go out onto the tarmac, where they walked to where their plane was parked. Brad stared at it, then turned to David. 'It's awfully small compared to the one we flew up on Sir. And it has propellers!'

'Don't worry Brad, it will get us to Coffs Harbour, no worries. Now, we leave our cabin bags out here and they will be loaded in with the other luggage, then we collect them when we get off the plane.' A Qantas official handed David four luggage tags, then Kate led the boys up the steps into the plane, and showed them their seats near the front, before she and David sat in the seats across the aisle from them.

'Will Jim be at the airport to meet us Kate?'

'I am sure that he will be there waiting with Donald, Colin. Wild horses wouldn't keep him away.'

Sure enough, Jim was standing with Donald near the door when the four travellers walked into the arrival area at the Coffs Harbour Airport. As the boys enthusiastically greeted each other, Kate noticed Jessie walking towards her. 'Hello Kate and David, welcome home. I have brought Donald's car, so you two can come back with me, as Donald has volunteered to take the boys and your luggage.' Once Donald and Jessie had been introduced to the boys and Jim had unreservedly embraced both Kate and David, everyone walked out to the two cars.

As Jessie headed out of the airport, David turned to see the SUV following. 'Donald deserves a medal for volunteering to drive those three home Jessie. How was Jim while we were away?'

'I really only saw him at mealtimes. He and Donald were away most of the time, fishing, swimming, and scouting around for things to do, and places to visit while Colin and Brad are up here. Donald loved it, and is like a big boy himself. Now, I don't think I need to ask how your time away was!'

'You are making my wife blush Jessie. We had a wonderful time thank you. The fireworks were spectacular, both outside and inside our room! Ouch, you have a wicked right jab Mrs Wilson!' David rubbed his upper arm. 'I seem to remember that it was Jessie's idea that we had a couple of nights alone in Sydney! We also went to Manly Jessie, and I rediscovered my love of surfing. So, now Kate is worried that she might become a surfing widow while we are up here!'

'Don't you surf Kate?'

'Not really Jessie. I am quite happy catching waves on a boogieboard, but won't go out to the bigger waves.'

'Do you think the boys might like to learn to surf while they are here? There is a surf school in Woolgoolga, and they would learn in the bay below us, on the smaller waves.'

'We will ask them when we get home.'

Jim had a wonderful time showing the boys around 'his new home'. They quickly decided which beds they would have, raced out to the back yard to check it out, then, after a quick change into their swim shorts and UV swim shirts that Kate had advised their mothers to purchase, went down to the pool.

'Do you mind if I take the boys out on the bay in the morning Kate? An SES pal has offered me the use of his boat, which is larger than mine, with plenty of room for the boys and it has a small cabin. I will hire life jackets for them before we set out for a couple of hours on the bay. If they like it, we can go fishing the next morning.'

'I am sure they would love to go out with you Donald, but are you sure that you are not taking on too much?'

'I will soon let you know if I have Kate, but I am sure that I will be fine. I love kids, well, the older ones, and wish I'd had a couple that I could share my interests with.'

'And you two can sit back and relax.'

David looked at Jessie. 'Yes Mum, we will, thank you!'

Jessie laughed. 'Get away with you. Why don't you sit on the balcony and supervise the swimming pool from on high, while I prepare dinner?'

Kate and David unpacked their cases, then went out onto the balcony, from where they could see the boys having a wonderful time together in the pool. 'I hope you don't mind Jessie suggesting that you do things David. She is the veritable mother hen, and just loves doing things for people.'

'No, I am actually enjoying it, having never really had much pampering from my own mother. I am not looking for that from you my love, but Jessie is old enough to be my mother, if she'd had me as a teenager!'

Kate had told David of her first meeting with Jessie and their consequent friendship. 'Jessie looks on this place as her home now, and regards me as a well-regarded friend, although she never oversteps the mark when it comes to decision making. Like you, I quite enjoy it when she fusses over me.'

When the boys arrive home after their trip out on the bay with Donald, they were eager to go out fishing with Donald and Jim the following morning. Brad and Colin were also keen to attend the surf school later that morning, so Donald took the three boys down to the beach to introduce Brad and Colin to their surfing instructor. When Jim saw where they would be learning to surf he decided to have a go too. All three were kitted out in wetsuits and given the appropriate size surf board, then spent the next two hours learning how to read the waves and how to stand up on their boards. By the end of the lesson, all three had managed to ride a small wave a few metres, before falling off, and were all eager to attend the next day's lesson.

David spent some of the time further out catching waves, and making friends with some of the local surfers, who invited him to join them at the back beach in the morning. This beach was on the other side of the headland and had more serious surf than Woolgoolga beach, where they were currently surfing.

When David came in, he persuaded Kate to have a try at surfing on his board. Seeing the fun the boys were having on the smaller waves, Kate decided to give it a go. After a number of futile attempts, she surprised both David and herself by riding a wave almost to the shore. David hugged her when she waded back out to him. 'You are a natural my love. Why don't you join the boys tomorrow, and learn the intricacies of surfing? As you can see, you don't have to go after the bigger surf to get a buzz from riding a wave.'

During the afternoon, while Donald took the boys back to the beach for a swim, David and Kate visited a board shop that David's new surfing friends had recommended. There he purchased a new board and sleeveless wetsuit, then convinced Kate to do the same!

When the boys came back from the beach, they happily sat out on their balcony chatting and reading. Before dinner Brad and Colin rang their parents and assured them that they were having a terrific time, and that Jim's new parents and Donald and Jessie were fantastic people!

Early the next morning the three boys and two dogs followed Donald down to the bay to launch his friend's boat, then had an exciting time hauling in a number of fish. David left soon after to meet his new friends and spent an idyllic few hours getting used to his new board. At first, he missed his great friend Ian, who had challenged him to keep developing his surfing skills, and they had entered into a friendly rivalry to see who could master the surf on the day. But soon he was enjoying the other men's company, and taking immense pleasure in regaining his former surfing prowess.

While they sat waiting for the swell to build, the men chatted and somewhere in the conversation David mentioned that he had been in the Scotch rowing eight when he was at school, and had competed in the Head of the River, and still rowed in an old boys eight when he had time. Kevin turned to David. 'Have you ever rowed in a surfboat David?'

'No, I've never had the chance, though I guess to some extent it would be similar.'

'Terry, Gordon, and I are local lifesavers, and are all in the Woolgoolga surfboat crew. Would you like to have a row with us tomorrow? We are always happy to welcome new members.'

'Don't forget that I don't live here Kevin.'

'Maybe not, but you and your wife own a house here, and I'm sure that you will be regular visitors throughout the year, now that you have experienced our surf!'

'Okay, I will come down tomorrow, because I would love to have a row in your boat.'

CHAPTER 39

——————>●<——————

WOOLGOOLGA NSW
JANUARY

The next two weeks passed in a blur of activity for the five visitors.
After meeting Kevin, Terry, and Gordon down at the lifesaving
club the next morning, David went out for a short row in their
lifeboat, and all were thrilled at his rowing prowess and how quickly
he adapted to rowing in the heavier, higher boat. David soon joined
the crews on their daily training sessions, filling in where required,
and thoroughly enjoyed himself. Although he felt slightly guilty at
leaving Kate, he also went out surfing each day, and was soon feeling
his usual robust self.

Kate was thrilled to see David become so involved and active
with some of the locals, and was quick to allay his feelings of guilt
at doing his own thing. He was tired at night like the rest of them,
but he slept well, and seemed to have shrugged off the lassitude of a
few weeks ago.

Jim, Brad and Colin were on the go from dawn till dusk, fishing,
surfing swimming and also they managed to fit in a visit to the Big
Banana, participated in a one hour all terrain Segway tour from
Coffs Harbour and visited the Dolphin Marine Conservation Park.
Kate and David took them up to the Forest Sky Pier, where they

experienced panoramic views over Coffs Harbour while standing on a cantilevered platform jutting out over rainforest, 15 metres above the forest canopy. They also went up into the hills behind Coffs Harbour to visit old gold mining areas and they were shown Russell Crowe's property, tucked into the forest at Nana Glen.

All four surfing novices were gaining confidence in surfing on larger waves, capably guiding their boards along most of the waves that they chose to ride. Kate and Jim were coping well with lager waves, providing they weren't dumpers, and were proud of their new found skills and self-confidence.

All too soon their time at Woolgoolga drew to an end, and they had to pack their bags, say goodbye to new friends and travel to Coffs Harbour with Jessie and Donald. To save an emotional departure, Jessie kissed everyone goodbye and Donald said goodbye to Kate and David. He then gravely shook hands with the boys, before enfolding each lad in a firm bear hug, wishing them a safe trip. The brother and sister then quickly left the building without looking back.

Everyone was quite subdued for the first leg of the journey back to Melbourne, but by the time the plane began the decent into Melbourne spirits lifted and the boys were discussing what they would do in the remaining days of their holidays. Carol and Annette had trouble getting a word in to thank David and Kate for having their sons for three whole weeks, Brad and Colin being so keen to inform their mothers of the wonderful time they'd had.

Eventually Kate, David Jim and their dogs arrived back in Spring Street and tiredly walked into the penthouse. To their delight Mrs Nash had left fresh milk, bread and butter in the fridge, and Mr Nash had left recently picked salad vegetables on the bench. There was also a welcome home card to the Wilson family from them both.

After a light tea Jim sat out on the balcony between his parents, with Toby and Mitty happily curled up on their beds. 'Thank you both so much for being my parents and for such a wonderful holiday, both at *Glen Rayne* and Woolgoolga. And especially for letting me have Colin and Brad to stay. I have had the best holiday ever. He hugged each of them, then headed off for bed. David moved into

Jim's vacated chair and cuddled Kate. 'I want to thank you too my darling, for being so understanding and reassuring. I must admit, I was feeling at a pretty low ebb when we returned from *Glen Rayne,* and wasn't really looking forward to travelling up north. By then, the realisation that Ian and Julie were gone had truly sunk in, and I just wanted to curl up and give up.

Then we had that glorious time in Sydney, and I realised that I had everything to live for now, with you and Jim in my life. And do you know what Kate? It felt as though an immense weight was lifted off me. I know there will be times I will miss Ian, but you Kate, are my beloved soulmate, who truly makes my life complete. Surfing again is helping me regain my normal vitality, but nowhere near as much as having your love, support and encouragement is my darling. I am now fit, healthy and raring to go, so you had better beware!'

Kate laughed. 'I am so relieved to hear that sweetheart. I must admit, that I was growing concerned about your increasing lethargy. Thank heavens for Jessie's perception and wise counsel. Let's say goodnight to our son, then have an early night to test your new stamina!'

With a few days left before David had to return to work, the Wilson's left Mitty and Toby with a delighted Mrs Nash and spent three days down at Torquay, a seaside town on the Great Ocean Road west of Melbourne, renowned for its surf beaches. They booked a two bedroom suite at a resort in Torquay, then went shopping for wetsuits more suited for the cooler water at the Victorian beaches, and a surfboard each.

For the next two days they had a wonderful time surfing together at the numerous beaches. David stayed with Kate and Jim for a lot of the time, helping them to further develop their surfing skills and confidence in various wave conditions. Occasionally he would test his proficiency in the bigger surf, while his wife and son sat on the beach praising his expertise on his new board.

Tired, but elated after spending such a wonderful time together, participating in an activity that they now all enjoyed so much, Kate and David both envisaged several family surfing weekends in the near future, before the weather became too inclement. Kate was overjoyed to see how she, David and Jim were bonding into a loving, unified family, delighting in each other's company as individuals, and in their three-way relationship. She and David decided that now that Jim was such an integral member of their family, it was time to act on adding to their family.

Scott and Belinda had returned from their Norfolk Island holiday by the time Kate and David arrived back from Torquay, after dropping Jim of at Brad's for an overnight stay. Kate invited them up to the Penthouse for pre-dinner drinks and both couples had a lot of holiday experiences to share. George for once was missing, having already started his ten day quarantine in Scott's apartment. 'I will have to work a bit more from home if that's ok Kate and will have to keep George away from Mitty and Toby for the next ten days. There may be some border security people call in at some time to ensure that we are doing the right thing. Oh, and we shouldn't have visitors, especially Jim, who spends so much time hugging the dogs.'

'That shouldn't be too much of a problem Scott, as Jim will be spending the rest of the holidays with Colin and Brad. Mrs Nash is happy to look after Mitty and Toby when David and I are both at work. Talking of Mrs Nash. Can you survive without her coming in each day for the ten days?'

'I am sure that I can Kate.'

Belinda joined Kate while she was putting together a platter of hors d'oeuvres. 'Kate, does *Windfall Holdings* have any constraints on employing couples? I think that you have guessed that Scott and I have fallen in love, but we both wish to remain working together for you if that is possible.'

Kate put down the plate she was holding and embraced Belinda. 'I am so pleased for you both Belinda. We certainly don't have such limitations on our staff, especially you and Scott.'

'Thank you Kate. We didn't want to make any definite plans for our future together until we'd spoken to you.'

'Does that mean an announcement is forthcoming?'

'Yes, Kate, and you and David are the first to hear it.'

The two women returned to the balcony with the hors d'oeuvres. Belinda smiled at Scott, who stood up and stood beside her. 'Kate and David, Belinda and I want you two to be the first to know that we are officially engaged.' He removed a ring from Belinda's necklace and placed it on her ring finger. 'We bought the ring not long after we arrived on Norfolk Island, but haven't told anyone else yet.'

Kate hugged Scott. 'I am so happy for you both. Have you thought of a wedding date yet?'

'We would like to set a date in early March if possible.'

'It looks like we will have a couple of wedding soon Kate. Aren't Julie and Tom looking at tying the knot sometime in April?'

'I think they are hoping the Littlejohn Chapel might be available sometime in April David. If not, they will probably marry in the church at Omeo.'

When Belinda and Scott left, Kate and David went down to Gaspare's for dinner. 'Will you have much to do when you go back to work tomorrow my love?'

'I hope not. With any luck I won't have too much to change on the timetable. Debbie usually does a great job preparing it, and I just do a tweak or two if necessary. As far as I know, all the staff will be returning this year, with the addition of Riley and a new teacher's aide. I will try to get home by the time you are due to finish your shift. The collar is going to rub for both of us I fear.'

'I will let you know if we have an emergency near the end of my shift. Unfortunately, holiday time can often be fraught with issues.'

'Well, you take care of yourself Mrs Wilson. Will you keep your maiden name at work Kate?'

'Do you mind if I do, darling? It would simplify things a lot if I do.'

'I don't mind in the least, my love. You are Mrs Wilson in my eyes, and that's all that matters to me!'

When Scott, Belinda, Kate, and Geoff met down in the office on their first day back, they contacted all the organisations that *Windfall Holdings* was associated with, to hear how their businesses were progressing and to confirm that more funds would be available, following further discussion on future projects.

Two rural prisons were now running the dog training program, where a professional dog trainer worked with prisoners, who were paired with dogs rescued from shelters. The dogs slept in the cell with their prisoner trainer, who was responsible for their feeding and upkeep, as well as specialised training. It was hoped that at the end of their training, most of the dogs would become service dogs to assist people with various disabilities. *Windfall Holdings* was also funding the training of a number of guide dogs and PTSD service dogs, as well as contributing to organisations assisting the homeless, especially in the city.

Belinda and Scott worked together in Scott's apartment while Kate was on ambulance duty during George's quarantine period, then one of them stayed with him for the other work days.

Kate, Geoff, and Sir Eric spent a morning together, going through the Company's financial spreadsheets and accounts. The companies that Geoff, with Sir Eric's support, had bought into on behalf of *Windfall Holdings* throughout the past eight months, were all now solvent, well run enterprises. Kate was pleased to see that the profits from these acquisitions were more than covering the outgoing funds to the numerous charities and the company revenue was growing. 'Does this mean that I can look for more charities to assist Geoff?'

'A couple more Kate, but don't go overboard! What do you have in mind?'

I thought we could assist some of the groups who are providing portable hot showers and washing facilities for the city homeless, and reimburse some of the costs the local vets incur, when treating the homeless people's animals for free.'

The Smythe Park renovations were completed on time, and late in January the first six women and their dogs took up residence after a very low key opening. A number of security personnel were employed to discretely protect the residents. One of their number was a qualified dog trainer, who made sure that the canine residents lived in accord with each other.

Jim returned to the penthouse the day George's quarantine period expired so there was a great reunion between Scott, Belinda Jim and all the dogs. Belinda moved into Scott's apartment the next day and Jim, dressed in his new uniform, went to school with David, to commence his studies in grade five with Colin and Brad.

Occasionally David ran through the gardens with Kate, although most days he preferred to swim with Scott and Jim, who was becoming quite a strong and proficient swimmer. David also used the fitness centre a few times a week to regain his previous robustness, and was pleased when Jim decided to join him when possible.

Early in February Kate and David received official notification of Jim's adoption. The adoption process had been accelerated due to Jim being an older orphan, Kate's guardian status and Kate suspected, Judge Thomas's testimonial. When Jim's official adoption certificate arrived, his legal name became James Harold Ross Wilson.

Francis, Eric and Judge Thomas called in to congratulate the elated family, and Francis informed Kate that Marjorie Hurston had been officially and publicly banned from representing any government body, in either a paid or voluntary position, and the humiliation of the ban had caused her to move overseas.

Unbeknown to Jim, the police had recommended his effort in saving Lionel Croom's life to the authorities, and he received notification that he was to be presented with a certificate by the Victorian Governor in early March. David and Kate proudly accompanied him to Government House, where he and nine other children were presented their certificates by Governor Linda Dessau, following an account of their courage in the face of adversity that had led to saving a life.

Kate was thrilled to see Jim's new name on the certificate. Lionel was introduced to Jim and his family, and expressed his deep gratitude for their efforts in saving his life. He was still in a wheelchair, but was hoping to be able to walk again in a month or so.

CHAPTER 40

———⟫●⟪———

VICTORIA

FEBRUARY – APRIL

Despite all that was occurring early in the year, Kate and David tried to get away surfing for some weekends, while the weather was warm. One weekend they took Brad and Colin with them to Phillip Island, where they rented a holiday house close to a recommended surf beach. After a great day's surfing they all went to see the Penguin Parade, where the three boys were enthralled to watch the little penguins waddle up the beach, seemingly oblivious of the spectators nearby.

The next morning Kate and David took them to the Nobbies where they could view the seals out on the rocks through binoculars. They walked along the boardwalk to the blowhole, where the large waves sounded like thunder as they surged into the spectacular sea cave. After a couple more hours surfing, they packed up and left the Island, stopping at the San Remo Fisherman' Co-op for a delicious late lunch of fish and chips, before they drove back to Melbourne.

Kate was pleased to see the three boys were so relaxed with David, despite them all being back at school again. Brad and Colin still called him Sir, but it was more as a name, rather than his more formal school title. Jim happily called him Dad when away from school, and Sir at school, and no boundaries appeared to be overstepped, despite their informal encounters. In fact, David seemed to be revelling in associating with the young boys, now that he had regained his normal vigour and was contentedly relaxed in his new family environment

Kate and David took the three boys up to Woolgoolga for the Labour Day long weekend, where the boys spent as much time as possible surfing, while Kate and David were happy to spend some time surfing, but mostly to relax on the beach supervising them, enjoying having a relaxing time together minus work restraints. Kate, Jessie, and Donald discussed the possibility of Scott and Belinda honeymooning at Woolgoolga early in March, and they agreed to have the house ready, then to keep a low profile during the honeymooner's stay.

When the weary travellers returned to Melbourne late on Monday night, the boys stayed in the penthouse, then travelled to school the next morning with David and Jim.

Scott and Belinda's wedding on the Saturday 16th March was suddenly upon them. They had decided on a small afternoon wedding in Scots Church in Collins Street, with an informal reception at Gaspare's. There was to be no dancing, just a meal and speeches. Kate was Belinda's matron of honour and David was Scott's best man. The wedding rings were tied on a white ribbon around George's neck as he sat with Scott and David at the front of the church as Colonel Peters walked Belinda down the aisle. Only twenty guests had been invited, but Scot and Belinda were astounded when they walked out of the church as man and wife, to be greeted by twelve of their former army comrades in dress uniform, with swords drawn, forming an honour guard on the church steps.

The wedding photos were taken in the Treasury Gardens, while Gaspare happily arranged seating for the additional twelve guests. Later that night the happy couple retired to Scott's apartment, then early the next morning David drove them out to the airport, where they caught a flight to Sydney, then the connection to Coffs Harbour to begin a week's stay at Woolgoolga. Scott and Belinda hadn't planned to take time off for a honeymoon, feeling that they'd had a honeymoon of sorts during their holiday on Norfolk Island earlier in the year. However, Kate insisted that they took a week off after their wedding, and paid for their tickets to Coffs Harbour.

Julie and Tom's wedding was planned for Saturday 8th June, at the local church at Omeo. As her mother's dress fitted her too, Julie was thrilled when her father asked her if she too would like to wear it to her wedding as Kate had for hers. Kate arranged for return tickets to England for their honeymoon, where Julie and Tom planned to spend three weeks touring around Great Britain, including a stop at the City of Hereford, and visiting numerous Hereford Studs along their way.

Kate, David, and Jim spent the first term holidays at Woolgoolga, where they revelled in surfing in the warmer weather. Jim now had his own board and wetsuit, and happily ventured further out with David if the surf wasn't too big. He also joined the Woolgoolga SLSC as a Nipper, and participated in their activities when David was out in the surfboat each day. Kate loved surfing but was happy to relax and chat to Jessie at times, to give David and Jim quality time together.

Brad and Colin's parents were delighted when told that their sons were doing well in grade five, working hard to keep up with Jim, and despite initial misgivings at having the 'three amigos' together again in class, by the end of term one, their teachers were happy to inform David that their reservations had been unfounded.

Before dawn on Anzac Day, David, Kate, Jim, Scott, and Belinda walked to St Kilda Road and caught a tram to the Shrine of Remembrance, where they waited in the huge crowd near the Eternal Flame for the Dawn Service. Scott proudly wore his medals on his left chest, while Jim wore his grandfathers on his right. At the completion of the service, they walked across to the Victoria Barracks for the traditional Gunfire Breakfast, then, while Scott and George went to wait at the start of the march, the others went back to an area near the Shrine, to watch the Anzac march, then listen to the service. Jim was thrilled to see the Scotch Pipe Band march past twice, then cheered loudly when Scott marched past with his regiment, his medals flashing in the sunlight.

That night after Jim had gone to bed Kate and David sat out on the balcony. 'Darling, you know that I never wanted winning the jackpot to change my way of life too much, and that I have refused to contemplate squandering it on pretentious items to impress people of my wealth. Apart from buying the Woolgoolga property and spending extra on travelling and hotels, I think that I have kept true to that aspiration. And through *Windfall Holdings* numerous agencies have assisted an abundant number of people and animals during the past year.

However, it has changed and enriched my life in a way that I could never have envisaged. I now have some wonderful new friends, but by far the most significant change, is the inclusion of you my love, and Jim into my life, and in a few months, we will also have Jim's little brother or sister!'

Kate laughed when David turned to stare at her. "Yes my love, I'm pregnant!'